INDELIBLE

INDELIBLE

A SEAN McPHERSON NOVEL

BOOK ONE

LAURIE BUCHANAN

This book is dedicated to authors,
their creative muses, and the craft of writing.

Published by SparkPress, a BookSparks imprint,
A division of SparkPoint Studio, LLC
Phoenix, Arizona, USA, 85007
www.gosparkpress.com

Published 2021
Printed in the United States of America
Print ISBN: 978-1-68463-071-4
E-ISBN: 978-1-68463-072-1

Library of Congress Control Number: 2020915729

Interior design by Tabitha Lahr

AUTHOR'S NOTE

While Bellingham and Fairhaven are
real towns in the state of Washington,
I've added fictitious touches to further the story.

PROLOGUE

"Everything must have a beginning... and that beginning must be linked to something that went before."

—MARY SHELLEY

MICK

A bullet explodes between his partner's eyes. The amount of blood that hits Sean McPherson, "Mick," is small in comparison to what covers the back of the squad car. The sharp taste of copper fills his mouth.

Mick watches Sam slump forward, the shoulder-belt prevents his weight from hitting the steering wheel, but not from gunning the accelerator. The car surges onto the right shoulder, and Mick braces himself for the inevitable impact of metal against the concrete abutment.

The snap of shattering glass mixed with the high-pitched scrape of steel fills his ears. He chokes on the scream lodged in his throat as the squad car collides with the bridge's unforgiving underpinning.

It hurts to open his eyes. Mick is aware that the underpass is lit by flickering red and blue lights shimmering on cement. He hears people shouting. "This one's alive, the other one's dead.

We're going to have to cut him out. Get the Jaws of Life," one of them yells. "Hurry; I smell fuel!"

Mick hovers over Sam. *Am I the one who's dead?* He wonders. *But I'm not levitating. I'm suspended, held captive by the seatbelt.* He sees Sam's eyes wide open and vacant, mouth parted. He swallows the bitter taste of bile that hits the back of his throat. Sam is more than a partner. He's Mick's best friend.

Five years have passed since the accident. Mick remembers the day when Chief Reynolds came to the hospital and said, "I'm sorry, but I have to put you on indefinite medical leave."

Mick's sister, Libby, and brother-in-law, Niall, pick him up at the hospital and take him to Pines & Quill, their writing retreat in Fairhaven, Washington, to live in one of their cottages. Libby assures him, "The Zen-like energy of the wooded acres will help you heal."

Fists clenching the sweat-drenched bedsheet, Mick sits upright in the dark, his body shudders. His heart races. His relief at the realization he's in his bedroom is palpable. Just yesterday, Dr. Fletcher assured him that nightmares are a typical side effect of post-traumatic stress disorder—PTSD.

Intimate with this now familiar routine, he knows there'll be no sleep tonight and heads to the bathroom to take a shower. He steps under the hot spray, tilts his head back, and closes his eyes. *Our shift was routine up to the moment the dispatcher sent Sam and me toward the I-280 bridge over the Lawrence Expressway & Creek in San Francisco to intercept a drunk and speeding driver that had been reported. We didn't know we were heading into the crosshairs of a telescopic sight on a sniper's rifle. A weapon designed for extreme accuracy. Perfect for an ambush.*

Hot water rushing over his body, he remembers the call to that overpass on a Friday night. It was their last ride together as police officers. Sam and Mick had just been promoted. The following Monday, they were to start their careers as homicide detectives.

He remembers the horrific crash and the helpless feeling at seeing his partner, Sam's, lifeless body.

He doesn't remember being life-flighted to the hospital. They told him afterward that he almost died during transport. The surgery that saved his life is a total blank. It left him with a limp and survivor's guilt.

The most heart-breaking memory he doesn't have is Sam's funeral. He was in the ICU.

Mick steps out of the shower and towels off. He can't make out his features in the steam-fogged mirror, but his clenched teeth inform him that his face looks grim. In a few hours, he'll head to the airport. He dreads it because every overpass he drives under opens old wounds and cuts fresh ones, triggering a grim reminder of what lays coiled inside him, ready to spring if disturbed.

JASON

Jason Hughes can't help but smile when he unzips the suitcase and sees two immaculate stacks of pristine white hotel towels. Both stacks contain five towels with a name badge pinned to each one. He touches the first rectangular name badge that's pinned with precision to the folded, thick white towel, and traces his finger over the name. *Rose.* That simple act, along with the scar on his left wrist, ushers a flood of sweet memories from New York.

After setting Rose's towel on the side table, Jason picks up the top towel from the second stack and winces a little in excruciating delight as he remembers Yolanda in Jacksonville, Florida. She left a small scar on his right forearm.

Jason checks his watch and sees there's still time to enjoy the rest. He chuckles as he remembers Teagan in Chicago. She's the first one he tested a zip-tie restraint on. *After all, I can't afford to get a scar each time I kill,* he muses.

While caressing his way through the rest of the towels and name badges, he revels in memories of Mai in Los Angeles, Teresa in Boston, Linh in Dallas, Amala—*oh she was feisty*—in Portland, Silvia in Kansas City, Veronica in Denver, and Devi in Philadelphia.

He remembers when Andrew, his fraternal twin, teased him, calling his suitcase "precious" and saying that he reminded him of Gollum. Jason smiles. *I don't have to worry about that anymore now, do I?*

After replacing the towels in the appropriate order, he zips the suitcase shut and gathers the other items waiting by the front door—another suitcase, a backpack, and two manuscript-sized boxes that he'll ship from the UPS Hub on his way to the airport. They're supposed to contain the manuscript he's pretending to work on, *Rearview Mirror: Reflections of a New York Limo Driver.* They don't.

Not one to leave anything to chance, he verifies, yet again, that "UPS accepts firearm parts for shipment, provided the part is not a 'firearm' as defined under federal law; the contents of the package cannot be assembled to form a firearm; and the package otherwise complies with federal, state, and local law."

The parts in either box by themselves can't be made into a firearm. It requires all of the pieces in both boxes. *Not a problem. I'll assemble my Beretta when they get to Pines & Quill.*

Jason loosens his white-knuckled grip on the steering wheel of the rental car and relaxes. *I'm not excited about the five-hour nonstop flight between Cleveland and Seattle, followed by a two-hour drive to the writing retreat. But I am looking forward to the in-air service. I always enjoy flying with my friend Jack Daniels.*

He keeps his backpack and watches as the airline representative at the ticket counter takes the rest of his luggage, tags it, then heaves it onto a conveyor belt. In moments it's swallowed by a fringed-rubber throat. He imagines its snake-like journey as it makes its way through x-ray machines with TSA officers looking for weapons, explosives, and drugs before passing the wet nostrils of trained dogs sniffing for the same. He's done this before and knows that no one will bat an eye; no hackles will rise, as his suitcase with ten folded, plush white towels passes through.

Jason's boarding pass is TSA pre-checked. *Unlike the other poor schmucks, passing through security should be fast and easy.* After stepping through the full-body scanner, he hears, "Sir, please step to the side."

"Is there a problem?" he asks.

"No, it's just your lucky day." The agent smiles. "You've been selected for a random check. Is this piece yours?" he asks while removing a backpack from the conveyor belt.

Jason mirrors the agent's smile and nods. "It sure is."

One by one the agent empties the innocuous contents onto the table, stopping when he gets to the stainless-steel flask. He gives it a slight shake. "Mind if I open it?"

"Not at all. Help yourself. I wish it had something in it, but I know that's not allowed."

With gloved hands, the agent twists off the lid and turns the empty flask upside down over the trashcan, then lifts it to his nostrils and inhales deeply. "I bet it was good to the last drop." He laughs at his joke. While replacing the items in Jason's backpack, the agent continues, "I hope to enjoy something like that when I get home tonight."

"Me, too," Jason says, smiling. "Am I free to go now?"

"Yes, have a good flight."

With deliberate calm, Jason walks away, savoring the sweet taste of victory. In the event he's being watched, he stops, and with practiced nonchalance fishes the burner he's carrying out of his pocket, ostensibly to check his messages. He smiles when he reads a new text. "c u soon."

CYNTHIA

I need time away after this last case, Cynthia Winters thinks. *The little girl was found where I said she would be, but they were too late. She was dead.* The look of devastation in her parent's eyes was gut-wrenching. She remembers her mother telling her, "Children are their mother's heart walking around outside her body."

Life is hard when your heart dies before you do.

In this morning's television interview, Cynthia said, "I recognize that it's difficult for some people to understand what an intuitive does."

The newscaster explained to the viewing audience, "Several law enforcement agencies use Cynthia's skill of *psychometry,* a form of extra-sensory perception that allows a person to read the energy of an object."

When asked to explain further, Cynthia says, "Every item has an energy field that can transfer knowledge about its history. As an intuitive, I can 'see' physical places associated with an object, in real time or the past. The detailed imagery I receive often helps law enforcement agencies to locate an item or a person."

After an impressive on-air demonstration, the newscaster asks, "What does it feel like to be an intuitive?" Cynthia responds, "The work of an intuitive consultant can be draining. In particular, when a missing person is found dead. However, it's rewarding when they're alive, or when the police find the perpetrator." She went on to say, "In addition to psychometry, I love to read people's palms. It's gratifying when I'm able to help someone by reading the lines on their hands." After another on-air demonstration, this time reading the newscaster's palm, she's asked, "What's next for you?"

"From here I'm catching a flight to a writing retreat in the Pacific Northwest to complete the book I'm working on."

In the limo that takes her from the news station to the airport, Cynthia smiles as she thinks about the title of her manuscript, *Guide Lines: The World in the Palm of Your Hand.* Close to the end, she's hoping to finish it while at Pines & Quill. She's not surprised there's a waiting list for the retreat, because she's heard and read rave reviews about the MacCulloughs, the husband and wife team who own it.

The glowing online praise says, "Libby provides guidance for writing that authors find inspiring. She offers insightful teaching and discussion of the writing process, as well as provides feedback on participants' writing. And she offers tai chi classes in the morning as a way to prime the writing pump."

The many enthusiastic reviews for Niall's cuisine agree. "He's an incredible gourmet chef who also possesses the working knowledge of a sommelier." One person wrote, "His food tastes like heaven!" And several people admitted to gaining weight during their month in residence because they couldn't resist his delicious meals, desserts, and wine pairings.

I'm looking forward to the nonstop flight from Tucson to Seattle. It's short at two hours and forty-five minutes. And I always enjoy picking up on the energy of passengers sitting near me when I fly. It's like "people watching," but at a much deeper level.

But there's something else about the destination. I can't explain it, but I feel drawn. I've never been to the location before, nor do I have any ties in that area, so it doesn't make any sense. Yet the sensation is intense; it's like I'm being summoned.

FRAN

I think it was Eleanor Roosevelt who said, "No one can make you feel inferior without your consent." Well, she was wrong, Fran Davies thinks, packing her suitcase. *My ex-husband took my self-esteem. When he found out that I can't have children, he pulled it right out from under me, just like a rug. And I fell flat on my backside and haven't gotten up since.*

Fran looked into surrogacy, but her husband said, "No." She looked into adoption. Again, he said "no." And that's when he also said, "No" to her. That's when he announced that he didn't love her anymore and that he wanted a divorce. *His disappointment in me—my infertility—trumped his love for me.*

"You can have the house, the car, and the bank account," he told her. "But you can't have children, and that's a deal breaker."

"But it's not my choice," she cried. "This is out of my control."

Do I hate him? No. Do I hate myself? Yes. But not for that reason. I'm angry that I've allowed myself to become a rigid, dried up old prune. I'm forty-one, but to look at me, you'd think I'm well into my fifties.

Upon learning that she couldn't have children, something out of her control, Fran became obsessed with controlling things she could. Her hair, weight, and wardrobe—precise and exacting—bear evidence of a choke hold, of being beat into submission.

Some people don't understand how hard it is for a woman to watch her friends and family members conceive and have babies, while she can't seem to. And when the attempts to conceive fail month after month and it becomes a case of infertility, it's even worse.

Fran thinks about being overwhelmed by failure. *That's when I started seeing a therapist, Traci Schneider,* she remembers. *One of the most important things Traci told me was,* "Fran, while you're dealing with infertility, you need support to help you vent your frustrations, worries, and fears." She went on to say, "Support is key for women struggling with infertility. It's a disease that affects a women's core, and it can affect their relationships with family, friends, and even people at work."

"Okay," Fran agrees. "I'll attend an emotional support group for infertility."

At Fran's first meeting, it becomes clear that the director, Maddy Shea, is a proponent of journaling. Maddy is fond of saying, "Writing your way to the heart of a matter is therapeutic." At the end of the session, she welcomes Fran, hands her a leather-bound journal with lined pages and says, "Write anything and everything that comes to mind."

A few months later, Fran shares her writing with Maddy. She's nervous about how Maddy might respond. Fran smiles when she remembers the conversation. When she handed the journal back to Fran, Maddy smiled and said, "This journal is full of helpful insights. It would make a wonderful book. So many women could benefit from it. I'd like to put you in touch with my friend, Libby MacCullough. She and her husband own Pines & Quill, a writing retreat in Washington state."

Fran is filled with nervous excitement because today she's catching a nonstop flight from Boston to Seattle. She doesn't enjoy flying, but she tolerates it. Travel is part of her job. Because it's a five hour and thirty-eight-minute flight, Fran is taking her laptop on the plane to focus on her manuscript, *Mother in Waiting: The Stigma of Childlessness*. If she's lucky, she might even make a bit of headway.

After zipping her suitcase shut, Fran thinks, *I'm giving myself this month away to scrape up the courage to remove the wedding band from my finger.*

EMMA

A year ago, I didn't know if a trip like I'm packing for right now would ever be possible again, Emma Benton muses, remembering what it was like to wake up one morning, paralyzed from the waist down.

She wanted to be a clay artist ever since she was a little girl watching her mother at her potter's wheel. When she grew up, she earned a Master of Fine Arts degree in Ceramics at Penn State School of Visual Arts, and then moved back to southern California to be closer to her family and open a small studio shop.

Last year I was delighted to be one of the artists invited to show my work at Gallery in the Garden—Celebrating Art in Nature, a two day, outdoor event. My best friend, Sally, helped me pack all of the materials in and back out again. It was hard work; pottery is heavy. But I felt that the opportunity for a wider brushstroke of visibility was well worth it. Sally agreed. The morning after the show, I woke up paralyzed from the waist down.

At the hospital, they run batteries of tests. "Have you recently been out of the country or had any vaccinations?" Dr. Christianson asks. Another member of the medical team, Dr. Davidson, thinks it might be the West Nile virus. "Have you recently been bitten by a mosquito or suffered any physical trauma?" After ruling these out, they test her for multiple sclerosis and Legionnaire's disease, but everything comes up negative.

By the second day, the symptoms Emma presents indicate that she has transverse myelitis, a neurological disorder caused by inflammation of the spinal cord. It can develop in a matter of hours or take several weeks. Emma's happened overnight.

It can occur in the setting of another illness, or in isolation. Emma's is isolated. When it happens like hers did, without an apparent underlying cause, it's referred to as 'idiopathic' and is assumed to be a result of abnormal activation of the immune system against the spinal cord.

Emma has been in a wheelchair since that time. Her medical team remains baffled. They tell her, "Your recovery may be absent, partial, or complete. At thirty-five, you're still considered young, and other than transverse myelitis, you're healthy. More importantly, you have a positive outlook."

"My friend, Sally, says that I'm 'unabashedly optimistic,'" Emma says, smiling.

At first, Emma stayed at her parent's home. It helps that she's from a family of creatives. They speak the same language and value the same things that she does. They understand that creativity is in her blood. Because of this experiential knowledge, they're supportive. Her dad and her brothers modified her home, art studio, and potter's wheel so that she can live independently and continue to throw pottery.

After adding the final items to her suitcase, Emma smiles, thinking about her family. *Mom's worried. Dad says he's not, but I can tell that he is. And my brothers are happy for me.*

In addition to physical therapy, part of the recovery work she's doing is writing a memoir, *Moving Violations: A Sassy Look at Life from a Wheelchair*. That's why she's excited to catch a flight today from San Diego to Seattle. She's looking forward to being a writer in residence at Pines & Quill. One of their cottages is designed for people in wheelchairs.

So far Emma's recovery's been partial. *I've regained some feeling in my hips, and I'm able to stand long enough, without collapsing, to transfer myself into a car, chair, or bed. One of my goals this month is to be able to stand at the bathroom sink long enough to brush my teeth. Who knows, maybe I'll even take a step.*

CHAPTER 1

"You take people, you put them on a journey, you give them peril, you find out who they really are."

—Joss Whedon

McPherson arrives at the baggage claim area with time to spare. He moves slow, weighed down by private burdens—the everyday struggle with profound loss. With regret. With guilt.

His piercing green eyes absorb the details of his surroundings, a habit he picked up on the force, one that kept him alive. His partner, Sam, hadn't been so fortunate. If the day's coin flip had come up tails, he would have been the driver. Not Sam. He would have been killed. Not Sam.

Mick has been "retired" from the SFPD five years now—if that's what you call being forced to quit because of line of duty injuries. He spent the first two years following dead-end leads trying to find his partner's killer. The last three years, he's worked with his sister and brother-in-law at Pines & Quill.

Libby was a freshman in high school when he was born. Always a sparkle in her eyes, Mick's mother calls him her *"iontas iontach,"* Gaelic for delightful surprise.

Swallowed by the unending tasks of groundskeeper and all-around handyman, Mick soon discovers that the Zen-like energy of the wooded acres works on him like a soothing balm, breathing life back into his weary soul.

He begins each morning with the same mantra, *Just make it through today.*

A monthly trek, the familiar Arrivals & Departures Board at Sea-Tac, the term locals use for the Seattle-Tacoma International Airport, indicates that the plane for the first guest, Emma Benton, will arrive in a moment from San Diego. The flights for the other three guests are staggered to arrive over the next hour.

Mick finds it interesting getting to know the guests who carve out three weeks of time from their schedules to write in near seclusion. Each one has a unique process for transferring ideas from their head to the page. They arrive on the first day of each month and depart on the twenty-first. This offers them a significant amount of protected time to work on their manuscripts.

The fourth week of every month—guest free—provides Niall, Libby, and Mick with time to relax and prepare for the next group of writers. It also affords the opportunity for the siblings to take turns visiting their parents in San Francisco; a two-hour nonstop flight.

Each month when Libby hands Mick the name-boards for their guest authors, she also shares a brief summary of what she imagines their personalities to be like based on the phone conversation or email correspondence she has with them. Mick enjoys indulging his sister because her predictions are darned close, if not dead on accurate.

"Let's see now. Emma Benton is arriving from San Diego. She's single, in her mid-thirties, and falls somewhere in the middle of several brothers, so I suspect she has a good sense of humor. Well-educated and artistic, she's our wheelchair guest this month."

"Do you know why, or how long she's been in a wheel-chair?" Mick asks.

"She didn't say, but I don't get the feeling that it's been long-term."

"There you go with your *feeeelings* again," he drags the word out while rolling his eyes. "I know. I know. You've told me time and time again that 'dogs experience life through their noses, and humans experience life through their *feeeelings*,' and that I should tune into mine more often," he ends with a cocky smile.

"If you'd listen to your big sister . . ." Libby trails off, shaking a finger at him. "Now, where was I? Oh yes, Cynthia Winters is arriving from Tucson. She's single, has refined taste, is eclectic, and cordial. If I had to guess her age, I'd say she's . . . hmm, let's just say 'seasoned.'"

"What do you mean 'eclectic?'" he asks.

"I get the *feeeeling*," she raises an eyebrow in teasing emphasis, "that she's well-traveled, which lends itself to a wide variety of interests."

Brows knit, Libby continues, "Jason Hughes is arriving from Cleveland. I wasn't able to get much of a handle on him." With a perfect imitation of Niall's Scottish brogue, she says, "He's tight as a camel's arse in a sandstorm!" Trilling the "r," she nails the burr in "arse." Both of them laughing, she continues, "That's what I get for being married to a Scotsman for thirty-two years." Libby composes herself. "That may not be a fair assessment of Mr. Hughes. He may just be shy, reserved, or private."

"Not everyone pours their heart out to a stranger," Mick retorts in mock severity.

Not stung in the least, Libby feigns aloofness, sticks her nose in the air and goes on. "Fran Davies is arriving from Boston. When we spoke on the phone, I didn't detect an accent, so my guess is she's a transplant." With a "So there!"

look, Libby continues, ticking attributes off her fingers. "She's proper, organized, thorough, and no-nonsense, while at the same time, polite."

Brow lifted, eyes narrowed, "What do you mean by *proper?*" Mick enunciates the word.

"Maybe 'stiff' would be a better descriptor. And I sense that she's sad," Libby ends with a perplexed tone in her voice.

———

Amid a busy hub of travel activity, Mick's thoughts return to his surroundings, his gaze sweeps the space, taking everything in like a dry sponge soaks up water. He'd learned at the beginning of his police training that, "It's all in the details."

Ever vigilant, he mentally notes people's hair color, facial expressions, body language, tattoos, jewelry, clothing, footwear, and baggage details.

His nostrils catch the smell of jet exhaust, fast food, and the heady mixture of perfumes and colognes that hang like an invisible cloud over the throng of bustling people. *Who among you is a killer?* he wonders.

Mick read in this morning's paper that Sea-Tac served over thirty-two million people last year alone. As each plane lands, passengers pour from the terminals, like human lava, into the baggage claim area.

He turns at the rapid slap of heels against linoleum and sees a woman running full speed from the baggage carousel area with a brief bag slung over her shoulder, bouncing against her back, and a carry-on biting her heels. She hangs a left. He continues watching as she gallops up the escalator, just missing people who also have luggage draped over their bodies, and wheeled carry-ons following disobediently behind. Mick shakes his head. *I'm glad I'm not part of that rat race.*

He returns to the task at hand, raising the name-board for "E. Benton" so it can be seen from a distance. Mick scans the crowd and spots Emma first. She's wearing a vibrant green, short-sleeved top, jeans, and ballet flats. Mick's surprised and impressed that she isn't using a motorized wheelchair. Instead, a manual wheelchair powered by her own suntanned arms. Libby neglected to tell him that she's beautiful.

Emma rolls to a stop in front of Mick. The delicate curve of her throat is revealed when she tips her head back to look up at him.

Something inside him flips.

Mick takes in dark auburn hair, reminiscent of deep Bordeaux wine, that frames moss-green eyes sparkling with devilish mischief, and an infectious smile. She extends her right hand and says, "I'm Emma Benton. You must be Mr. McPherson."

"I'm Sean McPherson, but please call me Mick, everyone else does," he says, noting the firm, self-confident grip of her handshake.

"If you give me your claim tickets, I'll get your bags from the carousel."

"I'll come with you and point them out. It'll be easier to spot them that way."

If she notices his limp as they make their way to the ever-circling conveyor belt, she gives no indication.

"When will the others arrive?" she asks, tucking thick, shoulder-length hair behind her ears.

"We're waiting for three more within the hour," he replies, noticing impudent freckles marching across the bridge of her tanned nose.

"There's one of my bags now," she points to a large suitcase.

He turns back to her with laughter in his eyes. "I don't think I could have missed that." He gives a pretend groan as he hefts the large, brushed aluminum case off the belt. "It's bright orange."

She looks up at him with an impish grin. "Pumpkin Spice," she counters. "The other two look the same, just a little smaller."

And he watches, heart beating a little faster, as a smile is born on her lips. *Pumpkin Spice,* he thinks to himself, *well I'll be damned.*

After collecting the other two suitcases and putting them on the baggage trolley, Mick checks his watch. "The next guest is about to land. Would you like to wait in the lounge while I gather the others?"

"That's a great idea. It'll give me a chance to check my voicemail and email. Should I meet you back here in about twenty minutes?"

"That'll be fine," he nods, tucking his hands in the back pockets of his denim jeans. And with that, she tilts her chair back, does a saucy little turn, and maneuvers toward the lounge.

Pumpkin Spice, he thinks again, smiling as he holds up the hand-calligraphed name-board for "C. Winters."

———

As passengers from the Tucson flight pour into the baggage area, a tall, slender woman with short white hair cropped close to her head like an elf cap, makes eye contact with Mick. Her liquid brown eyes have a faint slant and glimmer when she smiles. She's never known airports to be quiet. In her entire life, traveling is a buzzing, busy, energetic experience with a hive of people scurrying everywhere. And she loves it.

As she walks toward Mick, the gauzy fabric of her skirt swirls around her ankles, and metallic highlights wink from the folds of bright purple floral and striped panels. A jumble of silver bangles on each wrist—some thick, some thin—clank in unison with the rhythmic cadence of each purposeful step she takes on the buffed linoleum floor in strappy, Greek-inspired sandals.

"I'm Cynthia Winters," she says. Her easy smile, white against olive-toned skin, creases her eyes as she she extends well-manicured hands, bejeweled with chunky turquoise rings, to clasp one of his in both of hers. "You must be Mr. McPherson," she says while turning his palm up with practiced ease. As her hands hold his, she lets impressions of him come and go, to sort out later. Her intuition tells her that he is a man of integrity, someone you can trust and rely on.

"Please call me Mick," he says to the top of her bent head as she peruses his hand. Taken aback, eyebrows flirting with his hairline, he asks, "Are you reading my palm?" while trying to regain possession of his work-worn hand from the bohemian-looking woman.

"Oh, it's just a little hobby of mine," she assures him, hanging on, still gazing with deep interest at his hand.

With hesitation, he asks, "What do you see?"

She looks up with deep brown, knowing eyes and answers. "Each line makes a statement, but like words in a sentence, they must be read in context with each other. The shape of the hand, the flexibility of the fingers, the depth and color of the lines, all combine to form a statement about a person's character." *There's more than anguish*, she thinks to herself. *There's grief and a sense of guilt. For what?* she wonders. With a gentle squeeze from her warm hands, she looks with kindness up into his vivid green eyes and smiles before letting go.

Was that sadness in her eyes? Mick furrows his brow. *What did she see?*

As he's about to ask, Cynthia turns around as if on cue and points a red-tipped fingernail to designer luggage just belched from the fringed-rubber confines of the airport netherworld. And with that she sets sail, heels clicking across the smooth floor, her long, colorful skirt billowing like a wake behind her.

Not your typical "grandmother," Mick muses. Curiosity piqued, he scratches his head and follows. *How in the world did she know that her luggage just arrived?*

Ten minutes late, the Cleveland flight carrying Jason Hughes lands just ahead of Fran Davies' flight from Boston. Short, maybe five foot, six inches, but wiry and strong, his complexion is washed out, not just pale, despite the deliberate smudge of a three-day beard. With a crewcut of salt and pepper hair on his head and face, it's difficult to gauge his age. His nose, hooked and sharp, casts a shadow on thin, unsmiling lips. His ice-gray eyes are bottomless pools of seeming indifference.

When he shakes Jason's hand, Mick experiences a strange feeling of distrust, of instant dislike. *Maybe it's because I'm standing next to Cynthia and her hoodoo-voodoo's rubbing off on me.* Nonetheless, he has a disturbing feeling, like a warning, in the pit of his stomach, yet there is nothing to base it on. But if he's learned anything from his years on the force, it's to trust his gut instinct, another is to never show his hand.

"Jason, I'd like to introduce you to Cynthia Winters," Mick says, smiling. "She's another writer who's staying at Pines & Quill this month."

"It's so nice to meet you," Cynthia says. When Jason extends his hand, she takes it in both of hers, turns it palm up, and studies it, much in the same way she'd done with Mick's.

With a quickly erased dark look, Jason extracts his hand and excuses himself. "I need to get my luggage."

"I'll collect it," Mick offers, not missing the swift transformation from worried misgiving to a warm smile on Cynthia's face. *This woman knows things.*

She'd only held Jason's hand for a moment, but an instant's all that's necessary to receive a clairaudient impression. Inaudible to everyone else, Cynthia heard the distinct crash of waves growing in volume until it filled the air like thunder. She knows with certainty that it was precognitive in nature, a glimmer of something in advance of its occurrence. Something ominous.

"I've got it, man, thanks anyway," Jason says, backing away before turning to go collect his luggage.

As Mick watches Jason's retreating back, trying to decipher his own feelings, the incoming flight from Boston is announced.

———

Emma returns unobserved, taking in the way Mick's hands rest on his uneven hips—the left a few inches higher than the right. It would be hard to miss those masculine, denim-covered legs set in that determined stance. Hair, the wilder side of conservative, curls around his ears. His profile has a chiseled quality about it, with strong, imperfect features.

"Hi Mick, I'm back on time." Emma's smile is contagious as she rolls up and joins the group.

"That you are." He smiles, noting that her presence does something delightful to his insides. *Watch it, mister,* he reminds himself. *If you don't let anyone into your life, you won't have anyone to lose.* Past experience has been clear about that.

Emma turns to Cynthia and shakes her hand. "I'm Emma Benton. I just arrived from San Diego."

"Hi Emma, it's nice to meet you. I'm Cynthia Winters; I'm here from Tucson."

"I can see you brought the sunshine with you," Emma responds to the older woman who takes her hand in both of hers and turns it palm up.

"Oh, are you a palm reader?" A mixture of excitement and intrigue lace Emma's voice. "I've never had my palm read before."

"It's just a little hobby of mine," Cynthia says, studying the outstretched hand.

"What do you see?" Emma asks, an eager lift in her tone.

"The head line, here," Cynthia says, trailing her own finger along the lower of the two lines running horizontally across Emma's hand, "is bound to your life line, showing both caution and sensitivity. The forked end to the head line, here," she points, "indicates mental flexibility, plus the gift of seeing other people's viewpoints."

Holding high the name-board for "F. Davies," Mick feigns concern in locating the last arrival while at the same time, trying to overhear what Cynthia is saying to Emma about her palm. *Not that I believe in fortune-telling,* he assures himself.

Jason returns with a suitcase in each hand, and a backpack slung over his shoulder. "Should I put them here?" he indicates the baggage trolley with his head.

"Yes, that would be great," Mick answers, as the tall, willowy woman continues reading the volume that is Emma's hand.

Cynthia's forehead creases a little. She leans in close so that only Emma can hear and points to a line of tiny dots on her palm.

"That's odd. I've never noticed those before," Emma says.

"Dots aren't always this well pronounced on a palm. They can represent concerns about ill health or relationships, but that's not what I sense for you. They can also serve as a warning sign." Before releasing Emma's hand, Cynthia gives it a gentle squeeze. "We'll talk more later," she whispers.

Really God? Fran mentally asks a supposedly loving deity as the airplane wheels touch down. *I'm heartbroken that I can't have children and you seat me next to a woman with a toddler and a newborn on an almost six-hour flight?*

She turns to the exhausted woman in the window seat. "I hope the rest of your trip goes well. Can I get anything out of the overhead compartment for you?"

After placing the woman's bags and children's paraphernalia into the seat where she'd been sitting, Fran waves at the little girl, Sarah.

Sarah pries up three fingers on her right hand with her left hand and announces with pride, "I'm fwee."

With the back of her hand, Fran wipes a tear from her cheek and steps into the aisle, joining the crowd of passengers heading toward the front of the plane. Her head is pounding like a kettle drum. She doesn't enjoy flying but has learned to tolerate it over the years. When Fran started traveling for work, she discovered that sitting behind the first bulkhead in the aircraft eliminates another passenger reclining in your lap, you gain an extra bit of leg room, and are among the first to deplane.

Simple and straightforward, Fran is a practical woman. In fact, her most recent performance review at work indicates that she's "Terrifyingly efficient and organized." After hooking her glasses on the neck of her circumspect, navy blue sweater set, she heads toward the baggage area, stopping at the restroom along the way.

She catches a glimpse of herself in the mirror while waiting in line and mentally wrings her hands. *Dishwater blonde is an accurate term.* She gets an even closer view when she washes her hands. Her hazel eyes take in hair that looks like it's been beaten into submission and shellacked into place like a helmet with several layers of spray. *I don't want to do this anymore. I want something else—anything else will do.*

After pasting a smile on her face, she continues to the baggage claim area. From a distance, she spots her name-board and continues on. Stopping in front of the man holding the sign, she extends her hand and introduces herself. "Hello, I'm Fran Davies."

———

Their small group heads en masse to the parking area. Jason brings up the rear, taking mental stock of the females. *This group consists of an older, gypsy-looking woman; a woman so rigid she'd make a great prison warden; and a beautiful gimp in a wheelchair.*

Jason turns his attention to Mick, in front, pulling the baggage trolley. *It's evident that he's fit and strong and moves quickly despite a limp.* Focused on his gait, he watches Mick twist his left hip forward slightly, before propelling his right foot in front. *No problem,* Jason muses, with a self-satisfied smirk, *this is going to be easy.*

CHAPTER 2

*"Plot is people. Human emotions and desires
founded on the realities of life, working at
cross purposes, getting hotter and fiercer as they
strike against each other until finally there's an
explosion—that's plot."*

—Leigh Brackett

Much like a brilliant, multi-faceted gem nestled on the
ragged hemline of the northern Pacific coastline, Pines
& Quill, a wooded retreat for writers, sits Zen-like overlooking
Bellingham Bay in Fairhaven, Washington, holding space to
unleash possibility. The mango-colored sunrises and blood-
orange sunsets compete in their breathtaking showiness, each
vying for the rapt attention of would-be onlookers. One
heralding the beginning of day, the other bids adieu, sending it
off into the ink-black night sky.

Niall MacCullough brushes damp soil from the knees
of his pants. "Libby's going to kill me," he mutters under
his breath while snipping fresh dill for the evening meal and
adding it to the basket laden with garlic, basil, and potatoes
he's already gathered from his late spring garden.

"Hemingway! If I've told you once, I've told you a thousand times, don't bury your bones in the garden!"

A bustling, five-year-old, rough-coated, Irish Wolfhound, Hemingway tips the scales at just under one hundred and fifty pounds. Well-muscled, lean, and strong, his appearance is commanding. An ancient breed, Wolfhounds were bred to hunt with their masters, fight beside them in battle, and guard their castles. He possesses the ability of a fierce warrior, but he's gentle with family and guests, a magnificent combination of power and grace.

His dirt-crusted paws—giant earth movers with strong, curved nails—put the final touches on his buried treasure between the yellow pepper plants, before bounding over the rows of vegetables and herbs. Not quite stopping in the nick of time, they both tumble over as Hemingway collides with his constant companion and second-best friend, Niall.

Libby rounds the corner in time to see Niall's feet and Hemingway's wagging tail sail over the snap peas. Then she hears the deep, rumbling laughter of her husband of thirty-two years. She shakes her head and smiles to herself before calling out, "Boys, company's arriving soon, and we've got to be ready."

With that, two bushy eye-browed, bearded faces peek at her over lush, green foliage. Niall's hair is mussed like a boy's, but gray-hued in the late afternoon light. Libby shakes her head in false exasperation. *Humans do, indeed, resemble their companion animals,* then bursts out laughing at their twin, mischievous grins.

Set on twenty forested acres, the Pines & Quill writer's refuge provides respite from the distractions of everyday life so writers can focus on what they do best, write. An environment that offers peace, quiet, and inspiration, it boasts four secluded cottages, Dickens, Brontë, Austen, and Thoreau, each is handcrafted by a long-dead Amish man whose skill and devotion to his trade is still evident in his work. When the structures were modernized, painstaking care was taken to reflect the same excellence in craftsmanship.

Libby enjoys free rein expressing her natural flair for style and interior design in the main house, her brother's cabin, and the four writer's cottages. And while the original Amish builder saw that each cottage was similar in size and design, surrounded by its own type of tree, she ensures that they each have unique personalities: color scheme, furnishings, and hand-selected artwork created by local artisans.

In addition to electricity and internet access, each cottage has air-conditioning, a wood-burning stove, and a bathroom with a shower. They're also equipped with an efficiency kitchen that includes a mini-fridge, microwave, toaster oven, coffeemaker, and a fat-bellied tea kettle, ideal for a long day of writing.

On each desk is a phone. Retro, they're bulky and square, from an era before cell phones, even before cordless. Its sole purpose is to connect with the main house. A guest needs only to lift the receiver and dial zero to ring through to the MacCullough's kitchen.

The main house, large and rustic, is inviting in a down-home sort of way. Built for comfort, not grandeur, it sits at the center of Pines & Quill. And while each writer has the option to have breakfast and lunch delivered from the main house to their cottage door, they gather for dinner each evening at the enormous pine table Libby acquired at an auction in Seattle. Said to have seated a dozen threshers at mealtime in the early 1900s, it now serves the writers who've come to escape the distractions of life, who've come to this nurturing place for the sole purpose of writing.

Not a brick-and-mortar churchgoer, Niall believes that anything done with care and joy is an act of worship; that's why he strives to be a kind presence in people's lives; that's why the cookery and garden at Pines & Quill are his cathedrals. The casual atmosphere of sharing a meal in the spacious kitchen of the main house is conducive to *esprit de corps*—camaraderie.

Every scratch and divot, a history of purpose and bustling activity, reads like braille in the wide, buttery pine boards of the floor in his sanctuary.

With each group of writers in residence, Libby and Niall nod to each other under copper-bottomed pots that hang from the ceiling. In over thirty years of marriage, they've built an extensive repertoire of facial expressions that only they're privy to the meaning of.

Each month they settle back like satisfied cats washing their whiskers and smile as they watch a small community form, bonds deepening through conversation, as their guests share stories, histories, breakthroughs, and roadblocks, offering advice and feedback, and challenging each other to take risks. This month's group of writers should prove no different.

With its bevy of comfortable, overstuffed chairs, the living room is the after-dinner gathering place for guests to continue visiting over dessert while enjoying drinks from the small, but well-stocked main house bar, The Ink Well. The floor-to-ceiling bookshelves and massive fieldstone fireplace serve as an ideal focal point. The large mirror above the mantel gathers the entire room in its reflection.

The retreat's journal is housed in this community space; a journal in which each guest is invited to make notations during their stay. With entries dating from its inception in 1980, the Pines & Quill journal is a living legacy, a way for writers to connect with those who have come before, and those who will come after. And on more than one occasion, it's served as a way-shower, yielding clues that helped solve mysterious occurrences at this writer's haven over the years.

Between nonfiction and fiction, every possible genre has been penned here. From biography to self-help, and everything in-between: romance, business, humor, science fiction, children and young adult, political, crime, screenplays, essay, poetry, fantasy, history, and mystery. Dedicated writers come to Pines & Quill to gift themselves with time and space, to let go and connect with nature's muse, to find their creative rhythm, and to write about the many intersections of human activity, both real and imagined.

Seated on the periphery of Bellingham, a spot where urban civilization adjoins agriculture and wooded wilderness, this writing refuge is comprised of fog-kissed bluffs, great horned owls and red-tailed hawks, winding paths, solitude, and the blissful absence of noise, demands, and chores, an ideal place for contemplating many things.

In addition to Niall's gourmet cooking, another popular feature at Pines & Quill is Libby's movement meditation sessions—tai chi—a misty morning offering that many guests avail themselves of as a wonderful way to prime the pump for a productive day of writing.

"Niall, I'll take the ATV and put fresh linen in each of the cottages while you start prepping for dinner." With its rugged stance, canopied top, and knobby tires, their all-terrain vehicle is invaluable for getting around the property, regardless of the weather.

"Hemingway, you stay in the mudroom, I don't want muddy paw prints on the kitchen floor. Maybe you should leave your shoes there too," Libby says, pointedly gazing down at Niall's mud-crusted boots.

A cross between a utility room and a large walk-in closet, the mudroom is separated from the spacious, well-appointed kitchen by a Dutch door. Divided horizontally into two half doors, it allows either half to be left open or closed. The mudroom is the place where the MacCullough's stow outerwear, boots, and anything else they might need when venturing out-side, including Hemingway. It also houses his food and water bowls, leash, and bed.

Most people prefer not to have a curious, tail-wagging, pony-sized dog in their midst while eating, so they close the bottom, leaving the top portion of the Dutch door open during meals. This allows Hemingway to pop his head over—with its awning eyebrows and mop-like beard—and still be part of the gatherings without being in their midst.

Libby lifts her face skyward to feel the warmth of the elusory sun before heading north to Dickens cottage first. She smiles when she sees a weathered Adirondack chair on its covered front porch. A writer herself, she knows the value of not being confined, of being able to move around, and that nature's breath, fresh air, is an encouraging muse.

With this in mind, during the planning phase, she ensured that the porch of each cottage—Dickens, Brontë, Austen, and Thoreau—has ample space for quiet reflection. A handcrafted, bent-willow chair with a deep seat, the graceful lines of its arms open in welcome, and plump pillows is ready to receive a weary back at the end of a productive day of writing.

After making the beds with crisp, clean linens and setting out fresh towels and washcloths in each cottage's bath and kitchen area, Libby leaves a cheerful monogrammed notecard with P&Q, Pines & Quill's initials, on each kitchen counter. Inside is printed:

> *Pines & Quill offers writers a peaceful, inspiring, wooded setting in which to pursue the work they love. We aim to encourage artistic exploration, nurture creative thought, and forge bonds between diverse thinkers. Our vision is for you to find inspiration and make progress on your work.*

*Located between the main house and the garden
is a common area that includes laundry facilities and
supplies, a printer and paper, and assorted office supplies should you need them. There are also bicycles
with covered saddle-baskets if you feel adventurous
and would like to explore the surrounding area or
pick up sundries in town. Each basket contains a
map of the town, a brisk fifteen-minute walk, or a
five-minute bicycle ride from Pines & Quill.*

Satisfied that everything's in place for the arrival of their
guests, Libby returns to the main house under a saturated blue
sky dotted with white cushions of clouds.

CHAPTER 3

"My writing is a process of rewriting, of going back and changing and filling in. In the rewriting process you discover what's going on, and you go back and bring it up to that point."

—Joan Didion

Mick parked in Sea-Tac's area reserved for handicap pickup. He's thankful he doesn't have to jockey for position in the much busier central arrival section. After pulling curbside, he pushes a button, and both side panels of the van slide open for the waiting guests.

The MacCullough's had the body of their vehicle modified to offer three entry points and a rear lift-gate for wheelchair users. Guests using motorized wheelchairs that doesn't fold have different needs than those who are able to transfer themselves into a vehicle and collapse their chair.

Mick exchanges a glance with Emma, his jet-black eyebrows raise in query. She takes his cue. "Last one in, first one out," she says, rolling her wheelchair back somewhat from the rest of the group.

Without effort, Mick transfers the mountain of baggage from the trolley into the back of the spacious van.

While Jason sizes Mick up—*tall, fit, and strong*—Cynthia folds her willowy frame and eases herself onto the bench seat in the far back.

Fran uses the grip bar and enters the opposite door, sitting next to Cynthia on the smooth, gray leather seat.

"I'll ride up front with you," Jason says looking at Mick, not bothering to help with the baggage.

"That's fine," Mick nods.

The toned muscles of her arms and shoulders make it look easy as Emma transfers herself into the van. Seated behind the driver's seat, she collapses her wheelchair, stowing it in the space to her right.

Mick catches the faintest hint of vanilla and another scent he can't quite put his finger on. *Is it lime?* He looks at Emma in the rearview mirror. Whatever the combination, it wreaks beautiful havoc with his senses.

"Buckle your seatbelts, everyone, we've got a hundred-mile drive ahead of us. It could take a little more than two hours, depending on traffic. At about the mid-way point, Marysville, we'll stop for a few minutes so everyone can stretch, get a breath of fresh air, and use the restroom if needed. Once we arrive at Pines & Quill, dinner will be served within an hour."

Fran asks, "I'm curious to know why you have your guests fly into Sea-Tac in Seattle instead of Bellingham International Airport. Wouldn't it be a much shorter drive for you to pick us up there?"

Curiosity piqued, Emma leans forward a bit. *I wondered that, myself.*

Mick nods. "It sure would. But—" He holds up a finger for dramatic effect. "Experientially, we learned that it's the drive that cements the initial bond between our writers in residence." He smiles at everyone in the rearview mirror before continuing.

"As a captive audience, you get to know each other even before you arrive at the retreat. Added to that, you benefit from enjoying the beautiful scenery while I share a little bit about the surrounding area."

"That makes sense," Fran says, smiling. "Thank you."

When Mick eases the van out from under the enormous cement overhang, they're greeted by a vast arc of blue sky.

"Take a good look at that gorgeous sky," Mick says. "It's not raining. With an average of thirty-eight inches of precipitation a year, it's no wonder Washingtonians refer to rain as 'liquid sunshine.'"

With a look in the rearview mirror, Emma catches his eye and joins his playful banter. "Then it would be accurate to say that Washington is on the *wet* coast instead of the west coast." She throws her head back and laughs at her own joke.

Everyone joins in, except Jason who's looking out the passenger window, focused on the congested traffic on I-5. "Is traffic always this bad?" he asks.

Mick has to brake hard when an SUV swerves in front of their van. The jolt causes Jason's backpack to fall forward on the floor mat, spilling some of the contents. Mick notices him tuck two airplane-sized liquor bottles back in, then zipper the compartment. Brows knit, *I wonder if this guy's a nervous flyer and drinks to take the edge off?*

"Sorry about that," Mick answers, without letting Jason know he saw what spilled. "The traffic in the Seattle area is notorious, but the further north we travel, the better it gets."

Emma, Cynthia, and Fran talk like strangers do, sharing snippets and brief histories, putting the best light on things.

In the front seat, Jason sits quietly, listening for any weak links, noting hesitations and evasions, storing them for future consideration—ammunition. *Though I doubt their stories are anywhere near as fabricated as mine.* He smiles to himself.

Cynthia smiles at Mick's green eyes in the rearview mirror. "Should we be on the lookout for Sasquatch? I understand the Pacific Northwest is rife with them."

"It's true that a large number of Bigfoot sightings have occurred, but they're mostly in the area surrounding Mount St. Helens which is south from here. We're heading north. Pines & Quill is situated among the waters of Bellingham Bay, Mount Baker, and the Snoqualmie National Forest. Our village, Fairhaven, is considered a gateway to the North Cascades National Park."

With a grin, Mick continues, "I think the chances of us seeing a volcano erupt are greater than glimpsing a Sasquatch. Washington state is home to five volcanoes. From north to south they're Mount Baker, Glacier Peak, Mount Rainier, Mount St. Helens, and Mount Adams. These volcanoes, including Mount Hood to the south in Oregon, are part of the Cascade Range, a volcanic arc that stretches from southwestern British Columbia to northern California. The last eruption was in 2008 when Mount St. Helens blew."

Fran joins the conversation. "We'll be going past Seattle, won't we? Can you tell us why it's called the Emerald City?"

Catching her hazel eyes in the rearview mirror, Mick answers, "The city of Seattle lies between two bodies of water, Puget Sound on the west and Lake Washington on the east. In the mid-1980s the city was given the nickname by tourism officials promoting Seattle for its lush, green forests and more than six thousand acres of parks within the city limits."

As the silver van catapults north on Interstate 5, Jason's face is concealed, in part, behind dark aviator glasses. Catlike, he slits open his blasé, yet chilling eyes, keeping to himself while absorbing the conversation.

Every surreptitious forest-green glance Mick takes of Emma in the rearview mirror is met with an equally covert moss-colored glance. Finally, her grin blossoms into a beguiling smile. Contagious, he grins back like a fool.

What the devil's gotten into me? he wonders. *I feel like an enamored teenager, for God's sake.* With that, Mick takes in the snowy white, and dark blond crowns bent together clandestine-like behind Emma. *Cynthia's reading Fran's palm.* He smiles.

Fran can just hear Cynthia's whispered voice. It's warm and somewhat smoky, like oolong tea with a lot of sugar. "Timing is everything," she says. "You need time alone. Time to be quiet. Time to reevaluate. Fran, it seems to me that you're a woman who's allowing herself to be defined by biology."

Cynthia continues studying the map of lines on Fran's outstretched palm. Fran feels reluctant to speak, to draw her guileless brown-green eyes away from her palm nestled in the warm, tanned hands of another.

After a brief stop in Marysville, the conversation in the van turns to the indigenous Indian tribes of Washington. "The Lhaq'temish, the Lummi Nation, are the original inhabitants of Washington's northernmost coast and southern British Columbia," Mick tells them. "For centuries they've worked, struggled, and celebrated life on the shores and waters of Puget Sound. They're a self-governing nation within the United States. The third largest tribe in Washington state, they manage thirteen thousand acres of tidelands on the Lummi Reservation.

"Is it true that Pines & Quill is located on an ancient Indian burial ground?" Emma asks.

Theatrically lowering his ebony eyebrows, and with a melodramatic voice, Mick answers, "We're not on an Indian burial ground, but we do have our share of ghosts. Fairhaven Village was founded in the late 1880s, but it's now part of the city of Bellingham. The Mount Baker Theater is home to a woman, though long dead, who wants nothing more than to watch over her property and its current owners.

"The Shuksan Nursing Home has rooms with moving objects, call-lights going on and off by themselves, and they say that you can hear someone walking with a walker in the middle of the night."

In the rearview mirror, Mick sees a wide-eyed captive audience and continues in a hushed, eerie tone. "The Eldridge Mansion has disembodied voices and screams. People who work at the Old Town Cafe have seen dishes levitate for minutes at a time, then set back down. Some people have even heard piano music, but there's no piano. Others have seen the shadow-thin spirit of a woman looking down at them from a second-floor window.

"In the Sunset Theater, there's an apparition of an old woman who sits in the back of auditorium one, while a child-like waif roams auditoriums three and four. Employees have reported hearing unnerving noises and whispers and experienced cold sensations down by the screen while cleaning when no one's there."

Jason's tension-filled laugh erases the silence in the van. "You're making that up, right?"

In the rearview mirror, Mick sees time-etched tiny crow's feet at the corners of Cynthia's liquid-brown eyes. *She knows I'm not kidding.* And with that, they round a bend and stop at a massive wrought-iron entry gate, its overhead sign silhouetted against the cloudless sky beckoning, *Welcome to Pines & Quill.*

"If you wear a watch, you won't need it," Mick smiles. "The pace of life here is much slower. Libby, my sister, says that 'Time at Pines & Quill passes like a herd of turtles in a jar of peanut butter.'"

The three women laugh.

Mick presses a button on the remote attached to the visor over the driver's seat. The huge gate swings open and the vehicle sensor buzzes in the main house, notifying the occupants that their guests have arrived.

———

Niall turns the burners to simmer and removes his blue-and-white striped bistro apron. "Hemingway, our guests are here. Come on, boy, let's go find Libby."

Although well-traveled, this tranquil location, separated from the rest of the world by a long road and acres of trees, is Mick's favorite on the globe.

He notices the women's appreciation of their forested surroundings and uses the automatic controls to lower their windows as he takes the lengthy drive to the main house, slowing so they can drink in the beauty.

Tall trees flank the smooth road—like soldiers—their canopied shade expansive, with a few rays of light piercing the foliage in certain spots. The effect is mystical. The scent of evergreen fills the van as it glides around familiar curves. It carries with it a certain mellowness that only pines bestow.

At the end of the drive, the trees open into a natural space, and the main house comes into view. The two-story home sits on a gentle rise, accentuated by a large circular drive surrounding low, well-maintained shrubs and bushes.

Jason's gaze sweeps the area, taking everything in, as Mick eases the van into the roundabout. He makes a mental note of the side road off the circle leading to a large garage and what appears to be a workshop. He also notices the nearby, two-car parking space with plantings that integrate it into the landscape.

Casual yet elegant, the drive widens at the front door. It's here that Mick pulls to a stop and activates the sliding side doors on the van. Once open, Niall, Libby, and Hemingway step forward to greet the new arrivals.

Emma stretches out her hand and wiggles her fingers. Hemingway knows an invitation when he sees one. He shifts into a happy, full-body wag and steps to the open van door, plunging his whiskered muzzle into Emma's hand. She tosses her head back in laughter as his cold, wet nose makes contact. "I can see that we're going to be good friends."

Libby steps forward and takes hold of Hemingway's collar with her left hand while extending her right. In a rich, warm voice, like whiskey by a fire, she says, "I'm Libby Mac-Cullough." She nods her head toward Niall, and with a loving smile, continues. "And this is my husband, Niall."

Emma takes her hand. "I'm Emma Benton. It's so nice to meet you both."

"Let me introduce you properly to this big lummox." Libby turns to Hemingway, taps his rump, and says, "Sit." When he does—his wiry tail dusting the ground behind him—she continues, "Good boy. Now give Emma your paw."

Hemingway lifts his massive paw, and Emma takes it in her hand.

"Emma, this is Hemingway. If he becomes a nuisance, just point to the main house and tell him 'go home.' If you're lucky, he'll leave."

"You're like a small horse," Emma says to Hemingway while scratching behind one of his ears, the only unassuming thing about him. Within moments, one of his back legs starts twitching like a rabbit's.

"You've found his spot." Libby laughs. Under awning-like eyebrows, the now-delirious Hemingway's eyes roll back, and his long, pink tongue lolls out the side of his mouth. "You've got a friend for life now."

Cynthia and Fran walk around from the other side of the van. "I didn't know you raise livestock," Cynthia says, appreciating the Irish Wolfhound's massive size.

Libby's eyes regard a white pixie hairstyle, feathered around a face as tan and smooth as a child who plays in the sun. *If I didn't know better, I would have guessed she's yet to see fifty.*

As if reading Libby's thoughts, Cynthia looks into her eyes and smiles.

While Libby introduces herself to the other two women, Mick and Niall shift the luggage to the back of the ATV, and Emma transfers herself with ease from van to wheelchair.

Hemingway takes the opportunity to check out Cynthia and Fran while Emma's hands are busy elsewhere.

Not a fan of dogs, Jason uses this busy moment to exit the van. When he researched Pines & Quill on the internet, he learned about the resident dog. And while he isn't happy with that particular fact, there's nothing he can do about it. At least not yet.

Libby says, "Emma, you're in Austen cottage. Mick, here are the tags for her luggage."

"I won't need tags, sis. Emma's luggage is easy to distinguish from the rest. It's 'Pumpkin Spice,'" he says with exaggerated care, his grin bearing a hint of conspiracy as Emma laughs at their private joke.

Not lost on Libby, she notices the easy banter between her brother and the beautiful young woman.

"Fran, you're in Dickens cottage. Cynthia, you're in Brontë. And Jason—by the way, it's nice to meet you," she steps forward to shake his hand. "You're in Thoreau."

Then she turns and hands Mick the other color-coded luggage tags. "For those who'd like a ride, Mick will give you a lift in the ATV while he takes your luggage to the cottages, or you can come with me on the pathways."

Not wanting to spend any more time near the behemoth dog than he has to, Jason is the first to speak up, "I'd like a ride."

Cynthia chimes in, "I'm a bit travel-weary. I'd enjoy a ride too." *Travel-weary my ass*, Cynthia thinks. *I want to see if I can get more of a read on this guy. Something is wrong. Very wrong.*

"I'd prefer to come with you and get the lay of the land." Emma smiles at Libby while stroking Hemingway's anvil-sized head, now resting on her shoulder.

"If you don't mind, I'd like to join you." Fran smiles at the endearing picture that Emma and Hemingway make.

Niall glances at his watch. "While you folks are getting settled in your new digs, I'll put the finishing touches on dinner. We'll see you back here at six o'clock. That gives you just about an hour to catch your second wind."

Jason settles himself in the ATV. *I wonder if there's any booze in the cottage?*

CHAPTER 4

"Making people believe the unbelievable is no trick; it's work. Belief and reader absorption come in the details: An overturned tricycle in the gutter of an abandoned neighborhood can stand for everything."

—Stephen King

"Fran, Dickens cottage is located on the north end of the property and closest to where we are now, so let's head there first," Libby says, pointing in the distance to a thick curtain of Bigleaf Maple trees. "I think you're going to love it because the quiet is conducive to writing."

For a moment they stop to admire the surroundings in the tranquility of pre-dusk. The tinkling of wind chimes and the rustling of leaves from the breeze through the copse of trees surrounds them.

Fran brings up the rear as they continue. Her heart aches as she watches Emma roll herself forward with ease. *She's trapped in a wheelchair but is freer and more alive than I'll ever be.*

The moment is interrupted by a mighty "WOOF!" Something that looks like a cross between a Highland cow and a wookie barrels toward them through the trees. The muscles in Fran's body clench in fear as her brain scrambles to figure out where she can hide. Before she can move, the beast runs up to Emma, stops on a dime, sits down, and begins wagging its tail. Fran's racing heart slows down, and she laughs, realizing the giant furry thing is Hemingway.

Hands still at her chest, "Oh, my God, he's huge!" Fran exclaims.

Hemingway shakes his wiry head, causing his ears to flap.

"Yes, he's a big lummox," Libby agrees.

———

Emma reaches out her hand toward Hemingway. He moves his head under Emma's fingers so she can scratch behind his ears. "You handsome boy," she coos. When she bends forward, Hemingway moves even closer and leans against Emma's wheelchair.

Fran watches the scene and hopes he won't topple her over. She's sure the dog outweighs both Emma and the wheelchair, combined.

Fran looks up and inhales the earthy fragrance wafting from the forest surrounding them. As they continue toward Dickens cottage, Hemingway in tow, Emma and Fran admire the subtle walk lights that begin to shine along the path.

Libby explains, "All of the pathways at Pines & Quill have solar powered walk lights that come on at dusk and go off when their batteries are depleted. That time differs from day-to-day, depending on the amount of sunlight. We want our guests to feel as comfortable in the evening as they do during the day. Here we are." And with that Libby opens the door for Fran. "If there's anything I've forgotten, please let me know when you come to the main house for dinner. We'll see you at six o'clock."

———

Fran's arrival at Dickens cottage is like slipping into an old photograph of warm sepia tones—chocolate and ecru. The colors of unbleached silk and linen fabrics throughout the small space are welcoming and pleasing to the senses.

She remembers while researching Pines & Quill online that previous guests who'd resided in Dickens cottage wrote of their appreciation of the queen-size bed in the cozy sleeping loft, and the comfortable, overstuffed brown leather chair and ottoman with nailhead trim that welcomed them at day's end. More so, the large, smooth, walnut desk placed beneath a north-facing window, an invitation to survey the cool, quiet woods—Mother Nature's sanctuary.

Fran stands still in the center of the room and takes a deep inhalation. She follows her nose and finds a beautiful glass fragrance diffuser with a handwritten note: *Designed to comfort, the top notes are fresh pine sprigs and mandarin orange, the middle notes are pomegranate and cinnamon, and the base notes are roasted chestnuts and Madagascar vanilla. Enjoy!*

The room's warm embrace envelopes Fran. The walls seemed to whisper, "Come in and stay awhile. You can relax now and let your barriers down." The tension in her stiff shoulders melts, and an unexpected smile perches on her lips. *Libby was right. I'm going to love it here.*

Hand gliding over the smooth surface of the walnut desk, Fran gazes out the window into the woods. The shadows have grown more profound now. The spatters of red and gold giving way to the blues and purples of dusk.

She thinks about how her life has grown small and claustrophobic.

In an article she'd read in an in-flight magazine on the journey from Boston, there was a quote that brought her up short. "Whatever you are not changing, you are choosing."

Just eight little words, but they captured her attention, and she resolves that her time at Pines & Quill will be a catapult to change.

Unfettered, she rakes her fingers through her lacquered hair, the first of many changes to come.

On the way to the west side of the property toward Austen cottage, Emma tells Libby, "I knew that as a wheelchair-friendly facility Pines & Quill would have smooth surfaces, but this is exceptional."

"We learned so much when Mick was in a wheelchair," Libby responds, smiling. "And we've put everything we learned into practice."

Emma looks up in wide-eyed surprise. "Mick was in a wheelchair?"

"Yes, but that's his story to share, not mine. Here we are now."

Nestled in a glade of Blue Elderberry, Austen cottage features womb-like seclusion. Libby gives a hand signal to Hemingway that conveys, "Sit and stay." After he drops to his bottom, she activates a button on the outside wall and the door swings open. "There's a matching button on the inside," Libby says, "but it works manually as well."

Emma rolls up the ramp with ease, continuing right through the extra-wide doorframe.

"Oh my gosh," she exclaims turning around with a face-splitting grin.

But Libby is already stepping out, pulling the door closed with her. "See you at six o'clock," Libby says with a smile in her voice as the door shuts behind her.

Emma loves the welcoming, soft hues of sage and lavender. Her artisan's eye appreciates the wheelchair-friendly design with interior elements spaced for smooth transition. The wood floor reflects the same warm, honeyed tones of a massive beam that runs the length of the structure, parallel with the pitch of the vaulted ceiling.

Something smells delicious. Emma rolls to the kitchen following the scent. On the granite counter she finds a beautiful glass diffuser with a handwritten note: *Designed to enhance creativity, the top note is Caribbean pink grapefruit, the middle note is amber, and the base notes are Jamaican lemon, Tobago lime, and green florals. Enjoy!*

Emma feels warm with welcome. A battered and loved square oak desk with ample clearance space faces sliding glass doors that reveal a smooth-tiled patio of faded terra cotta. Outside the doors a wild profusion of potted flowers greets her. She realizes that with a west-facing view she'll enjoy an ideal vantage point from which to gaze at the sun as it bows farewell, making way for its alluring mistress, the moon.

After sliding the glass door open with ease, Emma wheels out and draws in a deep, invigorating breath. The pre-evening stillness is peaceful, a far cry from the hustle and bustle of San Diego. In the quiet, she hears the hum of a distant boat. From what she read online while researching Pines & Quill, she knows Austen cottage is near the water. If she remembers right, Bellingham Bay, a rather large inlet somewhat protected by Lummi Island, is to the west. *I wonder how close we are to the cliffs that overlook the bay?*

Back inside, canopied by the honeyed tones of the vaulted ceiling, Emma leans against the wheelchair's leather back and exhales, her eyes once again appreciating the soft hues of sage and lavender accents throughout. From the moment she entered the quaint space she loved it, knowing it will be the perfect place to finish her manuscript.

On the east side of the property, Mick pulls the all-terrain vehicle up to Brontë cottage. Like its namesake, Emily Brontë, the cottage is reclusive behind a wall of Douglas Fir trees. Their massive evergreen branches provide an occasional glimpse of light reflected from a window, like a knowing wink.

Mick carries Cynthia's luggage up the steps of Brontë's front porch. "Welcome to your home away from home," he says to Cynthia whose gaze is focused on Jason waiting in the ATV. "Is everything okay?" Mick asks, his forehead creased with concern as he remembers how Jason pulled his hand away from hers at the airport.

"I'm not sure," she responds. To ease his worry, she continues with a smile. "One thing I know for certain, I'm looking forward to dinner."

Setting her luggage inside the door, Mick reminds her, "We eat at six o'clock. Would you like me to pick you up in the ATV?"

"I'll walk, thank you," she says. "See you at dinner."

The wrought-iron spiral staircase leading to a sleeping loft is first to claim Cynthia's attention. She discovers a haven that strikes the ideal balance between Parisian chic and relaxed bohemian romance.

Second to claim her attention is the subtle fragrance flirting with her sense of smell. She follows the scent and finds a beautiful glass diffuser with a handwritten note: *Designed to enhance clarity, the top notes are Sicilian mandarin and Italian bergamot, the middle note is night-blooming Jasmine, and the base note is Tahitian vanilla. Enjoy!*

On the main level, Cynthia gravitates toward a cozy window seat with a thick, inviting, jewel-toned cushion and matching throw pillows of emerald, ruby, and sapphire. *How did Libby know those are my favorite scents and that I favor jewel tones? Is she an intuitive too?*

Cynthia's eyes feast on the gem-toned palette as she admires the beautiful space. She stops, crosses her arms and hugs herself. With a bow at the waist, she slips off her shoes and flexes her toes. After taking a deep inhalation, she returns to her full height, sways from sole to sole, and then executes a flawless pirouette, made all the more beautiful because of her tall, willowy frame.

In an east-facing pose, she curtsies toward a work-worn desk hugging the wall beneath a massive window. A proponent of supporting local artisans, one of Libby's favorite pieces—"A statement piece," she'd explained to Niall—sits on the wide windowsill. Created by a native glassblower, it's made from cast-iron and five transparent, gem-toned glass bottles that hang from hooks: carnelian, ruby, citrine, peridot, and turquoise.

Cynthia knows she'll rise at daybreak for the next three weeks to watch the sun's fingers grip the horizon and pull itself into the morning sky. Its natural mandala of inspiration is sure to stir her creative juices and not only help her complete the manuscript, but serve to lift the heaviness of her responsibilities as an intuitive consultant for law enforcement—even if temporarily.

Located on the south end of the property, one has to know where they're looking to glimpse Thoreau cottage. A double-take is in order because, by all appearances, it seems to have sprouted amongst the Western Red Cedar woods that surround it. Not much bigger than Henry David Thoreau's cabin on Walden Pond, it's the epitome of minimalism—simple, yet full—in natural surroundings.

"Thanks for the lift," Jason says, hopping off the ATV before it comes to a full stop. "I got this," he says, grabbing his luggage.

"Would you like me to pick you up for dinner?"

"No. I'll walk," Jason says over his shoulder, heading to the cottage door.

———

The moment Jason steps inside he freezes in his tracks. *Mother,* he thinks, lip curled in repulsion. He drops his luggage, steps in further, and shuts the door behind him. *It smells like Mother.* Disgusted, he sets out to find the source. It doesn't take long to find the odd glass container sitting on the kitchen counter accompanied by a handwritten note: *Designed to calm, the top notes are Moroccan amber and sweet patchouli, the middle note is heliotrope, and the base notes are bergamot and euca-lyptus. Enjoy!*

Patchouli. Jason hates that smell. His mother reeked of the stuff.

Before opening the door, he looks out the window to make sure McPherson is nowhere in sight. He steps out and rounds the corner of the cabin. When he reaches the steep drop-off to a canyon, Jason chucks the bottle as far as he can. *Designed to calm,* he sneers to himself. *What a crock of shit!*

Back inside, he takes in his surroundings. The fact that the furnishings are handcrafted pieces from a local woodworker, and that each creation is polished to accentuate its natural character and beauty, is lost on him. When she decorated the interior, Libby intended to convey the idea that "less is more." She designed the room to say, "Since you can't hide from yourself in a space this size, you might as well sit down and write."

The minimal nod to extravagance in Thoreau cottage is the south-facing wall, constructed entirely of glass. It frames a breathtaking view of the Bellingham Bay National Park and Reserve, home to *El Cañón del Diablo*—The Devil's Canyon. So named because of the boulder field at the bottom of a hundred foot rock wall. As for the caves, they're the nooks and crannies between the boulders and home to Townsend's big-eared bats.

This is the perfect location for what I've come to do. Elegant in its simplicity, inessentials had been trimmed away, leaving functionality. And although emotionally stingy, even Jason isn't immune to the breathtaking southern view. This bird's-eye perspective of a national park is beautiful, and should it become necessary, a quick sprint will provide safe hiding with its wooded, boulder-laden and sloping terrain leading to the canyon base. *If something's worth doing, it's worth doing well.* He smiles to himself like a Cheshire cat. *And I've done my homework.*

Jason settles himself in a chair facing the wall of glass and sets the suitcase across his lap. He feels a surge of exhilaration as tooth by tooth, he unzips it. It contains his keepsakes, sweet memories of power and total subjugation. He lifts the lid, drawing a deep breath of anticipation. He caresses the top two towels, their memories bring a swelling wave of pleasure. The soft leather chair back supports his head as he loses himself in thought, replaying his most recent conquest in his mind's eye.

He sees himself standing behind the shower curtain in room 414, holding his breath when he hears a knock—*tap, tap, tap*—followed by a voice calling out, "Housekeeping." Familiar with the routine, five seconds tick by before a louder knock—*tap, tap, tap*. Again, the call of "Housekeeping," followed by the sound of a keycard releasing the lock and a housekeeping cart being maneuvered. Knife fisted in his right hand, his heart races in anticipation.

And there it is. The look of sheer terror on her face as he pulls the curtain back when she straightens from collecting the liner in the bathroom trash can. He pushes the door shut, steps out of the tub and covers her mouth, turning the frantic, struggling woman toward the mirror. In the reflection, he reads "Devi" printed on a name badge pinned above her left breast. With the knife pressed at her throat, he whispers in her ear, "Devi, you get to watch and enjoy this as much as me."

A sudden ripple in the air breaks his reverie. Jason's muscles tighten. Ready to run, he looks behind him.

Nothing.

He closes his eyes and shakes his head to clear it. His knees almost buckle in relief. *All that talk about ghosts has me spooked.*

Jason wants a drink. No, he *needs* a drink.

A quick forage through the kitchen cupboards and refrigerator reveal the absence of alcohol. He'll remedy that on his first trip into town. For now, he heads up to the main house to gather information about Mick and to enjoy a before-dinner drink, or *apéritif,* as his mother liked to call their evening ritual. *Poor dead Mom,* he thinks, a self-satisfied smirk claiming his features. *There are so many ways to hurt women.*

CHAPTER 5

"The most important thing is to read as much as you can, like I did. It will give you an understanding of what makes good writing and it will enlarge your vocabulary."

—J.K. Rowling

Instead of heading straight to the main house, Jason takes a circuitous route to investigate the other cottages. Each one is surrounded by a copse of trees. His own cottage, Thoreau, is encompassed by Western Red Cedar trees. Brontë, Cynthia's cottage, is circled by Douglas Fir. Austen, Emma's cottage, is enclosed by Blue Elderberry trees. And Dickens, Fran's cottage, is surrounded by Bigleaf Maples.

Other than on the pathways, the forest floor is covered with lush maidenhair ferns. And while the wooded area provides the writers in residence with privacy, it also gives Jason camouflage. After noting the location of windows, doors, and each cottage's unique surroundings, he brushes bits of fern from his shirt sleeves and pant legs. At five minutes 'til six, Jason arrives at the main house.

Niall meets him at the front door and extends his hand. "Please come in, dinner will be ready soon. I'm headed back to the kitchen," he says over his shoulder. "Follow me, what can I get you?"

"It's been a long day. I'd like something on the strong side. Scotch and water."

"Make yourself at home, I'll be back in a moment," Niall says, turning toward The Ink Well, their living room and in-home bar.

Hemingway, observing their exchange from behind the Dutch door in the kitchen, lets loose a deep-throated growl.

Surprised by Hemingway's unusual behavior, Niall says, "Knock that off, big fella. You know we don't allow that kind of talk around here."

"I'll come with you," Jason interjects, throwing an icy-gray glare at Hemingway before following Niall. "By the way, I'm expecting two UPS packages tomorrow. I shipped my manuscript because I didn't want to lug it with me on the flight. I hope that's not a problem."

That's odd, Niall thinks. *It's been years since a writer brought a physical copy of their manuscript with them. The authors who stay at Pines & Quill bring their work on laptops.*

Seeming to read his mind, Jason continues, "I know it's a bit old school, but that's the method that works best for me; give me paper and a red pen for editing any day," he finishes with a smile that doesn't quite reach his eyes.

"No problem at all," Niall says, pouring two fingers of scotch into a whiskey glass and adding a cube of ice instead of pouring water in. "Let the ice melt. It provides the ideal amount of time to unlock the aromas and flavors."

Niall's advice goes ignored as Jason tosses back the drink. Then comes the obligatory grimace and purse of the lips. His eyes seem to melt a little, and his jaw relaxes as he extends his glass for another.

———

Fran and Cynthia arrive at the main house together. They climb the broad stone steps to the rustic, paneled oak door. Both women have changed from their travel clothes—Cynthia, into a sweeping marine-blue dress, its skirt creating beautiful movement with each step, Fran into a circumspect gray blazer and matching slacks made less rigid by her soft-combed hair and a touch of pink lipstick.

"I like what you've done to your hair," Cynthia says.

"Thank you." Fran beams at the compliment while Cynthia uses the heavy brass knocker that's polished to a subtle glow. Within moments, the big door is opened by Libby.

"Welcome to our home," she greets them with a warm smile. Libby steps back into the gracious foyer, inviting them into the casual elegance of the main house. "Niall says dinner's almost ready. Let's head back to the kitchen."

The aroma of grilled salmon mingled with mysterious spices teases their nostrils as they walk along gleaming hardwood floors, passing rooms on either side that feature wide windows boasting beautiful views. On the way to the kitchen, a dusk-filled, west-facing terrace leads to a garden of native plants where subtle uplighting exposes a handful of colorful birdhouses crafted by local artisans. The women stop and watch the sun bid its final farewell, casting deep purple shadows amidst vivid wildflowers sprinkled throughout.

When they arrive at the massive eat-in kitchen, both Fran and Cynthia appreciate the cathedral ceiling and large picture window with a southern exposure.

"Welcome to my domain," an apron-clad Niall greets them, bowing at the waist.

"This is where all of the culinary magic takes place," Libby adds. Pointing to the picture window that Fran and Cynthia are admiring, she continues, "When it's daylight, you'll be able to see Niall's garden. Much of the food he pre-pares comes from right here. The rest he sources locally."

In spite of his limp, Mick strides along the pathway toward the main house. Up ahead, he spots Emma's auburn hair caping her shoulders in silken sheaths. "Hey, wait up," he calls, pretending to be out of breath. "You're hard to catch, may I join you?"

"I'd like that," Emma says. "And your company ensures I won't get lost. That wouldn't be good, because I'm raven-ous." She laughs up into Mick's deep green eyes.

Mick leads Emma to the country kitchen where polished cutlery flanks sangria-red plates. Her artistic eye notices the hand-painted serving pieces. Swirls of sage and ochre in the gleaming stemware complement the glazed dinnerware. *Old-world style.* She smiles. *I love it.*

Hemingway's tail shifts into propeller mode letting God and everyone know that Emma's arrival hasn't gone unnoticed by him.

Emma rolls her wheelchair over to give Hemingway a scratch under his bearded chin. "Hello, handsome," she says. He stretches his neck further over the lower half of the Dutch door. "May I give him a biscuit?" she asks Niall, eyeing the clear container set out of Hemingway's reach.

"Yes, you may give the lummox one cookie," Niall answers from in front of the stove where he's stirring something that smells delicious. "Did you hear that, Hemingway? I said one. O-N-E." Niall spells it out for emphasis.

When Emma joins the others, she takes the opportunity to study the siblings, Libby and Mick.

Libby's shoulder-length hair, a captivating shade of sable with a few strands of silver, is tucked behind ears adorned with hammered-silver hoops. A silver necklace studded with moonstones lay on the neckline of her turquoise top, and a matching bracelet circles her wrist.

Emma turns her head to observe Mick, who's speaking with Fran and Cynthia. She takes in his striking green eyes and a cheeky little quirk in the corner of his close-lipped smile. A few silver threads at his temples looks distinctive in his otherwise jet-black hair. Emma's heart accelerates in appreciation for the way his body enhances his pristine white shirt and smart dark gray trousers.

Mick's gaze changes direction, catching Emma's. In her eyes, he sees undeniable appreciation.

Emma smiles, noting that the resemblance between brother and sister is strong, but there are striking differences. Unlike Libby's straight, delicate nose and flawless facial features, Mick's nose is crooked, making him look rakish. A thin scar creases his forehead at an angle, from his hairline down through his left eyebrow. Both imperfections compliment his square jaw and chiseled features.

Glass in hand, Jason stands near the others with studied casualness, appreciating two of his favorite things, alcohol and listening for information he can use to his advantage.

Behind the lower portion of the Dutch door, Hemingway watches with unveiled interest.

"Dinner's ready," Niall announces, adding two more covered dishes to the already-laden table. "Belly up to the bar, or table as the case may be."

Libby, adept at breaking the ice, primes the pump for conversation while Niall serves the meal. An author herself, she knows that part of a writer's job is reading. Turning to Cynthia, she asks, "What book are you reading?" Then she sits back in satisfaction as each person, in turn, shares their current book.

Niall takes great pleasure in pairing a vivid and citrusy chardonnay with dinner. After a toast to "Inspiration and the flow of creativity," they begin their meal. Between the *ooh's* and *aah's* of enthusiastic appreciation for the grilled salmon with mustard and crisp potato crust, steamed asparagus drizzled with lemon butter, garden-fresh organic salad, and aromatic garlic bread—homemade this morning—Libby orchestrates the conversation with ease. "If you were stranded on a desert island," she asks, "and can only have one book, which book would it be?" She smiles at the resulting avalanche of animated conversation.

Fran can't remember the last time she enjoyed a meal this much. "Niall, did you make the dressing, too? It's delicious!"

Niall smiles at Fran, who, to his way of thinking, is too pale and too thin. "Yes. It's barrel-aged balsamic vinegar blended with pomegranate-infused olive oil. I'm glad you enjoy it."

Fran continues, turning to Libby, "And I wanted to thank you for the beautiful scent you put in Dickens cottage. I love it. Did you blend it yourself?"

Before Libby can answer, Emma and Cynthia chime in, thanking her for the fragrance in their cottages, too.

"I'm glad you enjoy them," Libby says, smiling at the women. "I found the infusers at a local shop that carries a variety of handblown glass. And yes, I dabble a bit with essential oils. I couldn't resist."

Curiosity piqued, Fran asks, "Do we all have the same scent or are they different?"

"I try to create a unique blend for each writer in residence based on our email or phone conversations," Libby answers.

"You're right on target with mine," Emma says. "It's blended for creativity."

"Mine's blended for clarity." Cynthia smiles.

"And mine for comfort," Fran adds, a hint of pink touching her cheeks.

If it seems strange that Jason doesn't say a word about the scent in his cottage, no one mentions it.

Around the table, with strains of James Taylor singing "Carolina in My Mind" in the background, the formalities begin to slip away. The conversation expands and contracts, voices rise and fall, and faces flush with the exhilaration of the discussion and the wine.

Niall, the epitome of efficiency, interjects, "Okay, everyone, it's time to adjourn to The Ink Well. I'll join you soon."

"Thank you for the exquisite meal. I'm stuffed," Emma says, patting her stomach for emphasis.

"Yes, thank you," Cynthia and Fran say in unison, then look at each other and laugh.

Jason still doesn't chime in.

Does the man have no couth? Cynthia wonders. And though no one else seems to find it odd, she's on high alert for his glaring omissions. *Something is amiss.*

Jason watches Niall scrape some leftover scraps into Hemingway's bowl, observing how the dog devours what's put in front of it. "That dog's got a hearty appetite," he says to Niall.

"This fella will eat anything." Niall laughs. "And lots of it."

Before they adjourn to The Ink Well, Jason decides, *I'm going to poison that beast,* then wipes his mouth with a napkin to cover his smile.

CHAPTER 6

"All readers come to fiction as willing accomplices
to your lies. Such is the basic goodwill contract
made the moment we pick up a work of fiction."
— STEVE ALMOND

The living room, with floor-to-ceiling bookshelves on either side of the massive fieldstone fireplace, serves as the after-dinner gathering place for guests to continue visiting over dessert while enjoying drinks from the MacCullough's small, but well-stocked bar.

With her appetite satisfied, Emma surveys the large cozy room, enjoying its welcoming ambiance.

Mick notices red toenails peeking out of her sandals. The deep olive-green tone in the medallion pattern on her dress is a perfect foil for her dark auburn hair. That she tucks phantom strands behind her ears makes him smile. That, and the fact that the soft fabric of her dress caresses her curves.

"Didn't I read something online about a special journal?" Emma asks.

"Yes, you did." Libby walks to a thick book on an oak stand, rests her hand on the open page and continues, "We encourage guests to make entries during their stay. We have entries dating from 1980 when Pines & Quill opened its doors. It's become somewhat of a living legacy, a way for writers to connect with those who've come before, and those who'll come after."

From a deep leather chair, Fran asks, "And if memory serves me well, didn't it also say that on more than one occasion the journal has provided clues that were helpful in solving mysteries that occurred here?"

Jason, who seldom misses an opportunity for a negative barb or a cynical thrust, holds his tongue. *I don't remember reading about that.*

"That's right, Hemingway too," Libby says, smiling at Fran. "Snoopy as all get out, he's our resident Sherlock Holmes. But we'll share those stories another evening. I'm curious to know what each of you is working on." Directing her question at Jason, she asks, "What is your book about?"

Adept at redesigning the truth to fit the occasion, Jason answers, his words not quite slurred. "I was a limousine driver in The Big Apple for years, and the stories I can tell would curl your hair. My book is titled, *Rearview Mirror: Reflections of a New York Limo Driver.*"

"That sounds like an interesting read," they all agree.

"Do you share stories about famous people?" Emma asks.

Though sitting down, Jason's voice has a distinct swagger. "Sure. It's going to be a tell-all." He raises his glass high and swirls it before downing the rest.

"You've got something on your elbow." Emma points to the fern leaf she noticed on Jason's right elbow when he lifted his glass. "You must have taken the scenic route," she says, smiling.

Heads turn in unison when Niall enters the room with a large, dessert-filled tray. "Can I interest anyone in some crème brûlée?"

"I'm going to have to jog in the morning," Cynthia says, taking a colorful ramekin from the proffered tray.

"You offer tai chi classes in the morning, right?" Fran asks Libby in a hopeful voice, as she, too, accepts a calorie-laden dessert.

Emma moans as she lifts a ramekin from the tray. "If it went to my arms, I'd be okay. They get worked out on a regular basis. But this is going straight to my hips," she says, laughing.

"I'll pass on the dessert, but I'll take another scotch," Jason says.

Niall and Libby exchange glances. Libby says, "I'll pour you a short one, and then the bar's closed for the evening."

The look that passes between Niall and Libby doesn't go unnoticed by Cynthia.

Mick accepts a crème brûlée from Niall, knowing from experience that it's delicious. He doesn't worry about weight gain because he makes daily use of the workout equipment in his cabin. Mick looks into Emma's moss-green eyes and asks, "What's your manuscript about?"

"The working title is *Moving Violations: A Sassy Look at Life from a Wheelchair.* It's about observations I've made since finding myself in this chair." She pats the top of a wheel before taking a spoonful of the delicious dessert. After an appreciative moan, she returns Mick's question. "Do you have a work in progress?"

Mick clears his throat. "Yes, I've been working on it for some time now, and it seems to be going nowhere fast. It's titled, *Collateral Damage: Incidental Devastation,* but it's been years on the back burner."

"I noticed your limp." Jason's words have a faint slur. His fingers roll the edge of his cocktail napkin. "Is your book based on personal experience?"

In the now-quiet room, they can hear the wind-muffled sound of the distant surf.

"Yes," Mick answers. "Although it's a work of fiction, it's based on true events." The steel in his measured response warns Libby.

Accompanied by cold, gray eyes, Jason asks, "What are those events?"

Mick interlocks his fingers to avoid clenching his fists.

Aware of imminent disaster, Libby shifts gears, pretending she hadn't heard Jason's rude question. "Cynthia, what are you working on?"

Cynthia accepts the verbal baton with grace. "As a palm reader, I can tell you there aren't too many books that address that topic. I'm working on a book titled, *Guide Lines: The World In the Palm of Your Hands.*"

"That's an intriguing title," Emma says. "I've read that a book has less than thirty seconds to grab a reader's interest. Your title will do it."

"What are you working on?" Libby asks Fran.

Fran's soft words are directed onto her lap. "My manuscript is titled, *Mother in Waiting: The Stigma of Childlessness.* I want to share the lessons I've learned from my personal experience and how they've changed the way I see the world. And by extension, change the way the reader sees the world— for the better."

"That's a wonderful and worthy goal," Libby says, smiling at Fran. "And to help us all with our tasks at hand," she turns to the side table and lifts a small box, "I've brought *The Observation Deck: A Tool Kit for Writers* by Naomi Epel. I find it helpful in priming the writing pump."

"How does it work?" Emma asks.

"Most writers tailor it to their own needs, but at Pines & Quill, each evening after dinner, when we gather in The Ink Well to decompress, one of the guests draws a single card from the box. There are dozens to choose from. Each flash card contains a word or phrase that will be our focus—food for thought—for the next day's writing." Handing the box to Emma, she says, "You select the first card."

Emma picks a card from the middle of the deck.

"What does it say?" Fran asks.

"It says 'Flip it Over.'" With brows scrunched together, Emma turns to Libby and asks, "What does that mean?"

Libby opens the accompanying book, finds the correct page and begins reading. "It says, 'Jog yourself out of a rut by turning things around and doing something different. You don't need to make these changes permanent. Tomorrow you can return to your old routine, refreshed.

"'The opening chapter of *Midnight in the Garden of Good and Evil* was originally chapter nine. Chapter one became chapter two when John Berendt realized that he couldn't wait until the middle of the book to introduce the murderer, Jim Williams.

"'Truman Capote began writing *Answered Prayers* with what he thought would be the last chapter. He then wrote the first, fifth, and seventh chapters, claiming he was able to keep the threads of the plot straight only because he knew how each story ended in real life.

"'Phillip Roth told the *Paris Review*, 'For all I know I am beginning with the ending. My page one can wind up a year later as page two hundred, if it's around at all.'"

Libby looks up smiling. "There's more, but you get the idea. Start anywhere, just start."

"I like it," Cynthia says. "I can see how having a focus word would be helpful."

"Are the rest of you game?" Libby asks the room at large.

"Bring it on," Mick says, laughing.

"How about you, Jason?"

"Sure," he says, with a tight smile and curt nod. "Count me in."

Niall enters The Ink Well with a dish towel draped over his shoulder and Hemingway at his side. "Okay, everyone, you rise at the butt-crack of dawn tomorrow so you may want to get some shut-eye."

Emma bursts out laughing. "The butt-crack of dawn?"

After rolling her eyes at Niall, Libby explains, "For those of you who are interested in tai chi lessons, I'll see you at the pavilion at six-thirty. It's located on the east side of the property between Cynthia's cottage and Mick's cabin. If you walk toward the sunrise, you can't miss it."

Through exaggerated moans and groans at the suggested hour, the guests make their way to the front door.

"Good night, everyone. We'll see you in the morning," Libby says.

Jason breaks away from the others and appears to head toward Thoreau cottage. *Maybe not everyone.*

CHAPTER 7

"You learn to write the same way you learn to play golf . . . You do it, and keep doing it until you get it right. A lot of people think something mystical happens to you, that maybe the muse kisses you on the ear. But writing isn't divinely inspired—it's hard work."

—Tom Clancy

On her way to Austen cottage, Emma pauses to admire the night sky scattered with sparkling stars. She revels in the crisp air, inhaling the myriad of night scents before continuing. She hears the soft lap of water against the shore in the far distance and the call of the brown Barred Owl overhead. *"Who cooks for you? Who cooks for you?"* it seems to ask. When she arrives at her cottage, she rolls up the ramp, pushes the door-activation button, and smiles when it opens on a whisper.

After changing into her nightgown, Emma sets her toothbrush, toothpaste, and floss on the counter and prepares for her evening challenge—practicing standing and leaning against the sink long enough to brush and floss her teeth. Even though her legs shake from the effort, Emma smiles at herself in the mirror because she knows that means her muscles are hard at work. A little cocky now, she leans away from the counter, but grabs it again when she begins to tip.

That's okay, she thinks, sitting back down. *I'm further today than I was yesterday, and I'll be further tomorrow than I am today.* On that positive note, she pulls her hair up into a ponytail, and washes her face.

Emma wheels herself to the bed, pulls back the downy covers, transfers herself into the crisp linens and folds her wheelchair, slipping it next to the nightstand. With an air of contentment, she picks up the book she'd placed there earlier, leans back into the plush pillows, and begins to read.

"Niall, Hemingway and I'll take out the trash and make the rounds tonight. I need to clear the cobwebs in my head, and this big galoot could use the exercise." Mick teases the tall, lean dog, tousling the wiry hair on his head. "If he wants, I'll let him stay the night at my place. He makes pretty good company."

Hemingway shows his agreement with a near table-clearing wag of his tail.

"All right already, I'm coming." Mick laughs. With a bag of trash in either hand, he and his excited, four-legged companion leave through the mudroom. At this late hour, the temperature has dropped, the cooler causing a mist that swallows Hemingway's tall frame in the distance.

After depositing the trash in the raccoon-proof bin, Mick follows the pathway north to check on Dickens cottage. No light, not even a glimmer, pierces the tall curtain of Bigleaf Maples. *Fran must already be asleep.*

Little does he know that she's lying in bed, determined to ask Cynthia to go clothes shopping with her. After the palm-reading session and their whispered conversation on the drive from the airport, Fran knows this three-week retreat is going to be about more than writing a book. It's going to be a turning point in her life.

———

Where the heck is that dog? He's usually right by my side. The luminous mist slides ghostlike past the walkway lights as Mick continues. With a soft whistle and a pat on his thigh, he calls "Here boy, come on." He stops to listen and hears a woman's laugh. Faster now, he moves along the pathway and sees light streaming from the windows and open doorway of Austen cottage—Emma's cottage. "Oh no." He murmurs. "Hemingway's let himself in."

At the front door, Mick stops short. Through the open bedroom doorway, he sees Emma. Propped up in bed with her hair pulled up in a high ponytail, big moss-colored eyes, and the smattering of freckles across the bridge of her nose, Emma looks about twelve years old except he sees the enticing curves of her body. He'd have to be dead to miss those.

Hemingway knows Mick's there, but Emma—face now buried in his long, well-arched neck asking him how he got in—hasn't seen him. *She's beautiful.*

"Ahem." Mick coughs into his hand, not wanting to startle her.

Emma's head comes bolt upright. "Oh my goodness, you scared me!" She places a hand on her palpitating heart.

"I'm sorry, I didn't mean to. I'm also sorry that Hemingway barged in on you."

Hemingway's thick tail thumps like an overactive metronome at their exchange.

"We were just discussing that," Emma says, stroking the lanky dog's wiry coat. She turns to Hemingway. "I haven't figured out how you got in here, mister." Her impish grin tears Mick's insides, making something crack open.

Mick slips off his shoes and socks and steps inside the cottage. A cool snake of evening air wraps around his ankles. As he walks toward her, he nods toward Emma's wheelchair folded next to the nightstand. "May I sit down?"

"Sure," she says, smiling with appreciation as she watches him open the chair with expertise.

The vision that meets his eyes is breathtaking. Propped by a mountain of pillows in the sage-colored bedding, auburn hair shimmering in the lamplight that casts its glow across the now-forgotten book she'd been reading, Emma returns his look with inquisitive eyes.

Hemingway, satisfied they're going to stay a while, lays on the floor next to the bed and rests his bearded chin on top of his massive front paws.

"I lived in this cottage while recuperating from an accident," Mick says. "From puppyhood, as soon as he was tall enough, Niall taught Hemingway how to operate the door-activation button with his nose. He came and went as he pleased. It's obvious he's smitten with you." *He's not the only one.*

"Please tell me about your accident. What happened?" Emma asks.

Mick turns his pained expression toward the sliding glass doors and rubs the back of his neck as if reliving the fatal impact. Minutes pass lost in contemplation.

Emma waits in companionable silence while he gathers his thoughts.

"Five years ago, I was on the police force. Sam, my partner and I, were in a high-speed chase. We'd just radioed for backup when our windshield shattered. Sam lost control of the squad car, and we smashed head-on into a bridge embankment.

"When I came out of a coma a few weeks later, the first thing I learned was that Sam had been shot between the eyes by a sniper from the bridge. We'd been partners for over five years. He left behind a wife and two small children. The second thing I learned was that I was paralyzed, but they couldn't know the extent of the damage until I was conscious and could go through a battery of tests."

"Oh, my God," Emma whispers, pressing a hand against her throat. "Did they ever find the person who shot Sam? Did they ever find out *why* he was shot? I can't begin to imagine the heartbreak for Sam's wife and family, and then what you went through. But you're out of a wheelchair now, how did that happen?"

"The accident initiated a widespread response from law enforcement agencies and an exhaustive manhunt. A special crime unit followed hundreds of tips that failed to produce solid leads. As time wore on, the search scaled down and dwindled to nothing. Sam's assassin was never found.

"As it turns out, it wasn't Sam—specifically—that the elusive sniper was after. He could have shot *any* police officer. The high-speed car chase was a diversionary tactic to draw a squad car to the bridge so that a police officer could be killed. The sniper took out the driver, Sam. I was the collateral damage."

"The title of your book," Emma whispers in understanding as her moss-green eyes melt with emotion.

Mick nods and continues. "When backup arrived on the scene, they called in 'Officer down!' drawing just about every law enforcement officer on duty and within radio range. Not only police officers on patrol, but also deputy sheriffs, showing a united front and turning up even though the location is out of their jurisdiction.

"With an almost-empty stationhouse, a huge cache of heroin that had been seized from an expansive crime-ring bust was stolen out of lockup. The street value was well over ten million dollars.

"That seven-month investigation culminated in the arrest of eleven people, including one of two ringleaders. Fraternal twins. Since then, three of the eleven have died in jail. One was killed in the yard, another in the cafeteria, and a third, one of the twins, was found hanging in his cell. From the bruising and other marks on his body, it doesn't appear to be suicide.

"The brothers' rap sheets are a mile long. The charges include murder, aggravated assault, and conspiracy to transport, sell, and dispose of firearms. Added to that there's failure to appear, witness tampering, conspiracy to possess and distribute a variety of drugs including heroin and cocaine, and conspiracy to organize, finance, and manage a narcotics trafficking network.

"What makes this even more difficult is that the remaining twin is unknown. Their birth records were destroyed, and there are no fingerprints or DNA for him on file.

"The undercover operation determined that no one on the outside could have orchestrated this by themselves. They had to have help from the inside—a dirty cop. Unfortunately, the case has gone cold."

To lighten the mood, Mick pretends to look around, then slides Emma a sideways glance. In mock warning, he whispers, "I know you think that Libby and Niall are sweet, loving, kind, and thoughtful people. But let me tell you, they moved heaven, earth, and a little bit of hell, to get me well again. Sometimes their methods were downright vicious."

His voice returns to normal. "But as Libby will tell you, it's because I deserved it. They told me that I not only wallowed in my sorrow, but I also wasn't as cooperative as I could have been." He gives Emma a sheepish grin.

"Libby assures me that working and living here in the 'Zen-like energy,'" he says, making air quotes with his hands, "of Pines & Quill is therapeutic. Don't tell her, or I'll never hear the end of it, but it's breathed life back into my soul. Now it's your turn. Tell me your story."

Emma looks into Mick's eyes, a darker shade now, forest green. They'd changed with the low light of the evening. "I'm a potter. Last year I showed my work at a two-day, outdoor event. Because pottery is so heavy, my best friend, Sally, helped me pack all of the materials in and back out of the venue. My dad and brothers were on their annual fishing trip in Canada, or they would have done it. After the event, Sally and I lugged the boxes back into my studio, ate Chinese takeout, and then we crashed. When I woke up in the morning, I was paralyzed.

"After many tests, the doctors discovered that I have Transverse myelitis, a neurologic symptom caused by inflammation of the spinal cord."

Mick leans forward. "What is your prognosis? Will you ever walk again?"

"Every case is different. The doctors say that recovery may be absent, partial, or complete. At thirty-five, I'm still considered young. And aside from this," she says, patting the tops of her thighs, "I'm healthy and have a positive outlook." She smiles.

I want to touch that beautiful mouth so I can feel her smile.

"So far, I've regained some feeling in my limbs, and I'm able stand long enough to transfer myself into a car, chair, or bed without collapsing. My current goal is to be able to stand and lean against the sink long enough to brush my teeth. After that, I'll move on to a walker." She fist-punches the air for emphasis.

"Then I hope you'll come to tai chi in the morning," Mick says. "It was, and continues to be, a great part of my recovery. Libby's a terrific teacher. She has the patience of a saint. She has to deal with me." He smiles to encourage her.

"Isn't tai chi a whole-body exercise?" Emma asks.

"Yes, though when I started, I was in a wheelchair, like you are, and could only do the arm portion of each form. After I got that part down, it made it all the easier when I could add the leg movements," Mick says, in earnest, trying to convince her.

The eyelet trim around the scooped neckline of her white cotton nightie is like a magnet, drawing Mick's eyes first to the soft swell of her breasts under the sheer fabric, then to the delicate, pin-tucked bodice that seems to point to what lies hidden beneath the covers. He looks at her beautiful hands with their long, slender fingers now at rest on the thick sage-colored comforter.

Unbidden, the erotic potter's wheel scene with Demi Moore and Patrick Swayze in *Ghost* bursts in technicolor on the forefront of his mind, causing the fabric of his Levi 501's to pull taut against a burgeoning bulge in his pelvic region. *Oh, God!* He picks up her book from the bedside table, opens it in his lap, and asks, "What are you reading?" feigning great interest in the now-open pages.

"*Dinner with Anna Karenina*. It's about a group of six diverse women in a book club who are bonded by their love of literature. Do you like to read?" she asks.

"I do. In fact, this big lummox and I should go so I can get some in this evening." He nudges the sleeping dog with his toe. "I want to apologize again for Hemingway barging in on you, and now me disturbing your reading time as well."

"I enjoyed visiting with both of you," Emma says, looking first at Hemingway, now sitting up by the side of the bed, tail pounding the floor with glee at the mention of his name. Then she looks at his tall, handsome companion.

Mick bows from the waist, pretends to tip a nonexistent cap, and with a thick Irish brogue, says, "Promise me that once we leave, you'll throw the deadbolt on the door. Pines & Quill is safe, but once a cop always a cop, lass."

"So McPherson and MacCullough are Irish then?" Emma asks, laughing.

Her laugh is like sunshine.

"Well," he muses with a playful grin. "It's clear Libby's gone over to the other side. The general rule of thumb is that Mc's are Irish, and Mac's are Scottish. But there's always an exception to the rule. Remember that," he says, waggling his dark eyebrows as he backs toward the door.

When Emma reaches down to pet Hemingway's enormous head, she looks into his deep brown eyes. "I'm sorry, big guy, but you have to go now."

Hemingway looks at her for a second, stands up, and pads toward Mick. He stops and looks over his shoulder.

"It's okay," she says. "Go on home, now."

"See you at tai chi in the morning," Mick calls out before pulling the door shut. Then he and Hemingway step into the ink-black night.

Limp notwithstanding, Mick has a decided bounce in his step as he walks, dark hair ruffled by the cool breeze, to his log cabin on the southeast side of the property.

A pale moon illuminates the now-heavy mist, softening the silhouette of his cabin. "You deserve a treat, Hemingway."

The big dog barks his agreement and starts frisking beside Mick's leg in anticipation. Neither of them hears the quick crackling of dry branches snapping under solid weight.

Mick opens his cabin door. Its interior is welcoming with soft, worn leather furnishings, and natural, unrefined elements. His smile is slow, deliberate, and delightful. "If I had a tail," he says to Hemingway, "I'd wag it!"

CHAPTER 8

"Write what disturbs you, what you fear, what you have not been willing to speak about. Be willing to be split open.
— NATALIE GOLDBERG

The interior of Thoreau cottage is in shadows as the first tongues of morning light filter through the wall of glass. Jason wakes in a cloud of invective as he remembers last night's intent to kill Mick was thwarted by Hemingway's unexpected presence.

After a quick shower, Jason heads out to do reconnaissance. Aware that perception is often more important than reality, he takes his camera. In the event he encounters anyone who's suspicious of his activity, he does a quick mental rehearsal. *I'm a photography buff. I've learned that outdoor shots are best when the sun isn't bright—early morning or late afternoon is ideal.*

He's also learned that a powerful zoom lens proves almost as effective as binoculars without raising any suspicion. His excuse for not having his nose to the grindstone at work on his manuscript? *I shipped my manuscript so I wouldn't have to carry it on the plane. It should arrive today.*

Jason's shark-like gray eyes consume the details of his surroundings. The smell of wet earth, heavy with dew, assaults his nostrils as he creeps through thick woods. Simple young flowers, their blue heads still bent in the predawn light, add random flecks of color in nature's otherwise green and brown carpet. His ears are alert as he keeps well off the pathway.

No stranger to stealth, he chooses his steps with care. Snapping a twig, like he did last evening, would sound like a shot in the pre-dawn quiet. Similar to long sleeves, dark green moss with a faint hint of yellow envelops the surface roots of trees, and lichen covers jutting rocks with crust-like caps of pale grayish green.

Intent on the task at hand, the breeze, just a shimmering ripple on the air, carries a noise to his attentive ears. He freezes in mid-step. *What the hell?* With his head cocked like a dog, he turns to catch the sound. *There it is again.*

Jason eases his way toward the source of the sound and realizes that it's soft, contemplative music. Not wanting to give himself away, he crouches behind bushes and peeks through the thick foliage. In the distance, he sees a large, raised pavilion. It has a pagoda-style copper roof, patinated with age, and corners that flare out over Chinese-red supports. Its design is distinctly Asian.

As the sky grows lighter with the birth of a new day, Jason can just make out the silhouettes of five people, one in a wheelchair, in the spacious structure. He lifts the camera to his eye and zooms in for a closer look. What he sees reminds him of a trip he and his twin took to China to employ "mules"—couriers who smuggle narcotics—to avoid getting caught themselves.

He sees Libby, with her back toward the others, at the front of the group in loose-fitting, white silk pants and matching jacket. Jason remembers his brother snickering in derision at similar clothing with odd-looking front closures called "frog buttons," and short, unfolded fabric at the neck called a "mandarin collar."

Libby radiates confidence and control. Her color is high and her skin smooth, as she moves through the tai chi forms with graceful energy.

Jason can see her lips moving, but she's too far away for him to hear her voice.

Cynthia, Fran, and Emma are imitating Libby's lithe movements—Emma, using only her arms.

In the back of the group, Mick wears garb similar to Libby's, except his is black. His slow movements are impeccable.

Jason's attention is caught by a line of shoes next to the ramped entrance. He looks back at the group and sees that they're all barefoot.

This crack of dawn bullshit is going to cramp my style. That damn dog must be with Niall. He peers through the lens one last time. Jason gives the group a withering look before turning away, no longer careful with his tread. When he passes the garden area, he hears Niall's voice. "I'm going to the butcher shop this afternoon, Hemingway. I'll pick you up a nice big femur bone while I'm there."

Jason pauses behind a fifteen-foot wall of late spring, pink rhododendron, but doesn't hear anything further. Curious, he separates the dark green, oblong-shaped leaves for a better look and meets a pair of menacing eyes.

Hemingway lets out a deep-throated growl.

"Hey, what's the matter, boy?" Niall asks.

Smokey-blue eyes replace Hemingway's as Niall looks to find the cause of irritation.

"It's just me," Jason says, careful to erase the annoyance in his voice. He lifts his camera. "I'm trying to capture a few shots before my manuscript arrives this afternoon."

"Hold on a second. I'll come around."

Niall's easy smile and his firm grip on Hemingway's leather collar go a long way toward reassuring Jason.

"I guess you were admiring these 'rhodies,'" Niall says, nodding toward the giant shrub. "Coast rhododendron is the state flower."

Like Eddie Haskell—Wally's smooth-talking friend on the old *Leave it to Beaver* television show—Jason shifts gears to insincere charm. "I didn't know that, but I'll make a note. By the way, I'm heading to town to pick up a few supplies and take more photos. I'm glad I ran into you. Which way is it?" He feigns ignorance.

"We keep a full assortment of office supplies right here."

"Oh no. It's not those type of supplies I'm after."

"I'm heading into town later. I'd be happy to give you a lift," Niall offers.

"Thanks, but no. I'd like to get some photographs on the way," Jason says, raising his camera again.

"Would you like to take a bicycle? It's only five minutes by bike, but it'll take you fifteen on foot."

"No thanks, I'd prefer to walk."

"Well then, follow me," Niall says, then taps his thigh for Hemingway to come along.

Niall lifts the lid on one of the saddle-style bicycle baskets, pulls out a map, and hands it to Jason. "Magdalena's Creperie on Tenth Street has great food and coffee. If you stop in, tell Maggie I sent you."

"I'll remember that, thank you."

"If you wouldn't mind putting the map back when you return, I'd appreciate it," Niall says, nodding at the map. "Enjoy your walk. Come on, Hemingway, we've got work to do." And with that, the pair return to the garden.

"God-damned dog," Jason mumbles under his breath. As he turns toward town, aggravation glints in his moody gray eyes. Once again, he finds himself no longer wanting a drink, but *needing* one.

He gives a wide berth to the off-leash dog park and crosses Fourth Street to catch the Larrabee Trail. Fog hangs heavy on the path and the foliage framing it. The map shows that the trail cuts through the Dirty Dan Harris homestead where it connects with Harris Avenue. Once he turns right, the Visitor Information Center will be less than a block further on the left-hand side. Fueled by need, Jason makes quick work of the route.

He grasps the handle of The Farthing Bar & Grill while shouldering the door. It takes a moment for him to realize that the entrance is locked. Anger mounting, Jason spots the posted hours and checks his watch, painfully aware that it isn't yet seven in the morning. *Where the hell is that creperie? It's got to be somewhere in this God-forsaken town!* He yanks the map out of his pocket and recalculates his bearings.

Jason rubs his shoulder as he walks with steady determination to Mount Bakery Café only to discover they don't open until eight. Eyes blind with fury, he steels himself against the urge to smash his fist through the showcase window. He turns on his heel—the town's shops are little more than a blur—and strides back the way he came, stopping when he reaches a park bench at Padden Creek Lagoon.

He glares at his right hand, trembling, as it clenches the crumpled map in his balled fist. *Son of a bitch!* He extends his left hand, turning it palm up for closer inspection. It, too, is shaking. *I need a drink, but I have at least an hour to kill.*

Surrounded by a dozen historical markers, Jason walks from plaque to plaque reading. Not what he'd planned for the morning, but by the time he heads back to the café for coffee, he's learned quite a bit. Playing it back in his mind, he adds his own two cents worth:

"Fairhaven, Washington was founded in the late 1880s and is now part of the City of Bellingham. It's on the south side of Bellingham and borders Puget Sound on the west, and Western Washington University on the northeast. Its center is the Fairhaven Historic District." *Where I'm walking right now.* "It features a seasonal farmer's market." *Who cares?* "As well as numerous restaurants and shops." *Yes, but they're not open when you need them.*

"The district is a popular tourist destination." *God only knows why!* "All newly-constructed buildings in the historical district are required to conform in outward appearance to the community's traditional 19th-century style." *My task in life has been to conform in outward appearance to the rest of society.*

The tinkle of the shop bell announces his arrival. Jason's nostrils widen in appreciation of the heady smell of warm baked goods mingled with the rich aroma of fresh-brewed coffee. His stomach lurches. So focused on getting a drink—*a single drink goddammit!*—he hadn't realized how hungry he was. While placing his order, the pleasant woman behind the counter looks at him with concern.

"Are you okay?" she inquires, her glasses perched precariously close to the end of her nose.

"Yes, I'm fine," Jason says, smiling at the woman. "You must be Maggie. Niall told me to tell you he sent me. I'm at Pines & Quill this month and stayed up late following the thread of a good story. I ended up pulling an all-nighter." He shoots her a manufactured, embarrassed grin. "I didn't realize until this morning that I'm out of coffee." *I hope this broad doesn't know how well stocked the cottages are.*

Jason turns at the tap on his right shoulder and sees a man wearing a clerical collar.

"I couldn't help overhearing that you're staying at Pines & Quill. I'm Father Patrick MacCullough, Niall's brother.

Welcome to Fairhaven. I hope you'll join us at St. Barnabas while you're here."

When hell freezes over! "Thank you. I don't think there'll be time for that."

Maggie wipes her hands on a cloth, leans over the glass display case, and asks, "What are you writing about?"

"If I told you, I'd have to kill you." Jason winks. "It's cloak-and-dagger stuff."

"Oh dear! Well we can't have that now, can we?" Maggie says, with a conspiratorial smile as she fits the plastic lid on a large to-go cup of black coffee.

Jason pauses at the door and turns back. "If this tastes as good as it smells, I'll be back." He smiles. "By the way, can you tell me where the nearest liquor store is?"

"Old Fairhaven Wines is just up the street," Maggie says. "They have a large assortment of local vintners including Oregon and California, and a great selection that spans the globe."

"I'll remember that for my hostess," Jason says. He's seething with impatience, but his face is a mask of diplomacy as he continues. "I mean hard liquor like scotch, gin, and vodka."

Father MacCullough interjects, "Oh. That'll be Washington State Liquor out on Old Fairhaven Parkway." When he sees Jason's eyes widen in urgency, he adds, "But they don't open until ten."

"Is it within walking distance?"

"It's about a mile and a half from here." Father Mac-Cullough points west. "Near Interstate 5."

His words fall on deaf ears as the door shuts with a resounding bang and the tinkle of the shop bell echoes after Jason's retreating back.

It's eight o'clock now. The liquor store doesn't open until ten. I'll go back and hitch a ride into town with Niall. I can't waste any more time. I want to be there when UPS delivers my packages.

The walk back to Pines & Quill is much slower as Jason eats the baked goods and sips at his hot coffee. He sits on a fallen tree. His hawkish features are frozen in concentrated effort as he thinks about his next steps. *Buy alcohol and poison. Kill Mick and the damn dog.*

Buoyed by his thoughts, Jason arrives back at the retreat. Careful not to be seen, he slips behind the wall of Western Red Cedar trees and enters the confines of the simple, natural cottage named after Henry David Thoreau. He pauses in front of the all-glass southern wall. A glint of reflected morning sun winks at him through the foliage. He leans forward and squints to get a closer look. He can just make out two figures, one walking with a limp, the other in a wheelchair. He remembers how Mick and Emma talked, laughed, and looked at each other during dinner last night.

The coin drops.

Emma is Mick's Achilles' heel—his weakness, his vulnerable point. I can use her to get to him. Jason's slow smile is self-congratulatory, having nothing to do with the breathtaking view.

CHAPTER 9

*"The less attention I pay to what people want
and the more attention I pay to just writing the
book I want to write, the better I do."*
—Lawrence Block

Heading back to Austen cottage after the early morning
tai chi session, Emma says, "Mick, that was amazing! I
would have started tai chi a long time ago if I'd known I'd feel
like this afterward. My body's relaxed, my head's clear, and I
feel revved up and ready to tackle my manuscript."

"That's why it's called 'meditation in motion,'" Mick
says. "The combination of low impact circular motions, slow
movement, and deep breathing focuses attention. And because
nothing is forced, it initiates flow—in your case, creative flow."

"I think it should be called '*medication* in motion.' I feel
like I just drank a healing elixir. It's like I'm a new person."

Mick looks at Emma's dew-kissed face. *God, she's gorgeous.*
"You're glowing."

She scrapes a hand through her hair. Freed from the scrunchie, her dark auburn mane falls to her shoulders. "What I am, is burning to write. I want to dive into my manuscript while I still feel energized." The cloth-covered elastic gets a vigorous workout on her lap. A tell-tale sign of her excitement.

After passing through the glade of Blue Elderberry, they reach her cottage. "What's that?" Emma asks, pointing to something on her porch.

Mick picks it up and shakes his head. "It looks like you have an admirer. Hemingway's left you a gift," he says, holding a dirt-crusted bone out for Emma to see.

"The feeling is mutual." When they realize they're talking about each other, Emma tips her head forward to hide her blush behind a curtain of hair, and Mick uses the moment to activate the button on the outside wall. The door to Austen cottage opens, revealing the soft hues of its sage and lavender interior.

"If that big hairy galoot comes around and bothers you, send him home. Can I bring you anything for lunch?"

"I assume you're referring to Hemingway." Emma laughs. "He's welcome company. And Libby saw to it that my kitchen is stocked, thank you." She turns, looks at the sky, and notices cracks in the blue-violet clouds giving way to golden rays that cause the still-damp leaves to shimmer.

"If it doesn't rain, how about a picnic tomorrow afternoon?" Mick asks.

"I'd like that." Emma smiles.

"We can work out the details tonight at dinner."

Emma watches Mick's thatch of charcoal-colored hair until he vanishes in the distance.

He thinks about her clear green eyes and the vibrancy of her voice. *Her enthusiasm is contagious.* Mick whistles a merry tune, his feet barely touching the ground all the way back to his cabin.

Emma sits before her laptop and readies herself for a day of writing. Before starting, she picks up a smooth rectangular stone and runs her fingers over it. It makes her smile every time she handles it.

While attending a writing conference in Los Angeles, she and the other attendees were told that they'd encounter every author's nemesis. Writer's block.

Determined to make a preemptive strike and embrace this thing rather than run scared, she shifted her perspective and sought out a physical reminder when she returned home. She scoured San Diego to find what she was looking for and found it in a crystal shop near the beach in Encinitas.

A beautiful piece of jade, or "yu" as it's called in China, it symbolizes the five virtues of humanity: wisdom, compassion, justice, modesty, and courage. *I love my writer's block. It's all about flow.*

"Niall. Niall!" Libby calls from the mudroom before bursting through the bottom half of the Dutch door. "Where's that man gone off to?" she asks the empty room. "Niall!" she begins again with exasperation.

Niall pokes his head around the wall of the hallway entrance. "Where's the fire?" he asks, with mock fear in his blue eyes shining under bushy eyebrows.

With hands clasped in front of her chest in childlike glee, Libby says, "The fire's in Mick. He's hot for Emma." She laughs at her play on his word. "And I think the feeling's mutual. After this morning's session, they left together, and they didn't take the direct route to Austen cottage. They took the southern route behind Thoreau," she says, waggling her eyebrows suggestively.

Niall loves Libby's pixie nose that tends to wrinkle in disapproval or disdain. The same nose whose delicate nostrils flare when aroused.

"Good heavens, woman. It appears you got some extra exercise this morning."

"What do you mean?"

"You've been *jumping* to conclusions again. It's none of your business, Libby. Stay out of it."

"But—"

"No buts. I know how much you want Mick to be in a relationship again. But he's a grown man and doesn't need you to interfere."

It's difficult for Niall to hold a stern look while facing Libby. There she is, tendrils of hair spilling from the loose ballet bun she wears while working around the house. Now and then she raises her hand and fingers the rosewood hairstick Mick carved for her. A long and slender bird, he says it reminds him of Libby holding the crane pose in tai chi.

"I'm not interfering. I'm observing nature taking its course." And with that, Libby cocks her head haughtily, sweeps past him—hands on her hips—and sashays up the stairs for a shower.

Hot and bothered, all Niall can think of is following Libby, pulling the carved stick from her hair, and watching as it tumbles to her beautiful naked shoulders.

———

As she tucks through the Bigleaf Maples toward Dickens cottage, Fran thinks about the morning's exercise, the hospitality, and the protected time for writing. She thinks about last evening's conversation at The Ink Well. Cluttered and comfortable, it says home, family, and welcome. It dawns on her that Pines & Quill is like a balm to her soul.

She remembers on the drive from the airport, Cynthia, a complete stranger, taking her hand. After close examination of her palm, she whispered, "When you forget what you have, for what you've lost, grief is an indulgence."

Instead of stinging, that observation buoyed her, just as Cynthia knew it would.

As Fran opens the door of Dickens cottage, the warm sepia tones of its interior envelop her. Delicate splashes of mahogany, ochre, and rust vie for attention. *A safe harbor.*

After putting the kettle on, Fran sits in an overstuffed chair and lets her thoughts drift. *If I'm honest with myself, I've known for a while now that an internal storm has been biding its time, waiting to break loose.*

Moving to the desk chair, she turns on her laptop and selects a soft backdrop of music to appease her heart, then clicks on the document titled *Mother in Waiting: The Stigma of Childlessness* and begins to type.

This book is dedicated to all mothers whose hearts are held hostage by their unborn children.

While reading and rereading that first line, she twists her wedding band, removes it, and replaces it again. She admits to herself that she's become what Cynthia whispered on the drive to Pines & Quill, "A woman defined by her biology."

That's the moment the floodgates open and healing begins.

Except for sex, I can't remember a more enjoyable form of exercise, Cynthia muses, eyeing the wrought-iron spiral stairs that lead to the loft bedroom. *My muscles feel relaxed rather than tense, because as Libby explained, "In tai chi the joints aren't fully extended or bent, and the connective tissues aren't stretched."*

A tall, thin woman with a gamine crop of snow-white hair and eyes of far-seeing liquid brown, Cynthia thinks, *No matter how good my body feels, a feeling of unease—dread— has settled in the pit of my stomach.*

More than perceptive and insightful, she has an almost infallible gut instinct that most people refer to as premonition, intuition, or clairvoyance. Both a gift and a curse, Cynthia's learned to walk softly in other people's lives. But every time she thinks about, or is near Jason, she receives the impression of pure, unadulterated malice.

After taking a bowl from the kitchen cupboard, she fills it with water from the tap and sets it on her desk in front of the east-facing window. She smiles when she sits down, thinking of her mother, the woman who'd taught her to scrye. Her gaze, almost trance-like, rests on the water's surface. Within moments, the smile is wiped from her face by what she sees.

After a few hours of productive writing, Emma showers and then changes into a mint-colored cowl-neck tee and white ankle pants. With her feet still bare, she maneuvers her wheelchair across the honey-toned wood floor, gathers her laptop, and rolls out onto the terra cotta patio.

The overflowing pots of vivid flowers perfume the air with citrus, spice, earth, and sweet floral notes.

Moving her hair to one side, the angle of the sun hits the back of her neck at just the right spot, dousing her in a slice of warmth.

Taking a deep breath, Emma tips back her still-wet head to appreciate the cloudless, robin's-egg blue sky, a rare sighting in Fairhaven. She knows by the faint taste of salt that the ocean, framed by a wind-whipped bluff, is nearby. Closing her eyes, she remembers as a little girl when her family neared the beach, her mother would say, "If you lick the back of your hand, you can taste the ocean."

As if on cue, a large wet tongue licks her hand. Startled, Emma's eyes fly open. "Hemingway!" She laughs. "You're the size of a pony. How did you manage to sneak up on me like that?"

With what she knows to be a toothy grin beneath wiry whiskers, he circles a spot next to her and settles in. Within minutes his tongue is lolling, and his feet are twitching as he enjoys a dream-laden nap in the sun.

A vagrant wind ruffles Emma's now-dry hair. She's typing away, lost in thought. A mere channel for her contemplation. But there, drifting at the edge of her absorption, is a picture of Mick. In her mind, she likens him to the tall tree standing sentinel on the west side of the cottage. Deep-rooted, with a sturdy, powerful trunk that's able to bend in a storm and stand tall again after the battering winds have passed.

———

Mick circles his desk several times—like a big cat stalking its prey—keeping a wary eye on his laptop. It's been a long time since he's worked on his memoir, *Collateral Damage*. Not until his jaw hurts does he realize how tense the memories still make him. Pain flashes across his face as he remembers what the last attempt dredged up. Without conscious thought, he rubs his leg.

In his mind's eye he sees his partner, Sam, slumped over the steering wheel of their squad car with a bullet hole between unseeing eyes. *If the day's coin flip had come up tails, I would have been the driver. Not Sam. I would have been killed. Not Sam.* Guilt chokes him.

Unbidden, a picture of Emma comes to mind—intelligent, tenacious, witty, stubborn, passionate, unconventional, candid, and curious. *I can do this*, he thinks, pushing jet-black hair from his forehead. *I can, and will, exorcize the demons.*

White knuckled, Mick pulls out the chair, sits down, and begins.

———

True to his word, Niall gives Jason a lift into town. "So you weren't able to take care of everything this morning when you walked to town?" Niall asks.

"The liquor store doesn't open until ten. I'd like to go to the one out on Old Fairhaven Parkway."

"I've always prided myself on the selection we offer at The Ink Well." Niall smiles. A question in his voice.

"You have a fine selection. I'd just like to have my own stash, if you know what I me." He gives Niall a conspiratorial wink. "By the way, I met your brother at the creperie this morning."

"Yes. Paddy called to say he'd met you."

This town may be dead, but the gossip line is very much alive, Jason thinks.

Niall pulls into a parking space in front of the liquor store.

"This won't take long," Jason says.

Niall reviews his shopping list while waiting in the car. Lost in the task, he doesn't see Jason approach until he opens the back passenger door and places two brown paper sacks on the floor behind the front passenger seat.

"Well, that's done. Where to next?" Jason asks. "Will it take long?"

"Are you in a hurry?"

Jason works to keep the edge out of his voice. "I'm just eager to get back. I'm expecting my manuscript to arrive today, and I'm anxious to get started on it."

Niall pulls into a parking space at the butcher shop. "It'll just be a few minutes."

When he returns a short time later, Jason slips a thin, silver flask into his pocket.

"I'm sorry, but it's illegal to have an open container in the vehicle."

"It's just a few miles back to Pines & Quill," Jason says. "We'll be fine."

Seldom demanding, rarely confrontational, but a man who can hold his own, Niall says, "You can walk with what's open, and I'll drive with what's closed and put it on your front porch." His tone brooks no room for discussion.

"Well fine." Jason's voice has a petulant ring to it. After removing the sack with the open bottle, Jason raises it with a huff. "Cheers!" He turns away.

Niall heads home with an unaccustomed tight expression on his face.

"The goddamned goody two shoes," Jason grumbles. "What's a couple of miles with an open container? I do it all the time."

I'm going to tell Libby what just happened when I get home. She may well send Jason packing, and rightly so. We'd never keep a guest at the expense of others.

After refrigerating the items from the butcher shop, he takes Jason's brown bag to Thoreau cottage and deposits it on the front porch. On his return, Niall finds Libby in the circular drive in front of the main house signing for a UPS package.

"Hey, Niall. How are you?" the driver asks.

"I'm great, Tim. How's Mary? She's due any day now, isn't she?"

"She sure is." His chest puffs out a little more with soon-to-be-father pride.

"Keep us posted. And please give our best to Mary."

"I sure will." Tim waves as the truck follows the circular drive, then melts into the tree trunks in the distance.

Niall lifts his hands to Libby's dark brown hair and strokes it. He tucks a loose mahogany strand behind her ear, releasing a subtle and feminine fragrance of white jasmine, orange blossom, and a hint of sandalwood—a signature blend she created years ago.

His hands move down her back, homing in on the precise spot. His thumbs begin a circular motion, kneading the muscles on each side of her spine until they loosen and relax, bringing a helpless moan of relief from Libby.

"I'm sorry for what happened this morning," Niall says.

Unexpected laughter erupts from Libby. "You were right. Mick's love life is none of my business." She smiles into his smoky-blue eyes.

After Niall relays what happened in town with Jason, they look at each other. Libby's hackles rise, and her eyes transform to a glacial shade of blue, turbulent with storm clouds. She recognizes their commonality of thought. "We need to send him packing, but before we do, let's talk with Mick."

Just then, Jason rounds the bend and staggers toward them. "Did my packages come?" He enunciates the words to cover his slur.

"Yes, they just arrived," Libby says, handing them to him.

Jason gives them a plastic smile and tucks a package under each arm.

"We know you're anxious to get started, so we won't keep you," Libby says.

"I left your bag on the front porch of Thoreau. We'll see you at six o'clock for dinner."

Jason turns and walks toward his cottage. When he pauses to look back, he sees Niall and Libby watching his retreat.

He ignores the brown paper bag on the front porch of Thoreau and walks through the door with a single focus. The contents of his packages.

After releasing the tape with his pocketknife, he opens the first box and pulls back the wrapping to reveal his baby. His *Precious*. A 9mm Beretta Storm with a blued steel finish.

Gollum-like, Jason caresses its muzzle.

CHAPTER 10

*"Writing is about hypnotizing yourself into
believing in yourself, getting some work done,
then un-hypnotizing yourself and going over
the material coldly."*

— Anne Lamott

Emma inhales deeply. The air at Pines & Quill smells of blooms and earth. A ground squirrel darts toward the pathway and then back into cover. The sky blushes with the sinking sun. *It's a perfect evening.* She's the first person to arrive at the main house for dinner. Her outfit is a patterned tunic of multi-colored paisley. Its hem sweeps longer in the back, although seated, it's unlikely that anyone will see that artful detail. Paired with black leggings and matching sandals, she makes a beautiful picture.

Before ringing the doorbell, Emma notices its thoughtful placement—within easy reach for someone sitting in a wheelchair. *The MacCullough's have anticipated everything.*

Just then, Fran joins her.

"You look so nice," Emma says, admiring the lavender tailored shirt that Fran has softened by leaving the shirttail hem untucked over tan slacks.

"Thank you. Most of my clothes are for work. I hope to add some casual pieces to my wardrobe while I'm here."

"Oh, how fun! Have you been to the Pacific Northwest before, or is this your first time?"

"I've been to Portland, Oregon," Fran says, "but this is my first time to Washington state. How about you?"

"I've been to Seattle a couple of times, but I've never been this far north. It's beautiful."

"Yes, everything's so lush and green. It's quite different from the hustle and bustle of Boston."

"I love that town," Emma says. "I was there a few years ago to watch one of my brothers run in the marathon."

Libby opens the door. "Hello. You're right on time."

"Me, too," Cynthia says, joining them. Her tea-length raspberry dress looks stunning against her olive skin tone and white hair. "Something smells like heaven."

"Just wait 'til you taste it," Libby says.

Niall hears their *oohs* and *aahs* before the women reach the kitchen. Decked out in his bistro-striped apron, he greets them. "Ladies, you look like a beautiful bouquet. I can only hope this evening's meal does you justice." He gives an exaggerated bow from the waist while flourishing a wooden spoon.

"Do I detect garlic?" Fran asks, a hopeful smile on her face.

"Yes, you do. Tonight, we're having lemon garlic chicken paired with Sancerre, a white wine produced in the eastern part of the Loire Valley in France. But first, we'll enjoy a few appetizers. Please make yourselves at home. While you're seating yourselves, I'll bring them."

Awake from his nap, Hemingway takes the opportunity to pop his head over the lower portion of the Dutch door.

"Hi, big guy. It's nice to see you again," Emma says, rolling over to pat his large wiry head.

All eyes, including Hemingway's, follow the tray that Niall places in the center of the table. It's brimming with baked zucchini cups topped with gorgonzola cheese, mini pearl tomatoes wrapped in fresh basil leaves, and Tuscan tomato-basil-garlic bruschetta topped with diced artichokes, Kalamata olives, and capers.

The next tray he sets down has antipasto kabobs with Italian meats, cheeses, olives, and pickled vegetables skewered in bite-sized pieces, and grape gorgonzola truffles rolled in toasted nuts.

"Oh, my blessed word," Cynthia says. "This is the *appetizer*? There's enough food here to feed an army."

Mick and Jason enter the kitchen at the same time.

Libby, alone, is aware of the storm brewing behind her brother's calm facade. She flashes him a quick, questioning glance, unseen by the others.

Mick reassures her with an almost imperceptible nod that conveys, *We'll talk later.*

On the other hand, Jason's glib smile resembles the cat who ate the canary.

Both men are well-dressed in a casual style. Mick is wearing a salmon-hued T-shirt that sets off his green eyes, a sand-colored linen blazer, chinos, and topsiders.

Jason's navy blue shirt serves to highlight his gray eyes—pools of calculated indifference.

With them standing next to each other, it's hard not to make a comparison. Both men are well-groomed and radiate personal power.

Mick, at six-foot two-inches, has wavy, collar-length, charcoal hair. Muscular, his demeanor speaks of quiet self-confidence and protection.

Jason's five-foot six-inch stature is wiry and athletic. His salt-and-pepper hair is buzz cut. His bearing conveys arrogance and aggression.

Both men are capable.

Wine and laughter-peppered conversation flow as the group enjoy the delicious meal.

"Husband, this meal is cooked to perfection." Libby raises her glass. "To great food, great health, and a great chef," she says. Everyone around the table raises their glass, joining her toast to Niall.

After dinner, Libby suggests that everyone relocate to The Ink Well to continue their animated discussion. Before anyone can scoot their chairs back, Jason stands up and with a curt nod, says, "I'm heading back to my cottage. I've made great progress on my manuscript today, and I want to maintain momentum."

No one seems disappointed as he strides down the hall and lets himself out the front door.

"We'll join you soon," Libby says, as Mick ushers the women into the comfortable room. She turns to Niall and whispers, "What do you think that was about?"

"I don't know, but I'm glad he's gone," he whispers back.

"Me, too."

With his whiptail thrashing the deep sink in the mudroom, Hemingway gains their attention. The inquisitive look on his face says, *Hey, what about me?*

Libby gets him a biscuit from the jar. "No one forgot about you." After unlatching the lower half of the Dutch door, she says, "Now sit for your cookie." After scarfing it down, he gazes at her expectantly, hoping for another handout.

Libby digs her fingers into his wiry mane. "I know that Jason's not fond of you, but since he's gone, let's go ask the others if you can join them."

Hemingway gives a whole-body wag. After stroking his

head and rubbing his ears, Libby taps a hand against her thigh and says, "Heel," and they head into The Ink Well.

"Would it be okay if Hemingway joins you?"

"Who? That big galoot?" Mick asks, in a teasing tone.

"Yes, this big galoot."

Through a chorus of "Yes," "Oh please," and "Of course," Hemingway enters the room. He pauses to show off his best regal pose, eating up the attention of his feminine admirers.

"Hemingway, be polite," Mick says.

On cue, the big dog sits in front of each woman, one by one, and holds out his paw.

"Don't let him fool you," Mick says. "He's as much looking for treats as he is saying hello."

When Hemingway gets to Emma, she strokes his head. He leans against her wheelchair waving his tail back and forth. After a short while, he eases down onto the floor, letting out a soft *harrumph* as he settles in.

As the group in The Ink Well finish sharing the day's writing obstacles and triumphs, Niall enters with a bottle of Jackson-Triggs Vidal Icewine Reserve. "I think you'll enjoy the fruit-forward aromas of papaya, mango, and apricot in this dessert wine." After pouring, he says, "In Italy, a meal isn't over until something sweet, or *dolce,* hits the tongue. And while this isn't Italy, it is Pines & Quill, and the same holds true."

With that, Libby steps around him bearing a tray of tall dessert glasses of *gelato affogato.* While handing out spoons, she says, "The combination of hot espresso and vanilla ice cream is delicious. Dig in before it melts. And before I forget, how did focusing on 'Flip it Over'—last night's card from *The Observation Deck*—work out while writing this afternoon? Did it help anyone?"

"It gave me the freedom to just start," Cynthia says. "It was like I'd received permission to dive in."

Fran nods in agreement. "Me, too. I picked up a thread and moved forward from there."

"It wasn't quite that easy for me," Mick says. "But once I stuck my stake in the ground, I gained traction."

"Before today, I thought the story had to be in sequential order. I was a bit stuck," Emma says. "But when I swapped two chapters, the logjam let loose, and the story flowed."

"I'm glad it was helpful. Fran, would you like to pull tonight's card?"

Her enthusiastic nod was all it took for Libby to hand her the box. "I've removed last night's card, so we don't have to worry about repeats. Choose any card you'd like."

Fran's fingers go straight to the back where she pulls the last card. "It says, 'Eavesdrop.' What on earth does that mean?"

Libby turns to the corresponding page in the book and reads out loud. "'If you listen to people talk, you'll learn how to create better dialogue. Listen where people pause in their sentences and watch how their facial expressions change when they say certain words. Include this knowledge for the characters in your—'"

"Get down!" Mick shouts, a heartbeat before an explosion rips clumps of earth from the ground, sending them like projectiles against the house. The window shatters, spewing jagged shards of glass into The Ink Well.

———

Jason removes a vial from his pocket, uncorks it, and pours clear liquid into Hemingway's water bowl. He slips back out the mudroom door the same way he entered—with practiced stealth—and darts between the night-shrouded trees to Thoreau cottage.

———

As the group pours out the front door, Jason runs to them from the direction of his cottage. "What the hell happened? It sounded like there was an explosion."

"There was," Mick says. "Libby, call the police. Hemingway, stay!" After illuminating the flashlight on his cell phone, he continues, "Niall, come with me."

Niall turns his flashlight on, too, and they walk toward a smoldering area just off the circular drive. With the combined light focused on the charred remains, Mick says, "I'm no expert, but it looks like it was a pipe bomb."

"Who on earth would do such a thing? And why?"

"It was placed where no one would get hurt." Mick's voice is slow as he thinks out loud. "It wasn't a large enough charge to do much damage. But big enough to draw attention."

Heads lift as they hear the distant sound of a siren drawing closer. "I'll go in and open the gate for the police," Libby says. "Come with me, Hemingway. Ladies, why don't you come, too?

As the women wait in the kitchen for the vehicle sensor to buzz the arrival of a squad car, their rapid-fire conversation is speculative, circling back to the same two questions that Niall asked Mick just minutes earlier. "Who on earth would do such a thing? And why?"

Fran jumps when the buzzer sounds. Libby pats her arm reassuringly. "Between Mick and the police, they'll get to the bottom of this."

Mick's lean body is silhouetted against the headlights as he walks to meet the squad car. "Hey, Dan, thanks for coming out," he says, shaking the officer's hand.

"What happened, Mick?"

"Grab your flashlight and follow me. I'll show you."

After studying the gaping hole, Dan scours the surrounding area with an intense beam. Shaking his head, he says,

"Even with my SureFire it's still too dark. I'll come back in the morning when it's light. Hopefully, we'll find something then. And I'll bring a photographer with me. In the meantime, help me get this area roped off. I've got CS tape and stakes in the trunk."

After securing the area, Dan says, "You know the drill. Make sure nothing's disturbed."

"I'll keep everyone clear," Mick says. He hears the yellow plastic rattle in the sea breeze as a stray end waves like a torn flag.

"The wind's picked up," Dan says. "Let's go inside so I can meet your guests and take their statements."

Mick nods toward Niall. "I believe you know my brother-in-law, Niall MacCullough." Turning, he adds, "And this is Jason Hughes. He's one of this month's writers in residence."

After introductions are made, Niall suggests, "This could take a while. Why don't you all sit down at the table, and I'll make coffee."

Before they can move, all heads turn as a wind-whipped priest blusters into the room.

"Paddy, what are you doing here?" Niall asks, an expression of bewilderment on his face.

"I heard on the police scanner that there was an explosion at Pines & Quill. What the devil's going on?"

"You heard right," Niall says. He turns to his guests. "I'd like you to meet Father Patrick MacCullough of St. Barnabas Parish. He's also my brother." Niall turns back to Paddy. "I'm just about to serve coffee. Would you like some?"

"Yes, please. But make mine Irish."

"I'd like that, too," Jason says.

An hour later, and after paying particular attention to Fran, Dan says, "The way I understand it is that none of you, except Mick, saw a flash. You heard him shout, 'Get down!' then heard an explosion. That's when everyone went out the front door, where Jason joined you from his cottage because he heard the blast too."

They all nod in agreement.

Dan takes Mick's statement last. When he's done, Mick adds what he told Niall earlier. "I think the bomb was intentionally placed where no one would get hurt. The charge wasn't large enough to do much damage, only to draw attention. Now that I've had a chance to think about it, it seems like a diversionary tactic, but I don't know why. The last time I was used in diversion, my partner, Sam, was killed."

Mick pauses before continuing. "As you know, I was on the police force. Five years ago, my partner and I were intercepting a high-speed drunk driver. We'd just radioed for backup when our windshield shattered. Sam was driving. He was killed instantly. The squad car smashed head-on into a bridge embankment. The chase was a diversionary tactic to draw a unit to the bridge so that an officer could be killed. That diversion allowed for a heist from the evidence room at the police station. They got away with over ten million dollars of heroin."

After thanking everyone for their cooperation, Dan puts on his cap and starts to leave. "I'll walk you out," Father Mac-Cullough says. "I need to get back to the parish."

"And I'm heading back to my cottage," Jason adds. "I've had enough excitement for one evening."

Niall refreshes the coffee cups of the remaining group sitting at the table. As they continue to hash over the possibilities of who and why, Mick takes mental notes of the different scenarios that are offered up, weighing their plausibility.

Libby looks at each of the women, in turn. "I'm so sorry this happened. We're all rattled. If you'd feel more comfortable sleeping here this evening, we can have a slumber party in The Ink Well."

"I'll admit that I'm still a bit shaken, but I'll be all right," Fran says. "Thank you for the offer."

"Me, too," Emma says. "I'll be fine."

"As will I," Cynthia says.

"Okay," Libby assents, "but I think we should still do tai chi in the morning."

"Yes, keeping to a normal routine is helpful," Mick agrees. "Dan and the photographer will be here early. I'll meet you at the pavilion after they've gone."

As the women begin to leave, Libby lays her hand on Mick's forearm. "Would you mind staying? Niall and I have something we'd like to discuss with you."

"No problem. I have something to ask you, too."

After telling Mick about Jason's open container in the car this morning, and his subsequent drunk walk back to Pines & Quill from town, Libby and Niall ask his opinion about having Jason leave.

"Let's wait. He doesn't have access to any of the vehicles so he can't drink and drive, and so far, he's pretty much kept to himself." What Mick really has in mind is the old adage, *Keep your friends close and your enemies closer.*

"I'm going to make the rounds before I head to my cabin. Mind if I take Hemingway with me?"

"Not at all. We'll see you in the morning."

On his way to check Austen cottage first, Mick replays the conversation with his brother-in-law. When he'd asked Niall to make a picnic for him to share with Emma tomorrow, he couldn't help but notice the face-splitting grin on his sister's face. Still reeling after being slammed by this evening's event, it was a bright spot to focus on.

After changing into her nightgown and attending to her nightly routine, Emma transfers herself into the lavender and sage cloud that's her bed. She smiles that she was able to stand at the bathroom sink a little bit longer this evening. *I'm getting stronger every day.* Taking her book from the nightstand, she turns pages without reading them. Preoccupied with tonight's scare and tomorrow's picnic, nothing registers. Emma falls into a restless sleep with the light still on.

Fran feels raw in a shiny and new kind of way. Like the difference between a dying phoenix and one that's risen. She has difficulty falling asleep. It's not because her bed isn't the epitome of comfort, but because something is bubbling just beneath the surface. It's been a long time since a man like Dan has paid attention to her. And she likes it. She drifts off, dreaming about shopping with Cynthia tomorrow for clothes that are soft, feminine, and flowing.

Cynthia sits in the lotus position on her yoga mat trying to get a handle on Jason. It isn't often she encounters cold, soulless energy like his. Right now, however, it eludes her. *If I just had a piece of his clothing—anything of his—to tune into, it would be helpful. I'll see if I can remedy that tomorrow.* Before climbing the spiral staircase to the sleeping loft, she visualizes a sphere of protective white light. In her mind's eye, she steps inside, cloaking herself.

After the enormity of what happened, and the adrenalin rush begins to fade, Niall and Libby climb the stairs. Snug in their treehouse-like nest and delighted for her brother, Libby finally drifts into a dreamless sleep. She doesn't hear Niall slip out of their bedroom.

When Niall's upset, he cleans. Everything. He tiptoes down to the kitchen and starts with the mudroom, scrubbing everything to within an inch of its life—including Hemingway's bowls.

And though Jason has left a soft light glowing in Thoreau cottage to maintain the illusion of being hard at work, it's empty. Slipping into the dead of night, he uses the veil of darkness to set his plan into motion.

CHAPTER 11

*"The difference between the almost right word
and the right word is . . . the difference between
the lightning bug and the lightning."*
—MARK TWAIN

Sunrise brings with it Officer Dan and a police photographer. Mick and Niall are waiting for them. Mick's emotions are roiling just under the surface. Niall offers fresh coffee and hot blueberry muffins.

They scour the grounds again. The light of day reveals the same thing the previous evening had—nothing.

After bagging the charred remains of the pipe bomb, the two men leave with a promise. "We'll let you know if the lab is able to lift any prints."

***

Mick joins the guest authors, sans Jason, at the tai chi pavilion where a session with Libby is already underway. After slipping off his shoes and taking a position in the back, he begins the form, transitioning smoothly from one move to the next. The steps—done in a rolling motion, placing his bare feet with balanced weight one in front of the other—are soothing. Mick welcomes the relief as tension drains from his body. If stress were liquid, there would be a pool at his feet.

During Mick's recovery, Libby taught him that tai chi reduces stress, elevates moods, and opens the floodgates of creativity. In fact, many writers who stay at Pines & Quill resolve to continue the practice when they return home.

While putting their shoes on after the session, Libby hears Cynthia and Fran planning to meet at the bikes. They're going to peddle into Fairhaven for a shopping adventure.

"I have an errand in town. I'd be happy to drop you off. Then just call me when you're done, and I'll pick you up."

"That would be great," Fran says.

After glancing at her watch, Libby adds, "It's not quite eight o'clock. If you meet me in the circular drive at twelve-thirty, you'll still have the morning to write. Does that sound good?"

"It's perfect," Cynthia says.

That afternoon on the way to town, Libby shares with Fran and Cynthia the names of her favorite local clothing shops. After pulling up in front of the first one, she reminds them, "Just call me when you're ready, and I'll pick you up. I'm looking forward to seeing what you find."

By the time the two women arrive at the fourth store, one with a lovely selection of footwear, they'd already acquired several bags. When they leave the shoe store, they had yet another—a large, handled-bag containing boots, sandals, and heels.

"Before we call Libby," Cynthia says, "there's one more stop we need to make. Every beautiful outfit needs jewelry. Are you game?"

"I most certainly am."

Two hours later, as the exhausted women enjoy a celebratory glass of wine, Fran says, "I especially liked the last shop we visited. What's the name of it?"

"I did too," Cynthia says, while fishing a receipt from her purse. "It's called Hyde and Seek. I love their assortment of handcrafted jewelry. And did you see all of the other unique pieces made by local artists? They're gorgeous!"

"I agree. Do you think the tags on the pendants we purchased belong to *our* Mick? No one at Pines & Quill mentioned anything about it, but it says, 'Sean McPherson, Bespoke Wood: Handmade—Lovingly Crafted—Unique.'"

Cynthia places the ebony pendant she purchased between her hands, closes her eyes, and becomes still.

After a long pause, Fran whispers, "What are you doing?"

"I'm reading the energy in this piece. Yes, the artist who carved these beautiful pendants is *our* Mick."

Fran looks at Cynthia, hesitates a moment, and then continues. "You've been so kind, and not just in helping me shop for clothes. Thank you. I'm curious, and I hope you don't mind my asking, but what is your faith background? Are you like the Dalai Lama? Is *kindness* your religion?"

Cynthia leans forward, puts her elbows on the table, and steeples her fingertips before answering. "I believe in the common ground of shared humanity. Life is my cathedral. I embrace the idea that everyone is an extension of source energy, that everyone is a living church, a breathing sanctuary. And you?"

After a short pause, Fran answers. "I wish I had your confidence." She shifts her gaze to the table. "I don't believe in God anymore. I'd like to. I used to. But not being able to have children changed my mind. I can't believe in a God who would allow that to happen." She looks back up.

Cynthia nods, letting Fran know that she heard her, while at the same time, understanding she wasn't looking for a response. Fran was merely glad for the opportunity to voice what was weighing heavily on her heart and mind.

A short while later, Libby picks them up. The wind is whipping, and the sky is purple with near-certain rain as Cynthia and Fran dash for the car. Libby sees from the sheer number of packages that their outing has been a success.

"What did you buy?" Libby asks, with enthusiasm.

Fran repeats the old adage. "'A picture is worth a thousand words.' I'm excited to wear one of my new outfits to dinner tonight." Turning to Cynthia, Fran continues. "I'm so appreciative of your help today. I couldn't have done it without you. Thank you for coming with me."

"The pleasure was mine," Cynthia says. "I had fun, too."

At one o'clock, Mick knocks on the door of Austen cottage.

"Come in. It's open," he hears Emma call out.

When he opens the door, he sees her smiling face. His eyes can't help but take in her lithe body. Her feminine shape is accentuated in a dark blue shirt that she's paired with beige Capri pants.

After adjusting his collar and clearing his throat, Mick says, "You look lovely. Are you ready?"

"Thank you. You don't look so bad yourself. And yes, I'm ready. I've worked up a healthy appetite. How about you?"

"I didn't get any heavy lifting done with my manuscript, but I'm hungry too."

Closing her eyes and inhaling deeply through her nose, Emma says, "Whatever you've got in that basket smells delicious."

"I can't take the credit. Niall put this picnic together for us. We've got a basket of *gold* here—two of his world-famous panini sandwiches. If we hurry, we can enjoy them while they're still hot."

As they pass through the trees, sunlight dapples the walkway in front of them and wind whispers through the leaves overhead.

"The trees and smooth paving end soon," Mick says. "If you don't mind, I'll set the basket on your lap and push you the rest of the way. I'm taking you to one of my favorite places. The terrain's a bit bumpy, but doable."

Emma takes in the new landscape, intrigued that it could change so quickly.

They stop at a spot on the bluff a few yards from the cliff overlooking Bellingham Bay. Mick locks the wheels on her chair. The clear expanse offers them a breathtaking view. Rolling steel-blue waves shimmer beneath a cloud-flecked sky, the dark water bulging against the shoreline.

A seagull lands nearby and tips its head to ogle them. After ruffling its feathers, it jabs at a stone with its beak, shakes it, then continues on.

Mick takes a folded blanket from the basket. As he bends to set it on the ground near Emma's feet, a pendant on a black cord swings forward from the collar of his shirt. Before he can tuck it away, Emma says, "Oh, that's beautiful. May I?" She leans forward to take a closer look.

Slipping the pendant over his head, he hands it to her.

"It's a whale fluke," she says. Turning it over on her palm, she continues. "The craftsmanship is beautiful."

"Thank you. I enjoy carving."

"You made this?" she asks, with admiration in her voice.

"Yes," he answers, a little embarrassed. "After the accident, the only parts of me that worked for a while were my arms and hands. My surgeon suggested that I take up whittling as a way to work through my frustration and anger."

Mick reaches into his pants pocket and pulls out a knife. "This is called a deejo wood knife. I think it saved my life. I always carry it with me in case I have time on my hands—like waiting, *and waiting,* for Libby in town." He laughs. I just find a stick, and I'm happy as a kid with a cookie."

"This goes way beyond whittling," Emma says. "This is a gorgeous piece of jewelry. You're an artist. You could open a shop and sell these."

"Actually," he says, "there's a store in town that carries my pendants. They carry my walking sticks, too."

Astounded, Emma asks, "You mean like the ones with gnarly faces at the top?"

"Yes, that's the kind. Wood spirits, sorcerers, hobbits, and elves. That type of thing. But I'm starving. Let's eat."

After slipping the pendant back over his head, he opens the picnic basket and from a towel-wrapped bundle extracts two paninis, each wrapped in aluminum foil, and hands her one.

Mick watches Emma's perplexed face as she studies the delicious-looking grilled bread. He can see she's deciding how best to attack this feast with its moist and brightly colored mélange of vegetables for filling. She peeks inside and sees that it's filled with sun-dried tomatoes, mozzarella, grilled peppers, roasted eggplant, and spinach. She tries to bite into it without making a mess, but after a few seconds of dainty eating, she gives up and follows Mick's lead. He plows into his sandwich with gusto, leaning forward to let the juices drip to the ground.

"You need to eat it while it's hot," he advises, between mouthfuls.

When they finish, Emma breathes a sigh of pure content-ment. She tilts her head back and closes her eyes. They sit in silence, letting the breeze sweep through their hair, breathing in the salty air.

Turning to Mick, Emma asks, "Why a whale fluke? Does it have special significance?"

"I like the symbolism. Whales represent emotion, inner truth, and creativity. They embody quiet strength. But the association I like most is physical and emotional healing."

"That's beautiful," Emma says. "Thank you for sharing it with me."

An idea dawns on Mick. "Whale watching season just started. This month, May, they give narrated whale watching tours through the San Juan Islands each weekend. Starting in June, they give them daily. I take a tour at least once a season, usually not this early, but maybe you'd like to join me near the end of your writing retreat. I promise it'll clear out any writing cobwebs that might be hiding in there," he says, pointing to her head. *She's beautiful.*

"I'd love that. What kind of whales will we see?"

"The San Juan Cruises are part of a local whale spotting network," Mick says. "They look for resident and transient Orca, Humpback, and Minke whales. And on rare occasions, Gray and Fin whales. Not always, but many times, guests on the tour boats also see bald eagles, seals, porpoises, and sea lions. I've never been disappointed.

"After the cruise, we'd have plenty of time to wander around the seaside port. It's filled with shops, art galleries, brew pubs, and it's even got the largest whale museum in the Northwest. I hope I'm not overselling it. It's just something that I enjoy, and I'd love to share it with you."

"It sounds like a lot of fun, thank you. And thank you for such a lovely picnic. I'm thoroughly enjoying myself," Emma says. Looking directly into Mick's gaze, she makes him uncomfortable as he focuses on the color of her eyes. Tilting her head slightly, she says, "May I ask you another question?"

"You missed your calling. You'd make a great interrogator." He laughs. "But seriously, you can ask me anything."

With moss-green eyes that look as if they've pondered weighty matters with no conclusion, Emma looks into Mick's eyes, and asks, "How is it that a handsome, eligible man like you isn't married?"

"Well now," he begins, his facial features contemplative. As Mick takes a minute to gather his thoughts, they sit and listen to the wind and the sound of the waves receding and crashing below the cliffs. It sounds sad and plaintive, as if in sympathy with him.

"I was married for two years before the accident," Mick says. "We were happy. At least I was. After the crash when the doctors still didn't know if I'd regain consciousness or ever be able to walk again, Victoria announced that she wasn't up for the journey—the long hard road of my recovery."

"I'm so sorry," Emma says, sadness tinging her voice. Looking at her face, Mick sees tears fill her eyes, changing them from moss-green to shimmering peridot.

"I am too. But you know what? I'm glad I discovered the extent of Victoria's commitment. 'For better,' worked. But 'for worse,' not so much." Mick gets up and walks toward the cliff that holds Bellingham Bay captive.

Standing with his back to Emma, he wonders, *Do I dare risk another relationship?* Scratching his jaw, he realizes, *Oh hell, I've already fallen.*

After sitting down again on the blanket at her feet, Mick smiles. "Turnabout is fair play. How is it that a beautiful, eligible woman like you isn't married?"

"Touché." Emma laughs. "I enjoy dating, meeting new people, and having fun. But to be honest, I'm a little bit scared. One of my brothers was stunned to find himself in the middle of a divorce after two children and ten years of marriage. I don't want that to happen to me. So I'm working on myself, doing everything I can to ensure that I bring the best version of me into a relationship. When the time comes, I'll be open to someone who's done the same thing."

Mick sees a movement in his peripheral vision. He glances past Emma. "Oh boy, we're in for it now," he says.

Hemingway is racing toward them at breakneck speed.

From the crotch of a tree at the edge of the clearing, Jason, too, sees Hemingway. He's stunned with disbelief. *What the hell? I put enough poison in that goddamned dog's water bowl to drop an elephant!*

Emma watches Mick rake his fingers through his hair, then absently rub his left hip. She appreciates the masculine way he fills out his jeans and dark green shirt. *He looks devastatingly handsome.*

Hemingway stops on a dime at the edge of the picnic blanket.

Reaching out to pet Hemingway's sizable head, Emma laughs. "Hey, handsome. It's nice to see you again, big guy."

"I bet Niall doesn't know you're here. Did you give him the slip?" Mick directs his question into big, brown, soulful eyes. Hemingway stands up and shakes his massive head to clear the dust. They both watch as the shake ripples down his enormous body, ending with a final flip of his tail.

Emma crosses her arms and rubs them up and down with the palms of her hands. "The wind's picked up. It's starting to get downright chilly."

Squinting, Mick studies the horizon. "We don't usually get summer storms, but I think one's brewing. It's rare for this area to get thunder and lightning, but when it does, it's intense. A few years ago, we even experienced hurricane force winds. It was incredible."

Emma watches as Hemingway noses the picnic basket—hinting. After unlatching the lid, Mick finds a tidbit to share and then the three of them start toward home.

A rabbit darts across the open expanse. Never one to ignore a good chase, Hemingway bolts in pursuit. They're out of sight in moments.

When Mick and Emma reach the paved walkway, Emma looks up at the tree canopy.

Oh, shit! Jason's rapid-fire mind scrambles for a cover story should he be seen.

The wind rushes through the leaves, making them ripple like an ocean of greenery.

Closing her eyes and inhaling deeply, Emma makes out the loamy smell of leaves decomposing in the rich, dark soil on the forest floor.

"I had a lovely time," she says.

Kneeling, his face just inches from her, Mick draws Emma in for a kiss. Long, soft, and sweet, it brims with promise.

And though he suspected it before, now Jason has proof positive. *Emma is Mick's weakness, his vulnerable point. I'll use her to get to him. I'll make him watch as I kill her. And then I'll kill him. He'll die—twice.*

CHAPTER 12

"I would advise anyone who aspires to a writing career that before developing his talent he would be wise to develop a thick hide."

—HARPER LEE

Though the sun's shadows are lengthening by the minute, the day is far from gone. In the kitchen, Niall is brooding. A Scottish trait he inherited from a long line of MacCullough's. Stumped, he drums his fingers on the smooth, gray-veined marble pastry slab. He's a man who takes a great measure of pride in what comes out of his kitchen.

"Which would be the better appetizer to serve with grilled shark steaks in sage butter sauce?" he asks the room at large. "Cornmeal-crusted oyster mushrooms, or caramelized fennel and goat cheese?"

Like a third-grader with an answer—arm waving wildly—Hemingway's long tail thumps hard as if he has the answer to the question. "Ask me, ask me!" he seems to say.

"You think it should be the caramelized fennel and goat cheese? Well okay. But if you're so smart, what wine should I pair with the meal?" Niall asks Hemingway.

Now standing, Hemingway gives a whole-body wag.

"You think a medium-weight white with firm acidity, long finishes, and volcanic minerality would be sublime? Well now, that's where you're wrong, my friend. Granted it's unusual, but I've selected a red that won't overpower the shark while adding a range of earthiness, structure, fruit, and tannins. In town today, I stopped at Old Fairhaven Wines and picked up a few bottles of Molettieri 'Vigna Cinque Querce,' Riserva, Taurasi, Campania 2001," Niall says, punctuating each word with a fake Italian accent and hand gestures for emphasis.

"Hey good lookin' what cha got cookin', how's about cookin' something up with me?"

Niall looks over to see Libby leaning against the kitchen entry. "I didn't see you there," he says.

"I know you didn't. I've been watching you. I was admiring the way your hair falls onto your forehead and the way your rolled sleeves show off your forearms. With your shirt-tails hanging out over your jeans and the heat of the kitchen adding color to your cheeks, you have a boyish look that pulls at my heartstrings," she says, suggestively.

Niall, in turn, admires the way laughter erupts from Libby's unpainted mouth when she steps into the kitchen. While outside hanging laundry to dry, the wind had loosened her hair and sent it dancing around her face, causing Niall's molten gaze to search her features one by one. When his eyes drop to her lips, he feels a tug in his groin.

"How long have you been standing there?" Niall asks with mock severity, while thinking, *That woman could charm blossoms into blooming.*

The laundry basket is cocked on Libby's hip. Her sapphire eyes twinkle in merriment. "Long enough. I just finished hanging a load of towels out to dry, but the sky has repainted itself a slate gray. I expect rain clouds scudding overhead any moment."

Niall agrees. "The weather station revised the forecast a while ago. You're right, a storm is brewing. It's still well off the coast, but it's expected to arrive tonight or in the wee hours of the morning."

"It's going to arrive well before then," Libby says.

"You only use the clothesline when your soul needs soothing, Libby. What's wrong?" Niall asks.

She saunters over to him. "You know me too well." After pressing the soft red petals of her lips to his, she gives him a saucy, come-hither look and struts out of the kitchen.

With each languid step, the gauzy material of the billowing aqua and chocolate skirt whisper at Cynthia's ankles. Tall and willowy, the epitome of earthy, bohemian beauty, she's the first guest to arrive at the main house this evening. Stacks of silver and turquoise bracelets, perfect for her coloring, clink and clank together like a symphony, with each movement of her wrists. She's wearing her new, hand-carved pendant. Crafted from ebony, it's an intricately carved *patu,* the term for a club used by the Maori, the indigenous people of New Zealand—a symbol of protection, something to ward off evil.

Spacious and inviting, the main house at Pines & Quill is one you can enter as if it's your own. Further, the guests were instructed by Libby the night before to let themselves in at six o'clock and head straight to the eat-in kitchen. And that's precisely what Cynthia does. In addition to enjoying the company of these lovely people, her intent this evening is to discern something new about each one. Perhaps something she can help them with.

Cynthia watches as Niall bats flour smudges from the Paris bistro-striped apron he wears when cooking, then wipes his hands and begins.

"Cynthia, you've had a look at many of our guest's palms, I was wondering—"

"Oh my goodness, of course, I'd be delighted to look at your palm," she interjects before he can finish.

After taking Niall's right hand in both of hers, Cynthia turns his palm upright, tips her head forward, leans in, and gazes with intent.

A minute passes before she points a well-manicured, Ferrari-red fingernail to a place on his hand, touches it lightly and explains, "The outer edge of your palm provides the best view of the marriage line. See, it starts here and runs toward your ring finger. It's amazing that this tiny line has such a large impact on a person's life, but it does. And it's often overlooked because it's not as deeply etched into the palm as either the life or heart lines." She points to each line, in turn. "See how your marriage line is located so close to your heart line?"

Niall nods with wide-eyed interest.

"That means you married young. If it were closer to the base of your little finger," she says, pointing, "it would mean that you married later in life. And look here." She points at a single, vertical slash line. "This means you have one child."

"You're right," he says, astonishment lacing his voice. "Our son, Ian."

"And you're a good man," Cynthia says just as Libby, a captivating picture in a French-inspired, sage silk top, enters.

"I second the motion. But what makes you say that?" Libby asks.

She's worried about their son, Cynthia thinks. "Step over here and let me show you. See how this marriage line," Cynthia says, pointing, "doesn't have any lines running parallel to it?"

"Yes," Libby says.

"That means Niall is faithful. He always has been and always will be. Would you like to know why?" Cynthia asks.

"Yes, I would," Libby says.

"It's because he married the love of his life," Cynthia says, looking into Libby's vivid blue eyes. "For some, there's only one."

Hearing a noise, the three turn to see who's arrived.

Fran steps into the big, comfortable kitchen.

It's clear that the Zen-like balm of Pines & Quill is working its wonders, Cynthia thinks. *Her usually taut face is relaxed and smiling. Unsprayed, soft-combed hair frames her oval face.* "Oh, let me see you," Cynthia says with enthusiasm.

Fran turns around so Cynthia and Libby can both see the whole of her new outfit. She looks fantastic in the soft cream linen dress, sandals, and a vibrant lime-colored, light-weight, bolero jacket.

"You're beautiful," the women exclaim. Stepping closer, they admire Fran's new intricately adorned silver and burnished gold bracelet. It's decorated with a cornucopia of gemstones in a variety of different colors, each complimenting the next.

"I see you discovered Hyde and Seek," Libby says, pointing to Fran's new pendant.

"Yes, I bought one of Mick's hand-carved pendants. It's a *koru* design crafted from ash wood. According to the enclosure, it represents growth, new life, and new beginnings. It seems fitting."

Cynthia looks at Fran's left hand and sees that her ring is absent. *I'm glad that she's coming into her own.*

Just then, Mick arrives. Cynthia notices that his white shirt emphasizes his still damp, fresh-from-the-shower raven hair as he escorts Emma into a cloud of delicious smells that tease their nostrils when they enter the welcoming kitchen. Cynthia smiles. *They're falling in love. But I can sense Mick's fear. He's afraid of losing another important person in his life.*

A connoisseur of fine jewelry, Cynthia takes in the single pearls dangling from each of Emma's lobes. They're showcased by her upswept auburn hair. *They're like beautiful bookends, and if I'm not mistaken, they belonged to her maternal grandmother.* Cynthia's eyes follow Emma as she rolls toward the mudroom.

"Hello, handsome!" Emma directs the compliment at Hemingway, whose neck is stretched over the bottom half of the Dutch door. From a seated level, Emma can't give the attention to the now-beside-himself Hemingway that he wants.

Cynthia watches with smiling interest, as do the others.

After readjusting her position, Emma locks the wheels on her chair. With her well-toned, muscled arms, she uses the counter-like ledge on the closed half of the Dutch door to pull herself to a standing position where she is licked from chin to forehead for her effort.

Rubbing his whiskered face with her forehead, Emma turns to see a slack-jawed audience and declares, "I'm famished!" Seeing the shocked expressions on their faces, she grins and adds, "I've been practicing." Then she gracefully sits back down.

Cynthia's enthusiastic clapping is enhanced by everyone else's.

Not wanting to be left out, Hemingway joins their excitement, his ears shooting up in the air with each bark-laced jump.

Through hearty congratulations, peppered with questions, Emma explains. "Though I can probably bench press a Buick, I don't want the muscles in my legs to atrophy, so I work every day to strengthen them. And one day I'm going to move from this wheelchair to a walker. From a walker to trekking poles. And then on to hands-free walking," she finishes with a confident smile.

"This calls for a celebration," Niall declares. "I've paired our meal this evening with a red Italian wine. Who wants to try it?"

"Me," comes the chorused answer.

For the appetizer, Niall places a beautiful platter of caramelized fennel and goat cheese on the table. "Please help yourselves. Dinner will be ready soon. In anticipation of a storm, I prepared a variety of comfort foods. We're having grilled shark steaks marinated in a sage butter sauce, candied sweet potatoes with a pistachio crust, slow-cooked green beans, and cornbread topped with whipped honey butter."

"I'm in food heaven!" Emma exclaims.

"By the way, where's Mr. Hughes?" Cynthia asks, one eyebrow piqued.

"I'm not sure. We saw him earlier today. He must be running late," Libby says.

Worry strikes the pit of Cynthia's stomach. Her eyebrows draw together in private thought as she watches the red wine Niall is pouring purl against the glass inside her long-stemmed goblet.

———

Apart from the great horned owl perched on a high limb in one of the western red cedar trees surrounding Thoreau cottage, no one else is aware that Jason has company.

The owl watches the woman with short, dark curly hair step with care between tree trunks, stopping periodically to look around. After pressing his needle-sharp talons into the tree's flesh, he rotates his head on his flexible neck to get a better look with his large yellow eyes.

The owl isn't the only one schooled in the predator-prey dynamic. The man inside the cottage is well versed.

The Lhaq'temish, the local Indian tribe who live on the Lummi reservation, believe that owls think like humans—only far better.

The owl wonders if the woman tapping softly on the cottage door is predator or prey.

"That was a hell of a long hike," the woman says to Jason after stepping inside. "I need to pee."

Before leaving the bathroom, she checks the gun in her purse to make sure the safety is off. *I know him well enough to be armed and ready.* After placing the strap over her shoulder and adjusting the bag for easy access, she smiles at herself in the mirror then shuts off the light.

Stepping into the living room, she asks, "What's the plan?"

"All in good time," Jason says, raising his glass of Jack Daniels to her and nodding. "All in good time."

On the heels of a distant boom, Mick says, "It sounds like we'll need to batten down the hatches tonight." Raising his glass to Niall, he continues, "Here's to storms and comfort food."

After toasting their chef, Emma says, "I'm glad it held off until now. I enjoyed writing on the patio this morning." Then turning to Mick, she says, "And our picnic this afternoon."

"Me, too," Fran chimes in. "After tai chi this morning, I wrote, and then went clothes shopping in town."

Lifting her glass in acknowledgement, Cynthia smiles. "Me three. It was fun helping you shop. Thank you for inviting me along."

Turning to Fran, Emma says, "I love your outfit, it's beautiful. And your pendant is lovely. Did you buy everything in town today?"

While running her fingertips over the intricate carving on her pendant, a pleased blush blooms on Fran's face as she answers. "Yes, and more."

All eyes turn expectantly to Mick who'd remained quiet.

"What?" he asks the room at large. When no one responds, he says, "I see you found Hyde and Seek."

"The real question is, did *you* get any writing done today?" Libby asks, eyes dancing in wicked merriment over the rim of her wine glass at Mick's obvious discomfort.

"Earlier I saw laundry flapping on the clothesline. Did you have a chance to bring it in, or should I run out and grab it now?" Mick asks.

"I gathered it a while ago, but thank you for asking," Libby says.

Mick slides his gaze toward Niall. *Help me out here, buddy!* his dark green eyes plead.

"I read somewhere that writing is like painting images with words," Niall interjects in a rescue attempt.

Taking his cue, Fran responds, "I agree. I think that's why writing attracts me. I enjoy the mystery of it, the way words fit together on a page to paint an image."

"Words are important to everyone," Emma adds, picking up the verbal baton. "Left unsaid, they leave holes."

Cynthia adds, "I read a quote today by E. L. Doctorow. 'Good writing is supposed to evoke sensation in the reader, not the fact that it is raining, but the *feeling* of being rained upon.'"

And the topic of writing is off and running, taking on an animated life of its own. Strains of Norah Jones singing "Come Away with Me" float to the table as dinner is enjoyed, and what Mick did or didn't write today was forgotten.

The sky is ominous, dark with rumbling thunder, as they adjourn to The Ink Well for dessert, a wild blackberry custard tart topped with Niall's homemade whipped cream.

"Libby, with *his* delicious cooking," Cynthia says, nodding toward Niall, "why aren't you the size of a house?"

"Because I know there's more where that came from," Libby answers with a laugh. "And that knowledge allows me to enjoy his creations in small portions. I'm curious, who was able to leverage the focus word, 'eavesdrop' to help them write today?"

"Not me," came the unanimous response.

"But I'm going to pay closer attention to the conversations around me. I can see where it would be helpful in writing dialogue," Fran says.

Handing the box to Cynthia, Libby says, "It's your turn to select a focus word."

Closing her eyes, Cynthia reaches into the middle of the deck and pulls a card. "It says, 'Ribe Tuchus.' I wonder what that means?"

After finding the spot in the book, Libby reads, "'When, as a kid, I found myself unable to start or finish homework, my father would say, "Ribe tuchus!" Translated from the Yiddish, this means, "rub your bottom on the chair." Sometimes this is exactly what you have to do. Sit, even if you don't think you have anything to write. Sit until the muse says, "Okay, I guess you're serious. Maybe I'll drop in and dispense a little inspiration." If you're always running around, she may never find you. So put your seat on that chair.'"

With a deadpan twinkle in his eye, Niall asks, "Do any of you know what the best pen for a writer is?"

Everyone shakes their heads, no.

"It's a BIC pen. The letters stand for 'Butt in Chair.'" He doubles over with a hearty guffaw.

"Oh, brother," Libby says, rolling her eyes.

"I thought it was pretty funny," Mick says, shoulders still shaking with laughter at his brother-in-law's joke.

"And while I don't use a BIC pen," Libby retorts, smiling, "I do use a trick that keeps my bottom in the chair. I get the writing done by using a tea light."

Greeted by blank looks, she continues. "When I sit down at my desk, I clear it of everything except for two items, my laptop, and a tea light candle. Once lit, the flame is my 'contract' to stay seated, and I continue writing until it burns out."

"I love that idea," Emma says. "May I steal it?"

"Yes, I'm glad it resonates with you," Libby says.

"Scented or unscented?" Emma asks.

"I told you you'd make a good interrogator." Mick laughs.

After giving her brother a haughty look, Libby replies, "That's a good question, Emma. I use tea lights scented with peppermint essential oil. They're easier to come by during the holidays, so I stock up then."

"Any special reason you use peppermint?" Emma asks.

Ignoring her brother's *I-told-you-so* look, Libby turns to Emma and says, "It's a clean, fresh scent that boosts my concentration and keeps me alert."

"Oh, brother." It was Mick's turn to roll his eyes in mock retaliation.

"Now, now, you two," Niall interjects. "Break it up."

While fingering her hand-carved pendant, Fran takes the moment of camaraderie to ask Mick, "The enclosure that came with our pendants explains that the designs originated with the Māori culture in New Zealand. How did you become familiar with them?"

"After high school, I took a gap year in New Zealand before going to college. It was one of the best experiences of my life. I'm grateful that our parents," he says, nodding at Libby, "honored my request. I learned a lot about myself and did a lot of growing up during that year."

Also looking at Libby, Cynthia takes the opportunity to ask, "I know you help a lot of writers with editing, you write short stories for magazines, and a column for the local newspaper. But I'm curious to know if *you're* working on a book?"

Now it's Mick's turn to smile saccharinely sweet at his sister squirming in the limelight.

"Well," Libby hedges. "Why don't you tell me? You've read the lines on everyone else's palms, let's see what mine have to say." She holds up her palm for scrutiny.

After some consideration, Cynthia touches a spot on Libby's palm and says, "Do you see this split head line? It's often referred to as the 'writer's fork.' And if you look closely, this finger is slightly bent. That reveals that you're a spiritual person. This aspect, coupled with the intuition line that runs opposite the life line up to the base of the little finger, culminates in these four small lines," she says, tapping the spot. "These are known as the 'healing stigmata.'

"The lines in your hand indicate that you're driven to write a book. A self-help book. Now here, Cynthia says, pointing again, "can you see the deeper end of the head line and the upper one with a heavy middle zone to your little finger? That indicates you have a strong business mind as well. Perhaps your book will show people how they can create personal transformation at the intersection of business and spirituality, how they can enhance their profitability—body, mind, and spirit."

"Cynthia, I don't know what to say. You've floored me."

"Am I right?"

"Well to be more accurate, you hit the bullseye!"

Overhead, thunder crashes like balls of lead dropping on a floor.

Hemingway's bark is deep. His forelimbs are widely spaced on the floor, ready to protect. When the lightning flashes, they see rain lashing at the windows.

"Once it lets up, I'll drive everyone back to their cottages in the ATV," Mick says.

"I love a good storm," Emma says. "Once it lets up, I'll be fine to head back in my chair. I wouldn't miss a chance to dance in the rain for anything."

"Dance in the rain?" they ask in unison.

Emma's eyes are lively, and her mouth is quick to smile. "Yes. Ever since I was a little girl, I've danced in the rain. Whether on foot or wheels, my parents taught us that life isn't about waiting for the storm to pass, it's about dancing in the rain. We took every opportunity as a family to dance in the rain. And I still do, even when I'm alone."

"Well you won't be alone this evening," Mick says, eyes smoldering. "Once I return from dropping the others off, I'd like to join you if that's okay."

"I'd love to dance with you in the rain," Emma says.

CHAPTER 13

"Sometimes making a story is as easy as putting two characters in a room and seeing what happens."

—JIM TOOMEY

With a firm hold on Hemingway's leather collar and smiling goodbyes complete, Niall and Libby close the heavy door of the main house as the last of their guests leave. The brass knocker seems to wink in collusion as a flash of lightning illuminates the rain-slicked circular drive.

Mick gazes into Emma's rain-glistened, upturned face. "After dinner, you mentioned that you and your family dance in the rain." Looking up at the sky with his hands held out, palms up to catch the rain, Mick bows at the waist and asks, "May I have this dance?"

"Yes." Emma's face beams up at him. She begins to bob her head and tap a rhythm on the now-wet tops of her thighs. "Do you remember the Billy Joel song, 'For the Longest Time?'"

He looks into her eyes. "Yes. But there's something you need to know about me."

"What is it?"

"I can't carry a tune in a bucket."

"That's okay," she says, laughing. "I can." And with that, she begins a cappella.

Mick stares at Emma's upturned face bathed in rain. Eyes closed, her clear, low voice is rich. *It almost has a smoky texture to it,* he thinks.

His heart accelerates when she takes his work-worn hands in her soft ones and swings them back and forth in time to the upbeat tempo. Mick's eyes are held captive by Emma. Even on this stormy night, dimly lit by the subtle walk lights along the path, her expressive eyes remind him of the deep blue Bahamian pools he's scuba dived in. Her hair, darkened by the rain, is slicked to her head and shoulders; twin pearl earrings peek from the deep red, wet curtain.

Lightning jags across the sky, tearing it open to let the rain pour. Mick starts counting out loud. "One thousand one. One thousand two. One thousand three. One thousand—" thunder cracks. "The lightning's about three miles away," he says. He grasps the handles on Emma's wheelchair and moves them along the path at a rapid pace.

Head tipped back, Emma continues to belt.

As they whir past, the garden has a wild look about it. Its wind-whipped floral heads are ducking and bobbing as if in time to the water-slapped rhythm of Mick's fast-moving feet.

After Mick presses the exterior button, they enter Austen cottage with dripping clothes, wet faces, and rain glistened hair. Mick toes off his wet shoes, peels off his socks, then bends and removes Emma's shoes, giving her feet a quick rub while secretly admiring her sexy bare feet with toes sporting bright red toenail polish.

"You've got quite a set of pipes," he says.

"Back in the day, I was in a quartet. We called ourselves The Pastel Lollipops." She laughs.

"The Pastel Lollipops?" Mick asks with an arched eyebrow. "That has a British ring to it."

"It was our answer to The Beatles," Emma laughs. "Enough about that. I'm soaked to the skin," she says, looking down at herself.

"Me, too. Wait here just a minute," Mick says.

In the bathroom, Mick strips out of his sopping clothes and wrings them out in the shower. Grabbing a deep-lavender bath towel, he runs it over his hair then slings it around his hips and grabs another towel.

After checking her closet, he finds Emma's nightgown. Burying his face in the folds of the soft fabric, he inhales. *Fresh and citrusy, like lime, with a hint of vanilla,* he thinks. *But there's something more.* After inhaling again, *There's an earthy and exotic scent like sandalwood,* he decides.

The rain is pouring down now. Mick hears it lashing the roof and pelting the windows. Then a slash of lightning illuminates the interior of the cottage and is followed almost immediately by a crack of thunder.

When he returns to the living room, he hands Emma her nightgown. Holding a towel that matches the one he's wearing, he offers, "I can dry your hair." He waggles his eyebrows.

"I'll just bet you can," she says, with a smile. "I'll be right back." After snatching the towel, she wheels herself beyond his line of sight to the bedroom.

A few moments later, an ear-splitting boom and simultaneous flash are followed by inky darkness.

Mick opens the refrigerator door to verify that it's an all-power outage.

"Stay put," he calls out. "I'll light a candle and be there in a minute." Familiar with the cottage, he rummages in a kitchen drawer and finds the supplies.

With a lit candle in hand, he turns around. The air leaves his chest as if he'd been hit in the back with a two-by-four.

Illuminated by the single flame, there sits Emma, a vision in lavender, with the towel wrapped around her torso, ending at her thighs.

Their gazes meet and lock.

———

Oh, my God, he's handsome, Emma thinks. *Glowing in the candlelight, his face seems to be carved from stone, except his nostrils are slightly flared.* She looks down. *He's aroused.* She brings her gaze back up and looks into his intense eyes. She feels a sense of untamed suppressed just below the surface.

Mick walks toward her.

Emma's stomach knots in anticipation.

What the heck? Emma's eyes widen as Mick continues right past her, leaving in his wake a faint mixture of lime and healthy male that tickles her senses.

While throwing the deadbolt, he says, "That'll keep Hemingway from letting himself in and shaking out his rain-sodden coat in your cottage."

When he turns back, exhilaration shoots through her. She has an idea of what he's thinking, what he plans to do, but she's afraid he'll come to his senses and not do any of it.

She tries to swallow, but he's so close she can't even think.

After setting the candle on the end table, Mick bends down, picks her up in his arms, and carries her into the bedroom that's lit by intermittent flashes of lightning.

She hears roaring in her ears but can't tell if it's thunder or her heart galloping in her chest.

With care, he positions her legs on the comforter then tweaks her big toe as he goes back to retrieve the candle.

When he returns, he lays down with his full length next to hers.

This close, Emma sees the glow from the candle's flame reflected in the molten depths of his eyes. She can't help but notice how muscular his shoulders are, how full his lips look. She lets her gaze slip lower, to the rest of his body, noticing how his abs ripple down past the edge of the towel still draped around his waist.

He pulls his head back slightly to look into her eyes. "My God, you're beautiful," he breathes as his lips meet hers.

Emma responds in kind. His mouth is so warm, the caress of his lips softer than she imagined. She ignites when he tastes her lips tentatively with his tongue. Emma opens her mouth with a low moan. She feels his hand slip up and down her side, unwittingly hiking the edge of the towel up with every pass. She sees in Mick's eyes when that realization dawns on him, and he slides his hand behind and cups her firm, round bottom.

Emma's heart skips a beat as her entire body roars to life, eager for his touch.

His eyes are warm as they study her, and she feels her cheeks flush in response.

He moves his hand to the small of her back and draws her close. His mouth brushes hers, retreats, then brushes again.

Gazing into his green eyes, dark with intensity, Emma's about to speak, but before she can utter a sound, his long forefinger touches her lips, then he covers her mouth with his in a hungry kiss—a long, slow, lazy kiss. His tongue traces the outline of her lips, and she opens her mouth to him, her tongue dancing with his.

As the storm outside temporarily abates, it gains momentum inside Austen cottage.

After loosening the tuck in her towel, Mick pulls it aside, revealing her beautiful breasts. His eyes, warm to the point of smoldering, take in the view. He uses the pad of his index finger to trace an imaginary line from her temple, down her cheek, neck, and collarbone, then over the soft mound of her breast where he caresses the pink-tipped bud.

With a light touch of her thumb, she explores his lips before falling back to clear the way. Emma hears the catch in his breath, feels its warmth against her mouth. Yet she holds back, not quite kissing, sampling the excitement to be gained from waiting.

"Mmm, you smell good. Taste good," Mick says between lips that cruise up Emma's neck and skim her jaw before settling on her mouth. He drinks from her, his mouth languid, his tongue teasing, as she sinks her hands in his hair to keep him there.

Emma presses against him and moans into his mouth.

Mick gets the message. He shifts his weight, lifts her so that she's on top, pressed against the length of him.

"You're strong," she says, peppering tiny kisses all over his face.

"You're light." His dark hair rubs against her face as he raises his to kiss her neck, nibbling the sensitive flesh.

Oh, the man can kiss! So slow, so soft, so decadent. She cups his stubble-shadowed face in her hands and pauses his mouth's exploration to search his eyes. Deep green and naked with emotion, she sees what she hoped to find. Then her lips meet his, warm and wet with a whispered taste of wild blackberry.

Mick's lips touch her skin, igniting a quick flash of heat. When his tongue makes a trail across her collarbone, then caresses the silken divot in her throat, she shudders, setting loose a warm ribbon of need that unfurls in her stomach.

Fueled by desire, Emma untucks what remained of his barely-there towel. That's when she notices the silver scar on his hip.

Mick's eyes narrow as her finger traces the raised scar.

"Does it hurt?"

"The skin over my hip used to feel like it was burned, branded by a hot poker. The surgeon said the scar would calm down—the color—but he couldn't make promises about the pain. Some people find that wounds continue to throb for years. I'm fortunate."

Emma's heart nearly bursts from joy when Mick whispers, "I can't take it anymore."

She absorbs his warmth as he wraps himself around her—arms circling her shoulders, legs wound around hers—"Hold on," she feels him say into her neck as he rolls them both over, then braces himself above her with outstretched arms.

Emma sees his eyes, dark with desire, study her still-damp, deep red hair, fanned out across the pillow with abandon like a wanton stroke from a painter's brush. Her heart catches in her throat when Mick looks into her eyes. "Emma, I want you."

"I want you, too," she breathes.

She loves it when his lips graze her cheeks, her chin, and the tip of her nose. She parts her lips in a warm invitation, and Mick surrenders to his own ardent need. Her eyes encourage him as he lowers himself into her waiting arms, his body covering hers. *A perfect fit.* His hand traverses her skin, paying homage to her naked body.

Emma is struck again by the firmness of him, his long, lean length. Electricity shoots through her with every feather-light touch.

As his mouth takes possession of her lips, now swollen from his welcome attention, Emma runs her hands along his back, her fingers finding more raised scars. She moans into his kiss as his hips press into hers, and her body, excited by his presence, answers his. She is, she realizes, unmoored by his touch.

―――――――――

Mick shifts so he can cradle Emma. They doze, still wrapped together, still content. His heart beats against the softness of her back. When he's sure she's asleep, he repositions himself so that he can see her face. Her hair is tumbled onto her cheek, her lips unpainted and just parted.

Pull yourself together, Mick. He closes his eyes and rests his forehead against Emma's as though he can make her calmness sink into him by sheer willpower. *As long as you just stay away from her until she goes home at the end of the month,* he says to himself, *she can live her life with a happy ending. Not me. My best friend, Sam, died. My ex-wife, Victoria, divorced me. If I've learned anything in life, it's that there are no happy endings—at least not for me.*

Why have I thrown myself at Emma? I should have known better. I do know better. I got caught up in the rain. In the storm. In Emma. And I didn't think at all. Because I'm a damned idiot. That much is clear. But it's not the end of the world. The only thing I need to do is steer clear of Emma. He sighs. *If only I can convince myself. A little willpower and self-discipline, that's all I need.*

He opens his eyes and looks at Emma's sleeping face. He can't help but kiss the tip of her nose. That is when all of his resolve flies out the window, carried on a gust of wind to the howling surf of the storm-ravaged bay.

CHAPTER 14

"Close the door. Write with no one looking over your shoulder. Don't try to figure out what other people want to hear from you; figure out what you have to say. It's the one and only thing you have to offer."

—Barbara Kingsolver

Grazing the back of his fist over his jaw, Jason feels the night's growth of beard—each bristle standing at attention like an undaunted soldier. *So far, my moves have been smart and careful. I can't slip up now.* Bleary-eyed, he lifts his heavy head to peer through the wall of glass in Thoreau cottage, now weeping with rain, and sees morning clouds sloppy in a drunken sky.

He struggles to sit upright as he pulls fragmented pieces of yesterday's events out of his foggy brain to examine.

I remember the UPS truck delivered my packages. I brought them to the cottage, opened them, and celebrated their arrival with my good friend, Jack Daniels. Oh shit! I missed dinner at the main house.

Gingerly turning his head, Jason spots an empty fifth lying on the floor, its shiny black cap lost to abandon at the side. He blinks as he turns his head with deliberate care and sees his Beretta laying on the counter of the small, well-lit kitchen. He adjusts his gaze downward, his line of vision now level with the top of the almost empty desk. Its well worn surface is interrupted by the solitary presence of a speed loader.

He exhales with relief, then smiles as he considers the ease with which he can load magazines to maximum capacity, *Thirteen, my favorite number.* With tentative caution, he rolls to all fours and pushes himself from the floor. The room swims in gentle waves around him. Once he's upright, another memory comes to the forefront of his mind. *A woman—that woman—was here last night. Who am I kidding? She's not a woman, she's a viper. Lethal. She said, "You've gotten predictable, Jason, and in this business, predictable is one step from being dead."* Jason shivers.

———

Second to Libby, Fran arrives at the tai chi pavilion and removes her shoes before ascending the steps. "Last night when you said, 'rain or shine,' you meant it, didn't you?"

"I sure did," Libby returns with an easy smile.

"How long have you been doing tai chi?"

"Niall would tell you, 'since the day after dirt,'" Libby teases, "but the truth is, I've been practicing tai chi for about thirty years. I started in my early twenties and fell in love with it. It's become a way of life."

"Well, I can understand why. I've only tried it a few times, and I'm hooked. If for no other reason, it makes the words flow when I sit down to write," Fran says, her voice tinged with delight.

"It has a way of dissolving blocks—energetic and otherwise," Libby says. "I've learned that with regular practice, tai chi provides me with a complete workout, deep relaxation, a clear mind, inner peace, and it leaves me feeling both rested and invigorated."

Over Libby's shoulder, Fran watches Cynthia moving toward the pavilion with graceful purpose. She arrives under a head of steam, accessorized with a thick, turquoise cuff bracelet on her left wrist and its more-slender twin on her right. She slips out of her shoes, climbs the steps, and announces, "I'm ready and rarin'."

Fran admires the way Cynthia's short, choppy hairstyle accentuates her elfin face, although tall and willowy, she is anything but.

Fran turns toward the movement in her peripheral vision.

Like a shaft of happiness piercing a dull pewter sky, Emma's and Mick's arrival illuminates everything in its path. Hard to look away, Fran, Libby, and Cynthia watch with keen interest as Mick removes Emma's shoes, pausing to pinch a painted little toe, before removing his own and ascending the steps two at a time.

Emma rolls up the ramp with ease.

Buoyed by joy, it seems that neither of them touches the ground.

Fran, riding a wave of happiness generated by those around her, watches as Libby faces the group and begins the class with the gesture of *Namaste*—a slight bend at the waist, hands steepled together in front of her heart—an expression of respect and goodwill.

Fran and the others follow suit. Libby turns around, and with her characteristic calm and casual authority, begins leading the class in a slow, graceful routine that combines movements from martial arts with stretching and balancing. Fran is glad to let go of her need to control and allows herself to become absorbed by the flow.

From the back of the tai chi pavilion, Mick watches Fran, Cynthia, and Emma move in harmony, looking for proper posture, stepping in subtly to help refine body mechanics when needed.

He remembers the first time he saw tai chi. He was about seven years old, and from his young perspective, it looked more like a dance than exercise or a martial art as Libby practiced the smooth and slow motions in their backyard. To his young eyes, it was impossible to tell when one posture ended and another began.

An almost imperceptible ripple in the air lifts the hairs on Mick's arms. Raising his eyes, he sees a thin, silvery curtain in the distance—a line of rain. *There won't be much outdoor work today. Maybe, just maybe, I'll hole up in my place and continue working on the manuscript.*

Thanks to Libby's artistic flair, the interior colors of Mick's cabin—indigo and cream, with a few splashes of soft yellow—welcome him home at the end of each day. Libby was careful to keep his masculine taste in mind.

With reading as a favorite pastime, his well-used books fill the built-in shelves. A French club chair and ottoman with worn leather upholstery sit on a muted rug facing the stone fireplace. The exposed logs and wooden beams of the rustic interior create a restful atmosphere, a perfect retreat for encouraging the flow of thoughts.

It also places him a stone's throw from Thoreau—Jason's cottage. *I wonder what he's been up to,* Mick thinks, as Libby brings the session to a close.

Blinders on, heads bent with focused determination, each of the guests—except one—work on their manuscripts. Sedulous wordsmiths, they hunker over laptops in their cottages throughout the day.

The sky with its sleepy shade of gray-blue and the intermittent rain is conducive to creativity.

Taking brief, periodic breaks to stretch and grab a quick bite from their well-stocked kitchens, thousands of words assemble themselves on pages, some orderly, others haphazard, as the writers in residence paint vivid word pictures.

Fran sits at the large, smooth, walnut desk in Dickens cottage baring her soul in the pages of *Mother in Waiting: The Stigma of Childlessness.* Even though she pauses now and then to wipe tears from her eyes, she finds the view of the woods gentle and encouraging. She's glad she's here at Pines & Quill where she feels positive internal and external changes taking place. She looks at her left hand and smiles at the white line on her finger, sans wedding ring.

In Brontë cottage, Cynthia slips her "writing pendant"—a beautiful, multi-faceted piece of blue topaz—over her head. While doing so, she speaks out loud. "I invite the energies of inspiration and creativity to flow. Thank you, and so it is."

She stretches out her long legs on the cozy, jewel-toned window seat cushion. Now and then her toes wiggle with excitement as her manicured fingernails breeze across her laptop keys, breathing life into the pages of *Guide Lines: The World In the Palm of Your Hands.*

With brows knit in concentration, Emma's eyes are laser-focused on her laptop screen. Her fingers are a blur of movement. She's glad to have Hemingway's company.

He's laying on the floor next to her wheelchair at the battered oak desk in Austen cottage. Whimpers and twitching paws are sure signs that Hemingway's enjoying a dream adventure while Emma forges ahead in *Moving Violations: A Sassy Look at Life from a Wheelchair*.

———————

After being left high and dry by Hemingway who apparently doesn't appreciate his pacing, Mick settles himself at his desk. At first, it feels as though he's taken two steps backward in *Collateral Damage: Incidental Devastation*. But then he finds his footing, gains ground, and makes significant strides with the refrigerator's strangely mellifluous noise keeping him company.

———————

Smelling of shaving cream, coffee, and a ghost of whiskey, Jason is the first to arrive at the main house at ten minutes to six. Dressed in a fresh shirt and cargo-style khaki pants, he enters the kitchen and extends Libby a bouquet of breathtaking flowers: orange roses and alstroemeria, yellow Asiatic lilies, pink Matsumoto asters, hot pink miniature gerberas, and green button spray chrysanthemums—accented with oregonia and solidaster—arranged with care in a substantial crystal vase.

Libby is taken aback. "Oh, my goodness," she says.

Not one to miss details, Jason notices her polish-free, well-manicured hands as she accepts his offering. She's dressed for comfort in leggings and a knee-length, tropical print tunic with turn-back cuffs and a shirttail hem.

"Thank you so much. To what do we owe this beautiful arrangement?"

"It's my way of apologizing for having missed dinner last evening. I got caught up in my manuscript and ended up burning the midnight oil. I found Belle Flora in town today, and hopefully, they've helped me save the day," he says through a carefully assumed, penitent smile.

Fran arrives as Libby's accepting the rippled crystal vase with a scalloped pewter rim.

Jason's pleased with Fran's response to his gift.

"It's the most exquisite bouquet I've ever seen," she gushes.

Jason also notices that Fran's a softer, more relaxed version of herself than when she first arrived. He takes in her hip-length, cotton gauze tunic in dusty aqua over wide-legged, chocolate gauze pants and sandaled feet. *She would be a delight to eliminate.*

Clearing the centerpiece and replacing it with the stunning, flower-laden vase, Libby looks up when Mick and Emma arrive, their faces still bearing sunshine. The artistic side of Libby appreciates Emma's taste in clothes. She's wearing a scoop-necked willow-gray tank paired with a soft, drapey avocado topper that sets off Emma's auburn hair and moss-green eyes.

Turning to Mick, Libby's heart nearly bursts at the happiness shining from her brother's eyes. Sliding a knowing, sideways glance at Niall, her eyes say, *See? I told you so!*

The floor-length, relaxed elegance of Cynthia's West Indies caftan underscores her statuesque figure as she enters the kitchen. The dark taupe fabric accents her liquid-brown eyes as she takes in her surroundings without effort. Notwithstanding the chunky necklace around her slender throat that seems to dance with bedazzlements, her intuitive radar kicks into overdrive.

Something is wrong. Something menacing. I can't quite put my finger on it. How imminent, she can't tell. Positioning herself next to Jason, silent warning bells begin to clang, putting her heart and head on red alert. Keeping her face a pleasant mask, she accepts the proffered glass of wine from Libby and says, "I've never had wine on ice."

Apron-clad, Niall turns from the stove. "I think you're going to enjoy it, Cynthia. You'll find this vibrant wine exudes notes of ripe apple and a hint of lemon citrus. A crisp white, it has a modest fizz. And the wedge of lime I squeezed in serves to enhance the fruitiness, making it even more refreshing." He places a towel over his arm and bows from his waist like a waiter.

Laughing at his antics, Cynthia asks, "What smells so heavenly?"

"That would be dinner," Libby answers. "Niall's made spicy cornmeal-crusted scallops with wild sweet fern butter, lobster creole-stuffed eggplant, and yellow water lily leaves stuffed with purple rice."

"That sounds delicious," Cynthia says.

"But first, we're going to enjoy double tomato bruschetta," Niall says, carrying a large platter and setting it on the table.

After an avid conversation comparing writing accomplishments and obstacles, they adjourn to The Ink Well for after-dinner drinks. Jason's abstention from alcohol throughout dinner hasn't gone unnoticed by anyone, least of all, Cynthia.

During the meal, Cynthia took the opportunity to "listen between the lines," homing in on the energetic impressions she received. And though she can't explain why she feels compelled to lead the conversation back to Mick's manuscript and learn more, it seems imperative.

"For dessert this evening we're having apricots, raspberries, and goat cheese with blackberry drizzle." Niall's announcement is greeted by *oohs* and *aahs* as he sets the dessert-laden tray on the center coffee table.

Looking at Mick, Cynthia asks, "If I understand correctly, the sniper who killed your partner, Sam, was never caught. Is that right?"

The pain in Mick's dark green eyes overshadows his mouth, bracketed with sadness. "Yes, that's correct."

All eyes are on Cynthia. If anyone had bothered to look at Jason, they would see that an alert, extremely attentive demeanor has him sitting ramrod straight, at full attention.

"Did your department enlist the aid of a forensic intuitive to help with the case?" she asks.

His curiosity piqued, Jason leans forward and asks, "Hire a psychic?"

"Yes. I've been involved in many cases throughout the southwest including Arizona, New Mexico, Colorado, Utah, and most recently in Nevada." She has everyone's rapt attention.

Jason asks, "Under what circumstances does a police department decide to involve an intuitive consultant in an investigation?"

"It varies by state and department, but in the most recent case, I was brought on board two days into the search for a kidnapped child. The parents were out of their minds with fear and grasping for anything to find a trace of evidence."

Jason's more than intrigued. His tongue darts out to wet his lips. He asks, "At any point did you feel that the child could be dead?"

"Yes. I've worked several kidnapping and homicide cases. After about forty-eight hours we're typically looking for a body."

"If you don't mind my asking," Mick says, "what is it, *exactly*, that you do?"

"I don't mind at all. Normally, I use a photograph of the missing person or an item that belongs to them."

"What happens then? What do you do with it?" Jason asks.

Choosing her words carefully, Cynthia answers. "I use

what's known as *psychometry*. I hold the photograph or item in my hands and tune into the personal energy signature of the individual. Much like a radio station, I fine tune my frequency to the frequency of what I'm holding and receive information. I can usually tell if they're alive or dead, what they're feeling emotionally if they're alive, and what's happening to them. I don't have the means of solving the case, but I can give the police some guidance, a place to look, or an avenue they didn't know existed."

"Can you tell where the person's at? Their geographic location? Is that something you can sense?" Mick asks.

"Not always, but many times. In the most recent case, I sensed that the child was still alive and saw him with men— one in particular. When I confirmed that I could describe him, they brought in a police sketch artist."

White-knuckled, Mick's hands are knit together tightly. "What happened next?"

"I described the impression that I received. The boy was abducted from the parking lot of a store. He was bound, gagged, and hidden under a camouflage tarp, like hunters use, in the back of a truck, then driven to a cabin. I could see what it looked like and described it and the surrounding area. Then I saw an impression of a ridge. It turned out later that the cabin was located on Ridge Road.

"The part that helped the most, however, was a large, distinctive belt buckle one of the abductor's wore. The police artist's rendering of my description confirmed it was a rodeo prize and they were able to narrow the search considerably."

"What was the outcome?" Jason asks.

Cynthia looks into his ice-gray eyes. Her intuition is on high alert. *The something that is wrong, the something that is menacing, is Jason.* "Because he had sexually molested the child, the ringleader, the man with the belt buckle, received a life sentence. The other men are serving twenty years each."

"Cynthia, I'm very impressed. What you've shared with us is incredible. I'm curious to know if you've ever worked on any cold cases?" Mick asks.

"Yes, I work on those periodically."

"What's your rate of success with those types of cases?" he asks, barely suppressing the hopeful excitement in his voice.

"I don't know for sure, but I'd say just about half the time, about fifty percent."

Hemingway enters the room and saunters over to Emma. After circling a few times, he settles down on the floor near her feet.

Jason leans back in his chair. His face is impassive. *Fifty percent accuracy on a cold case is too close.* Sweat trickles down his skin on the inside of his shirt. He remembers as a young teenager eavesdropping on a conversation not meant for his ears, between his mother, a social worker, and the school psychologist, after yet another "incident," this time involving a dismembered dog. His ears perked up when his mother said, "I don't understand all this psychobabble. Are you saying that my son, Jason, is a psychopath?"

Clearing his throat, the psychologist tried again. "Mrs. Berndt, psychopaths lack the neurological framework to develop a sense of ethics and morality. Violent and cruel, they show no remorse for their actions because they don't feel emotion."

"But my son can be charming."

"Yes, I'm sure he can be. And while psychopaths don't feel emotions, they learn to mimic them to gain people's trust. They're highly skilled at what's known as 'impression management.' That's part of what makes them so dangerous, Mrs. Berndt. That, and the fact that they don't have a moral compass, a sense of right and wrong."

Those words left an indelible impression that Jason has used many times over the years as a gauge, a measuring stick. *I'm not a psychopath,* he reassures himself. *If I were, I wouldn't feel satisfaction every time I kill. Psychopaths don't feel emotion.*

He looks at Cynthia, his face a composed mask of indifference. *And tonight, I'm going to break your pretty little neck.*

CHAPTER 15

*"With most of my books, I'll actually go out
and look at the setting. If you describe things
carefully, it kind of makes the scene pop."*

—JOHN SANDFORD

Walking together part of the way to their cottages, Fran turns to Cynthia. "Wow, this evening was intense."

"Yes, it was." Cynthia nods her head in agreement.

"I've never known anyone who does what you do. I'm impressed that you use your intuitive gift to help families who've lost someone."

Eyes bright, lips trembling, Fran fears that at any moment she might weep. She looks at Cynthia through pain-filled eyes. "I want to thank you for what you said after reading my palm the other day. It's made me realize that I've sacrificed my life on the altar of my inability to conceive."

With a keen sense for another's wellbeing and the evening's conversation fresh on her mind, Cynthia responds, "It's left to the living to miss those who aren't—including those who've never been born."

Fran reaches for Cynthia's hand. "I'm beginning to under-stand that I'm *enough* just the way I am. Thank you." She squeezes Cynthia's hand in a parting gesture. "We've both had quite a day." Stifling a yawn, she continues, "I'm heading to bed. I'll see you at tai chi in the morning. Good night." And with that, Fran turns onto the path that heads north to Dickens cottage.

Cynthia is restless. She needs time alone, time to be quiet, and time to reevaluate. In the distance, the low rumble of the sea—like a siren's song—beckons her. Instead of veering east to Brontë cottage, she heeds the enticing plea and the main house falls from sight as she winds her way through thick tree trunks with a ghostly sheen to their bark. Between the sound of the wind-whipped leaves and the surf, she is soothed. The gulls are down for the night, so there's no screeching. And if there is the sound of boats rocking at their moorings, it's muffled by the lashing wind.

Tucked behind an unpruned hedgerow of photinia, a natural barrier Niall planted to ensure privacy, a line of perplexion creases Jason's compact forehead. *What the hell?* Shifting slightly, he continues to watch Cynthia. He'd counted on her heading straight to her cottage.

Treading over pine needles that have been years gathering, and gnarled tree roots that have been decades growing, Cynthia walks with unfailing certainty, guided by her inner compass. Her nostrils catch the scent of Douglas-fir, cedar, and the unmistakable rank scent—like rotten parsnips—of drying hemlock needles. Years ago, she'd learned from her mother that while hemlock and fir needles both have two white stripes, fir needles can be rolled between your fingers, but hemlock can't because the needles are flat.

Unbidden, thoughts of the past come flooding forward. Cynthia had been relieved when her father died, guiltily and honestly relieved. It was her mother's death that had devastated her. She wished her mother was here now. This forest is muddy green, drab, in comparison to the vibrant, lush foliage of her youth. *Life is so much shorter than we realize.*

The clouds are low and threatening. The air is drenched and salty. Thunder booms in the distance, but Cynthia continues, drawn to the sea.

Jason follows Cynthia at a safe distance. A stealth and panther-like predator, he relies on quiet and strategy. His slit-like eyes, iced silver in the night, are coldly calculating, piercing, as he watches Cynthia turn, this time down a rutted dirt path.

So intent on his quarry, Jason doesn't see the exposed pine root and falls with bone-jarring intensity. With heart leaping in his throat, *Goddamnit!* rings through his head as he balls a fist to keep from releasing a sound, nails digging bloody crescents into the palm of his right hand. Bitterness curdles his thoughts, making him almost blind with rage. Resisting the urge to use his other hand to smash the bottle of wine he's taken from the main house, he remains quiet.

Cynthia steps out from the thick forest onto the bluff, a large clearing that borders the wind-whipped cliffs. Crossing the vast expanse, she notices the ground is barren except for intermittent chunks of fist and boulder-sized rocks. It looks as if the area has been bombarded by a meteor shower.

Peering in tension-filled silence from the camouflaged space of shoulder-to-shoulder trees, Jason watches Cynthia as intermittent flashes of lightning illuminate the night. She seems to glide, not walk, over the uneven ground.

He remembers Niall's remark during dinner about their storms. "Lightning and thunder are rare in this part of the country." *Well then what the hell is going on?*

In the eeriness of the night, Jason doesn't doubt for a moment that Cynthia's a witch. *I bet she brought the storm with her.*

Cynthia is a sight of understated elegance in the now-soaked caftan hugging the shape of her body. She stops next to a boulder at the cliff's edge, tips her head back, raises her arms skyward, and sways from sole to sole. A mixed feeling of exhilaration and dread fill her heart.

A blast of wind roars in from the west, only to discover it has no place to go. The area, much like a fortress, is surrounded by mountains. Turning back on itself, the wind rages, the ground rumbles, the cliffs brood, and the indigo skirt of the sea billows, shamelessly displaying white foam petticoats as wave after wave crash against the sand.

Like a tick in dog flesh, Jason burrows into a mossy nook of exposed tree roots. His back is pressed into the rough texture of bark. Other than absently turning the bottle of wine in his hands—his thumbnail periodically scrapes the label's edge—he sits statue-like amid the smell of rich earth and watches Cynthia. *Is she performing some type of sorcery? All she needs is a hooded cloak, a dagger, and an animal sacrifice.*

Just then, a billowy whiteness wafts into his line of sight. It gives off an agitated feeling.

Skin tingling, Jason watches, mesmerized, as the shimmering form goes slightly out of focus, like an old-time photograph. Moving closer, it congeals into a form—a woman with brilliant white eyes, silver skin, and the smile of a predator.

Heart crashing against his ribcage, he wonders if this is his mother, or one of the ghosts they'd talked about in the van on the way from the airport. Hearing the nursery rhyme his mother use to sing-song to him and his twin, he freezes. The ending always scared them witless. "Here comes a candle to light you to bed. And here comes a chopper to chop off your head! Chip chop, chip chop, the last man is dead."

Jason raises a hand to ward off its approach.

It stops and smiles. "Have you come to play?" it asks. The smile becomes a snarl, baring teeth like a wolf. As it drifts closer, Jason bolts into the clearing toward Cynthia.

Thunder booms and lightning jags through the midnight sky. Looking over his shoulder, the apparition is gone. If he didn't know better, he'd think that Cynthia is the one who arranged that ghoulish display and who is orchestrating the storm.

Like a ripe melon, heaven's canopy splits open, and rain falls in sheets. *Perfect!* he thinks, kicking into action.

The air cringes. Cynthia feels a hot clench in the muscles of her throat as she senses, rather than hears, soft footfalls behind her. With a calm she doesn't feel, she lowers her arms, turns around slowly, and says, "Hello, Jason, I've been expecting you."

Jason's uneasy that Cynthia sensed his presence before he'd made a sound. He produces a rare smile, though disingenuous. "I've been watching you," he grunts. "You look like a sorceress or Druid casting a spell."

"Maybe I am," she says, smiling. "Why did you follow me?"

"Because you know about me, don't you?"

"I don't know anything about you. You never let me look at your hand."

In the next flash of lightning, Cynthia sees a movement in the far distance, behind Jason's head. "What is it you think I know about you?" she asks, drawing him out.

"You're the psychic," he sneers. "You tell me."

"I don't know what you're talking about."

"Don't toy with me." Turning, he raises his right arm high, then slashes it down with fierce intensity, smashing the wine bottle against the boulder next to her.

The fractured sound of shattering glass mesmerizes Cynthia. She stares at the shards glittering like teardrops on the ground and wonders if her blood will soon mingle with the wine and the rain in the mud.

She sees the movement behind Jason drawing closer. To hold his attention, Cynthia looks directly into his eyes.

Hemingway is the epitome of power and swiftness as he charges across the vast space. His stride is long and smooth with great reach and a strong, powerful drive that eats up the ground.

"And so close to the edge here," Jason continues, waving the bottle's jagged glass at Cynthia. Jutting his chin toward the cliff's edge, he sneers, "Anything, a gust of wind, could cause you to keel over the edge and plunge to your death."

Speaking with an even voice, Cynthia asks, "Why do you want to hurt me?"

"Oh, but you're mistaken. I don't want to *hurt* you. I'm going to *kill* you. But it's got to look like an accident." His cruel wink looks like a grimace in the flash of lightning.

A deep-throated growl that vies with the storm's grumbling causes Jason to look over his shoulder. His emotions shift as panic rises.

There stands Hemingway, feet planted in a fighting stance, one hundred and fifty pounds of menace, a terrorizing sight of strength and savagery. No longer the friendly mascot of Pines & Quill, his ears are tucked to the sides of his head, hackles raised, and lips pulled back revealing teeth that can tear the flesh of formidable prey.

Grasping at mental straws to buy time, Cynthia lets out a cackle-like laugh and says, "And here you thought I was a sorceress or Druid. I'm neither." Pulling herself up to her full height she continues in what she hopes is a foreboding voice. "I'm a witch. And this," she says, pointing a long, slender finger at Hemingway, "is my familiar."

Jason looks at her blankly, without comprehension. She smiles indulgently as if he were a child, and says, "You should have done your homework. Let me enlighten you. Familiars are animals that work with a witch during spell casting, rituals, and for psychic guidance. Any animal a witch feels a spiritual connection with can be a familiar."

Eyes narrowed against the rain, Jason looks at Cynthia and Hemingway with wariness.

Playing on his fears, she continues. "Jason, you saw me, arms raised, orchestrate this storm didn't you? And then Hemingway appears. You said yourself that I know who you are and what you've done. I drew you out here intentionally and you followed. Can you explain that?"

As the sinister implication dawns on him, Jason reacts, wide-eyed. He swings the bottle, its jagged edges hissing through the air in an arc, catching Cynthia's thigh. Slicing through the rain-soaked material, it lacerates the tender flesh beneath.

Cynthia sucks in air as burning pain sears her leg. Falling against the boulder, she presses the wet fabric of her dress against the wound to stop the bleeding.

Wheeling around, Jason squats with both arms out. "Come on you son of a bitch, try this on for size." He taunts Hemingway, thrusting the broken bottle at the imposing dog.

Hemingway, with well-muscled dexterity, side-steps the weapon, all the while maintaining eye contact as he circles his prey.

Jason springs toward Hemingway's withers. The serrated glass meets shoulder bone with a resounding shudder as it penetrates hair and skin.

Cynthia falls to a sitting position on the ground where her hands search desperately for a rock. Finding one she can palm, she eases herself back to a weak-kneed, standing position. In her entire life, she's never seen anything like this. She wishes it was a nightmare but it's grimly real. She doesn't know if her uncontrolled shaking is from fear or the frigid cold wafting off her rain-soaked clothing.

What she does know—this is a fight to the death.

Jason reaches a hand up to wipe pouring rain from his eyes. In one swift, powerful lunge, Hemingway's head catches him in the solar plexus, knocking him off balance. Pinning his opponent to the ground, he fastens his teeth—designed to tear, shred, and grind— on Jason's right forearm.

———

"Release the bottle," Cynthia commands.

Jason's gray eyes ice over. "Not on your life," he spits through gritted teeth.

Cynthia looks at Hemingway and nods.

Clenching his powerful jaws, he pierces Jason's flesh with unrelenting strength until Jason lets go of the broken bottle.

———

Laying on his back, Hemingway still over him, Jason tries to gain purchase with the soles of his shoes on the rain-soaked, slippery bluff.

Darting a glance at Cynthia, Jason lifts his head while continuing to deliver heavy blows to Hemingway's neck, chest, and belly—anything in reach. "You'll pay for this," he growls at her through anger and excruciating pain.

It's then he realizes with horror that his head, no longer supported by the ground, is entirely over the precipice. With his good arm, Jason gouges at Hemingway's eyes. Redoubling his efforts, Jason tries to sit up, succeeding only in sliding yet further past the muddy edge.

———

Hemingway's long muscular legs step away from Jason and toward Cynthia. With a hard, wiry outer coat he seems impervious to the downpour. Standing guard in front of her, his broad chest thrust forward, he's the epitome of courage and protection.

Jason manages to get to his knees, then maneuvers to unsure feet just as a large gust of wind comes tearing from the north. He loses his footing on the slippery edge. Sheer terror consumes his face as he plunges over the cliff.

Spoken only minutes before, Cynthia remembers Jason's threatening words. "Anything, a gust of wind, could cause you to keel over the edge and plunge to your death."

CHAPTER 16

"Always write as if you are talking to someone.
It works. Don't put on any fancy phrases or
accents or things you wouldn't say in real life."

—MAEVE BINCHY

Cynthia crumples to her knees as a searing pain shoots through her thigh like a red-hot bolt. At Hemingway's gentle nuzzle, she turns and wraps her arms around his neck, sobbing in relief.

He answers with a soft whimper as her hands touch his injured shoulder and pummeled body.

"Thank you for saving my life," she whispers into his fur. As she pulls away with an iron-like taste on her lips, she realizes that his wiry coat is soaked with a mixture of rain and blood. "We've got to get you home."

Cynthia struggles to her feet. After grasping Hemingway's collar—as much for support as guidance—they start to make their way across the rock-strewn bluff. With every footfall, a flash of white sparks burst into Cynthia's vision, a familiar precursor to her recurring cluster headaches, but somehow this seems worse. *Please God, not now,* she thinks, as panic flirts at the edge of her mind.

She remembers what her doctor said about the correlation between stress, dehydration, and these debilitating headaches. She tips her head back, opens her mouth, and lets the rain sluice over her face, willing the pain away. *I'm in the middle of a rainstorm, yet I need to hydrate.* Under different circumstances, she'd find it humorous.

With her head tilted back, she drinks in the night sky. Like a vast black sea, its depth is unfathomable.

Hemingway looks at Cynthia—a question in his eyes—when she stops walking. There's nothing he can do as darkness pulls its velvet corners tightly around the edges of her consciousness and she collapses to the ground.

With his long, wiry-haired muzzle, Hemingway nudges his fallen companion. Puzzled by the lack of movement, he paws the ground next to Cynthia, tips his head back, and lets out a long, doleful cry. A twin to the howling surf of the storm-savaged bay.

Still no movement.

Furrowing his brows, he licks her face, then sits quietly and watches for any sign of motion. Even in the raging wind, his nose catches the metallic scent of human blood. Moving closer he finds the open wound on her thigh.

Infinitely devoted to the people he likes, Hemingway runs for help, blood oozing from the serrated gash in his shoulder, his broken ribs screaming in pain.

As his left hand clings to a small horizontal sill, Jason knows he's losing his grip on one of the slight projections on the side of the cliff. His right arm dangles at his side. He uses the next flash of lightning to get his bearings. As he looks down, he sees a shelf-like outcropping about six feet below. *I hope it'll hold my weight,* he thinks, as his fingers lose their purchase and a forceful impact evicts the air from his lungs.

The rock shelf he hits is like a coffin, just wide enough to hold his frame. Below, he hears the crash of waves smashing against the cliff. He turns with care to look over the edge. With minimal light, his guess is a hundred-foot drop to the storm-whipped water of the bay. *Shit!* Mind racing, he lays still and stares at the cauldron-black sky. *If I can make it to the canyon, I can hide. I'm glad I stashed my backpack there yesterday when checking out the caves.*

He remembers the way Mick looks at Emma and knows his weakness. With that in mind, he'd set out to locate the perfect, yet private, place to hold Emma hostage while he drew Mick out. *God damn that bitch Cynthia, and God damn that bastard dog!*

The rain continues to lash his face. The next bolt of light serves to unveil tiny lichen and moss clinging to the cliffside with tenacity, like barnacles on a ship's hull. As the storm brews overhead, each flash of light reveals more of his surroundings. Depressions, humus-covered rock shelves jutting out in varying shapes and sizes, and cracks splayed every which way—like on his mother's gray-veined porcelain. *It's too bad I had to remove her from the equation, but she just wouldn't cooperate.*

In his mind's eye, he rereads the headlines of *The Plain Dealer,* northeast Ohio's largest newspaper.

"A Cleveland woman who was discovered dead Wednesday night has been identified. Sybil Berndt died from blunt force trauma to the side of her head, according to the Cuyahoga County Coroner's Office. The incident is being ruled a homicide.

"The Cleveland Police Department on Thursday announced in a release that officers are investigating the death of a 70-year-old woman and a dismembered cat, found next to the body, according to a press release.

"Around 5:30 p.m. Wednesday, police responded to a welfare check in the 1200 block of Italy Street, where they found the deceased woman and cat. Neighbors reporting a 'foul odor' coming from the home, prompted the welfare check, police said.

"Neighbors said that Ms. Berndt was apparently the mother of adult sons—twins—who they never saw. One is allegedly incarcerated, the other's whereabouts is unknown. These details have yet to be confirmed.

"'It's a tragedy, and we're digging to the bottom of it. In the meantime, with Canada just across Lake Erie, we've also notified US Border Patrol, Immigration, and Customs Enforcement in connection with the incident,' CPD spokesman Andrew Smith stated."

Agonizing pain brings Jason back from his mental reverie. *I won't die! I won't die until I've had the pleasure of sending McPherson to hell!* Blind with rage, intent on revenge, Jason views the dips, divots, and outcroppings. In his mind, it looks like a craggy, pockmarked face. One that he can descend to freedom.

He's done rock climbing on numerous occasions with his brother. He's aware that even at his best it's a physically demanding sport. But with a wounded arm and no equipment, it's going to test every bit of his strength and resiliency. As he examines the prospect of what lays ahead, he grits his teeth. *I need a stiff drink to calm my nerves, just a shot.* He gathers his resolve, waits for the next flash of lightning, then makes his move.

"What on earth has gotten into Hemingway?" As he barks incessantly, Libby turns to Niall with a look of concerned surprise.

"Hold your horses," Niall shouts as he makes his way through the mudroom to the outside door where the barking continues as if the house is on fire. As he opens the door, Niall steps back and catches himself on the deep sink when Hemingway rushes him, wild-eyed, continuing his frantic barking.

"What is it, boy?" Niall pats Hemingway's rain-soaked coat, trying to calm him. The big dog's skin flinches at Niall's touch. Drawing a blood-soaked hand away, Niall yells for Libby. "Come quick, Hemingway's hurt, and it looks bad!"

Always cool under fire, Libby makes a quick assessment and moves into action. "Niall, bring me the first-aid kit and help me lay him down."

Backing toward the still-open door, Hemingway continues to bark.

"I'm not going to hurt you," Libby says in a soothing tone. When Libby reaches for Hemingway's thick, leather collar, he bares his teeth and continues to back up.

"Niall, aside from the gaping wound, something's terribly wrong. Mick lived with him from puppyhood and understands his every move. Call his cell phone and tell him to hurry."

Still running high on adrenaline from his after-dinner conversation with Cynthia, Mick pushes Emma's wheelchair through the rain to Austen cottage at almost a run. "When we get there, I'm making you a hot cup of tea, then tucking you into bed," he says with a wolfish grin, waggling his eyebrows suggestively. "But first I want to talk about what Cynthia said."

The warmth of the cottage envelops them. Emma asks, "You mean about her work as a forensic intuitive to help solve cases?"

"Yes, even long forgotten cold cases," Mick says as he brings two lavender towels from the bathroom and hands one to Emma.

As he dries his face and hair, his rich masculine scent fills Emma's nostrils.

When Mick tosses the plush fabric over his shoulder, Emma notices that his wet shirt is stuck to him, like a second skin.

He walks into the kitchen, ignites one of the burners on the gas stove, fills the tea kettle with water, and places it over the low flame. While waiting for the water to boil, Mick forages for mugs in the cupboard.

"I find it fascinating," Emma says. "I don't know Cynthia very well yet, but what I do know, I like. She's a straightforward woman who shoots from the hip. I appreciate that in a person." Bent forward at the waist drying her hair, Emma sees rain-drenched jean cuffs resting on the tops of two masculine feet come into view.

Mick's fingers weave into Emma's wet hair, savoring its dark luxuriance.

Looking up, she finds herself drawn into his smoldering gaze.

"Then I'm going to shoot from the hip. You're beautiful and I'm going to kiss you." Leaning forward to deliver on his promise, the peal of his cell phone wrenches them both from his intent. "Who on earth would be calling at this time of night?" He fishes the phone from his pocket, brows furrowed in puzzlement, as caller ID indicates that it's Niall. *He rarely calls, and only if it's important.* "McPherson," he answers.

Emma hears an indiscernible voice on the other end and watches as Mick's eyes, moments earlier smoky with intent, register alarm. Then the color drains from his face, baring dread. "I'll be there in a minute," he says, then hangs up. "Hemingway's hurt. Niall says it's bad. I've got to go."

"Oh, my God, run. I'll follow, just go," Emma urges.

Mick puts on his shoes and bolts out the door while Emma follows as quickly as she can. She's grateful for her upper-body strength. Like steel coupling rods on an express train of days gone by, her well-toned arms pump rapidly. The wheels of her chair make a hissing sound as rubber speeds over the smooth, wet pathway where subtle walk lights vie with lightning to show the way through the unrelenting rain.

As Mick rounds the corner at a dead run, hip aching, his frantic mind tries to reconcile the scene presenting itself in what seems to him, slow motion. The doorway of the well-lit mudroom looks like a gaping hole in a jack-o-lantern's smile, with Hemingway's body silhouetted against the humorless grin.

When Mick squats down, he asks Hemingway, "What is it boy?" His voice thick with concern.

The burly dog turns and gently wags his tail, a poor imitation of his usual enthusiastic greeting.

Mick draws closer to his friend.

The shaft of light from the doorway reveals a blood-sodden coat and an eye that's swollen almost shut.

First nuzzling Mick's hand, then licking it anxiously, Hemingway takes Mick's wrist in his powerful jaws and gently tugs.

"Do you want to show me something?" Mick asks his companion of several years.

Hemingway gets to his feet.

"Niall, throw me a flashlight. Libby, call the police and the vet. Get them both out here. Now!" he bellows.

"Where are you going?" They ask in unison.

"I'm following Hemingway," he says, catching the flashlight. "I've got my cell."

Hemingway let go of Mick's wrist and walks away, looking back only once to make sure Mick's following.

"I'm coming boy. I'm coming."

When Emma rounds the corner, she sees Libby's and Niall's shattered expressions watching an empty space where the dark had just swallowed both man and dog.

"What happened? Is Hemingway okay?" Emma asks between gulps of air, trying to catch her breath.

"Come inside and we'll talk in the kitchen once we've called the police and the vet."

"The police?" Emma asks, hand-to-heart, wide-eyed in alarm.

"Yes, Mick told us to call them both before he followed Hemingway into the woods."

Hemingway pants ahead. He turns periodically, his soulful eyes urging Mick to catch up. When they reach the clearing at the end of the forest, he bolts across the expanse, stopping when he arrives at a dark mound on the ground. He turns back to Mick and barks urgently.

Mick ignores the mud sucking at the bottom of his shoes and runs. As he draws closer, he sees Hemingway hovering over a person. A woman in a dress.

Reaching them, he recognizes Cynthia. "Oh, my God!" Dropping to his knees, he checks her pulse. "She's alive," he says with relief as much to himself as the big dog. He gets out his cell and calls the main house. "Niall, Hemingway led me to Cynthia. She's alive, but unconscious. She's covered in mud from head to toe."

"What happened, Mick?"

"In this merciless wind and rain, it's hard to tell, but she's bleeding." With great care, he pulls the fabric of Cynthia's dress away, and continues. "She has a deep gash on her thigh. I don't think whatever caused it severed an artery, or she would have bled out by now. But still, she's bleeding a lot. It'll be impossible for an ambulance to make it out here, and they can't airlift her in this storm. Bring the ATV to the bluff by the cliffs and hurry!"

Mick's medical emergency training from his years on the police force kick into high gear. He rips off his shirt and staunches the flow with a shirt sleeve. After containing the wound, he assesses the rest of Cynthia's body to see if she has any other visible trauma. "Cynthia, if you can hear me, it's Mick. Help is on the way."

The rain pelts his flesh, the wind whips his hair, but he's focused and impervious.

Mindful of inflicting further harm, Mick positions Cynthia so that her wounded thigh is up. He tilts her head back to keep her airway open, knowing that an unconscious person can't cough or clear their throat. In doing so, her clenched hand falls open, exposing a smooth rock. *What on earth? Was she going to use this as a weapon?*

Ignoring his own, he sees goosebumps on her flesh. *She needs to be kept warm. I wish I'd grabbed my jacket.*

As if reading Mick's mind, Hemingway lays on his side with his back next to Cynthia's, letting out a tired sigh.

"Hemingway, you probably saved Cynthia's life. You're a hero, big fella." The usual whip-like force of his long tail is replaced by a gentle thumping on the ground.

As he looks at the surrounding area, Mick's eyes catch a flash of splintered glass, registering a broken bottle several feet away. Careful not to tamper with the scene or touch anything that might be evidence, he makes mental notes and remains where he is.

Head cocked, ears alert, Mick takes Hemingway's cue and follows his suddenly alert gaze. In the distance, two headlights dance in unison over the rugged landscape as the ATV nears the forest's edge. With its rugged build and knobby tires, it makes quick work of the terrain.

Before it reaches the clearing, Hemingway is up on all fours barking for attention.

Mick stands and waves his arms, hoping not to be a lightning rod in the wicked storm.

"Kära Gud!" Niall says, scrambling out of the all-terrain vehicle.

"I don't think she has any broken bones," Mick responds. "I'm going to lift her and lay her in the backseat. Then I'll get in and hold her for support."

"She's got to be freezing in this wind and rain," Niall says. "Libby sent a wool blanket."

"Thank God for Libby. She thinks of everything. Niall, I don't want to bump Cynthia's head, so help me guide her in and bundle her up, then Hemingway can ride up front with you. Instead of heading straight east the way you came, let's head south. I know it's a longer route, but in this weather, it'll be faster and smoother."

Niall looks puzzled. "I didn't know there's another route," he shouts over the roaring wind.

"It's more of a wide path, but wide enough for the ATV. The trees there are younger so there aren't as many exposed roots. I used to take my wheelchair through there."

"Well, I'll be damned."

As the all-terrain moves forward, the bluff falls behind, leaving the mysterious scene in its wake. Mick calls ahead to say they're on their way and adds an ambulance to his original request of police and vet.

With his guidance, they enter the property just south of Austen cottage. Then, like a switchback on a mountain trail, they head north on the smooth, wet pathway between the copse of blue elderberry trees and the main house.

Around the next bend, welcoming light from the main house emerges ahead. As they connect with the circular drive, they're greeted by flashing blue, red, amber, and white lights from a patrol car, ambulance, and what seems sedate in comparison, a pickup truck and horse trailer with *Fairhaven Veterinary Hospital* stenciled on the side.

Someone in the main house must have been on the lookout because their arrival doesn't go unnoticed. As the all-terrain enters the circular drive, a wave of umbrellas bears down on them at once—Libby, two paramedics, two police officers, the vet, Emma, and Fran.

The paramedics transfer Cynthia from the all-terrain to the ambulance on a stretcher board. Mick hops in beside her as they pepper him with questions and check her vitals.

Skip, a seasoned paramedic with silver hair that commands respect, breaks open what looks like a glow stick. He wafts it back and forth under Cynthia's nose as several pairs of curious eyes watch from the back end of the well-lit, efficient space.

Her forehead draws into a puckered frown and her nose wrinkles. She coughs, splutters, then coughs again. Cynthia's eyes fly open, and she tries to sit up, but can't. Gripping Mick's hand she looks him straight in the eyes and says, "It was Jason. He fell over the cliff and he's dead." Then she passes out cold.

CHAPTER 17

"When you write suspense, you have to know where you're going because you have to drop little hints along the way. With an outline, I always know where the story is going."

—JOHN GRISHAM

Libby hears rapid-fire conversation coming from the kitchen as muffled voices rise and fall like the rhythmic ebb and flow of a tide, punctuated now and then by a sharp staccato as someone slaps the well-worn pine table for emphasis.

Different from the comfortable atmosphere of conversation and laughter that usually fill their home, the air is charged with a prickly edge born of interrogation as the two police officers, Herb and Chris—short for Christine—ask and re-ask their questions, trying to piece together the evening's events after briefly checking Thoreau cottage to verify that Jason isn't there.

Niall is one of the warmest people on earth, and Libby knows with certainty that he, ever the diligent host, is in the kitchen dispensing Scottish coffee—an antidote as effective as any.

When his mother passed away, he told Libby, "Sometimes it's the rituals that get us through."

She remembers how he looked. Niall had a dish towel fisted on one hip as he explained—his Scots burr coming thicker—"Scottish coffee is a wee bit different than the Irish kind. The main difference is that Irish whiskey is distilled three times, whereas scotch, only twice. That means we use half again as much. Are you followin' the mathematics of it all darlin'?" he'd ask her with a big smile and a deep wink.

As if in a classroom instead of a kitchen he'd continued, "Now we start by brewin' a pot of espresso. You know, espresso is as much an art as it is a science." This bit of knowledge he'd delivered while using the dish towel to wipe an imaginary smudge from his shiny espresso machine.

"Now measure the scotch and sugar together in warmed glass mugs with handles. Add the espresso and stir until the sugar's completely dissolved. Don't skip this step,"—he'd lifted a warning finger—"even if you don't normally put sugar in your coffee. You see, lass, the sugar helps the cream to float above the coffee. Then top it off with a big dollop of freshly whipped cream. Once the cream's in place, don't stir. It's imperative to drink the coffee through the cream." He'd ended with a flourish, bending at the waist and handed her a delicious cup of freshly made Scottish coffee.

Libby shakes her head to clear her mental reverie. Given the gravity of the situation, she knows that to soothe frayed nerves, the doses in Niall's coffee this evening are more liberal than usual. And as sure as the sun will rise, she also knows that she'll soon smell the heavenly goodness of his homemade biscuits, as much to ease himself as everyone else. The warmth of this knowledge helps dispel the chill she felt moments before.

Sitting on the tiles in the first-floor bathroom with Hemingway's head in her lap, the length of his body across the cold, hard flooring, Libby distracts herself from watching Dr. Sutton gather instruments from his bag. As she looks up, her gaze takes in the lights above the mirror over the sink. Her thoughts take a welcome, mind-numbing turn as it wanders to a piece of homemaking advice her mother had given her as a young bride.

"Always use soft pink lightbulbs in your bathrooms dear, especially the guest bathroom. The subtle pink color coating enhances everything with a slightly warmer tone that detracts from flaws and compliments any face, delighting your guests."

Looking down at Hemingway's lacerated body she knows full well the lighting isn't complimenting anything, and it can't come close to easing the harshness of the situation.

"Is he going to be okay?" Libby asks Dr. Sutton, watching his rough, old hands feel through Hemingway's blood-soaked, wiry coat and then insert the bevel of a needle into a vein in his neck.

Hemingway flinches slightly but holds his doe-eyed gaze—filled with trust—on Libby's face as the vet's calloused thumb slowly pushes the plunger down the syringe barrel, easing sodium pentobarbital into the bloodstream where it travels swiftly throughout his system. Eyes too heavy to keep open, Hemingway closes his lids and drifts off to sleep.

"He'll be much better off anesthetized while I wash and tend to his wounds. And so will we for that matter," he says, his eyes smiling through craggy brows. "You're holding up well," he continues encouragingly. "Care to help me get him cleaned and stitched up?"

"I'm at your service. Tell me what to do."

The hospital is shockingly bright compared to the storm-tossed evening outside. Mick can't seem to sit still. He needs to *do* something. With a thin green ambulance blanket draped over his shoulders, he wears a path in the highly buffed linoleum floor of the emergency waiting area, his limp more pronounced than usual. Frustration mounting, Mick realizes that repeatedly checking his watch doesn't make its hands move any faster. As he walks, he clenches and unclenches his hands. Just hours ago, they'd been holding Emma's.

Taking another lap around the waiting area, his mind replays Cynthia's voice. *"It was Jason. He fell over the cliff, and he's dead."*

Using the combined processes of experience and elimination, Dr. Alice Zimmerman approaches Mick, her low heels tapping across the worry-paved flooring as she enters the waiting room.

The space is designed to calm. Neat and tidy, of course, but with a comfortable, open style, quiet colors, and soothing music meant to tranquilize frayed nerves.

As she extends her hand, she asks, "Are you the person who escorted Cynthia Winters in the ambulance?"

"I am. I'm Sean McPherson," he answers, noting the doctor's firm, professional handshake. "Is she going to be okay?"

Seeing the deep lines of worry creased in his forehead, she asks kindly, "Are you a relative?" as she guides them toward two overstuffed chairs angled companionably toward each other and they sit. Her lap is holding a no-nonsense clipboard stayed by the flat palms of her hands. His lap is supporting two fists that he clenches and unclenches in an unconscious effort to relieve anxiety.

"No. Cynthia's one of our guests at Pines & Quill."

"The writers' retreat out by the cliffs," she says, more as confirmation than a question. "I've heard of it. First let me say, Ms. Winters is going to be okay. But in addition to suffering from a cluster headache, she's lost a lot of blood from the wound on her thigh. Thankfully, her femoral artery was only nicked instead of cut or severed. Can you tell me about the circumstances around that?"

"I don't understand, what's a cluster headache? Is it like a migraine?" Mick asks.

"A cluster headache is one of the most painful types of headaches there is. In fact, they've been described as 'suicide headaches,' a reference to the excruciating pain and resulting desperation that has culminated in actual suicide. They can be debilitating and last from weeks to months, or vanish as quickly as they arrive and stay in remission for months, even years before recurring."

"How do you know that's what she has? Can you help her?"

"When I was stitching her leg, she came to long enough to tell me before passing out again." Cool, calm, and collected, the doctor continues. "Unfortunately, there's no cure for cluster headaches, but they can be treated with medication to decrease the severity of pain and reduce duration. Right now, we're treating Ms. Winters with pure oxygen through a breathing mask. The effects of this are usually felt within minutes and provide dramatic relief for most patients.

"Once she comes around, we'll get an accurate medical history. If we can rule out high blood pressure and heart disease, we'll give her an injection of triptans. But Mr. McPherson, you still haven't told me why Ms. Winters arrived looking like she was tattooed in blood, and how she sustained the trauma on her thigh."

"Dr. Zimmerman, all I know about the gash in Cynthia's leg is that Hemingway"—noting her quizzical look under raised eyebrows, he explains—"he's my dog," and then continues, "came and got me. I called my brother-in-law and told him to bring the ATV," and we took Cynthia back to the main house where an ambulance was waiting to bring her here. That's the extent of what I know."

"What was Ms. Winters doing out in the storm?"

"I have no idea, but I'm just as anxious to find out as you are."

"We're going to keep her overnight. She's been through quite an ordeal, and there's always a potential for shock. Plus, I want to keep an eye out for infection in her leg, and also see if she's a potential candidate for triptans. By the way, that was some pretty impressive work you did with the sleeve tourniquet," she says, pausing to look pointedly at his missing shirt. "I'm grateful I didn't have any resulting complications to clean up after someone who doesn't know what they were doing. Where did you get your training?"

"I was on the police force."

"*Was,* as in past tense?" she asks, standing as Mick stands too.

"That's correct, I'm no longer active."

"It's their loss," she says, smiling and extends her hand. "I'm sorry about the circumstances, but it's a pleasure meeting you."

And with that, she turns around and retraces the path on the well-worn floor until double doors shush closed behind her retreating white lab coat.

Mick's tired step triggers sensors hidden under the massive, black rubber mat and the automatic sliding doors of the emergency room glide open. As he steps between them, he's welcomed by a blast of fresh night air and a gravelly smoker's voice. "Hey, buddy."

Mick turns to see Skip, the lead paramedic on Cynthia's ride to the hospital, also a poker-night friend. His head is shrouded in cigarette smoke.

"Even though it stopped raining, I figured you might want a ride back home."

"Thanks. I appreciate it."

The sole of Skip's shoe pushes him away from the wall he'd been leaning against while waiting for Mick, and the two men fall into step as they head for the ambulance.

They ride in companionable silence most of the way. Arriving at the massive wrought-iron entry gate—*Welcome to Pines & Quill*—Mick thanks Skip for the ride. "I'd prefer to walk the rest of the way to clear my head before answering what's sure to be a boatload of questions when I get to the main house."

Watching the taillights, extinguished by the dark distance, Mick opens the gate that separates hearth and home from the rest of the world. Before starting down the long road, he stands still and draws in the peaceful, after-storm calm.

A trio of deer wander silently as ghosts on a berm behind rain-drenched trees.

When he looks up, he sees a sliced moon through leafy branches.

Inhaling deeply, he breathes in the night air appreciatively and contemplates. *In all of the busyness, a person can forget that there are times and places so wondrously still.*

With that thought buoying his mind, Mick walks home through the night-dark woods.

"Oh, my God!" Emma's hands fly to her panic-stricken face. "The tea kettle. We were waiting for it to boil when Mick got the call from Niall and we bolted," she says over her shoulder, already halfway out the door. "I'll be right back."

She rushes down the ramp, arms pumping the pushrims on her chair as she barrels toward Austen cottage, grateful for the glow of the subtle walk lights along the way. The rhythmic slap of rubber wheels against the rain-soaked path is hard-pressed to keep pace with the pounding of Emma's heart.

———

Fueled by hate, Jason transitions his heels over the edge of the horizontal surface. *Without a rope, my only chance of reaching the bottom in one piece is to stay upright.*

With his back against the sheer rock wall, he uses his heels for leverage, pulling closer, then lowers his legs over the side until his calves are against the cliff face.

He knows that gravity is going to work against him as he slides, gaining speed, to the bottom of the precipice. And with that knowledge, injured arm tucked tightly to the front of his torso, he shoves off.

———

It feels like someone's tightening a vice-grip on my head and holding a hot iron to my thigh, Cynthia thinks. Through barely slit eyelids, she scans the dim room illuminated by a soft light over a door with a small window. Her gaze takes in a raised bedside table playing host to a short stack of individually wrapped clear plastic cups, a yellow pitcher, and a matching, kidney-shaped emesis basin. Next to the bed, two upholstered chairs stand sentinel, and a partially opened door reveals a handicap rail attached to the wall next to a toilet.

Her continued inspection drifts down, taking in her hands—fingers and wrists absent of jewelry—resting on top of a sterile white sheet, and a thin green blanket folded neatly over her legs. From an IV pole, a clear bag of fluid hangs half empty with a tube running to the inside of her right arm. A call button attached to the metal railing around the bed confirms that she's in a hospital room.

———

"Where's Emma?" Libby asks when she and Dr. Sutton enter the kitchen.

"She'll be right back," Fran says. "She remembered they left the tea kettle on in their hurry to get here." Shifting her gaze from Libby's tired face to Dr. Sutton's, Fran asks, "Is Hemingway going to be okay?"

The vet nods. "Yes. With Libby's help we got him cleaned and stitched up, and now he's sleeping comfortably until the anesthesia wears off. He'll be very sore for a while, but right as rain in a few weeks."

Dr. Sutton turns to Libby. "Do you still have the Elizabethan collar from Hemingway's last adventure?"

"Yes," Libby confirms.

"When he wakes up, you'll need to put it on him, so he'll leave the dressings alone."

"What's an Elizabethan collar?" Fran asks, her brows scrunched.

Niall answers. "It looks like a big plastic funnel from his neck, outward, like a giant halo around his face. We called him 'Bucket Head' the last time he wore it. It kept him from getting at ointment he would have licked off otherwise."

Turning to the vet, Niall says, "Hey, Doc, can I get you some coffee?"

"I thought you'd never ask. And are those biscuits I smell?"

"They sure are, let me get you a plate."

"Libby," Officer Chris says, patting the empty seat next to her, "I know you're tired, but Herb and I need to ask you a few questions to get your perspective on the situation. We've already taken statements from Niall and Fran. We'll try to keep it brief."

"Okay. But first, is there any word from Mick?" she asks, looking at Niall.

Setting a frothy cup in front of both Libby and Herb, Niall says, "Mick called a while ago to let us know they're keeping Cynthia overnight for observation. He's catching a ride home with Skip. He said he'd fill us in on the details when he gets here."

Through the steam of her cup, Libby watches Chris flip open her notebook as she prepares to take her statement.

Jason, a strong swimmer, holds his breath when he shoves off the ledge.

Then he hits the frigid water.

It feels like glass cutting into his skin when he cannons beneath the crashing waves. Jason knows better than to fight the descent. As the current pulls him deeper, his heartbeat stabs his chest.

Once the downward progression stops, he uses powerful scissor kicks to follow the barely discernible phosphorescent bubbles from his plunge, back up. He realizes, too late, that being fully dressed is working against him. When his head breaks the surface, he empties his lungs and draws in deep gulps of fresh air.

As he treads the churning water with one arm, he gets his bearings and makes a quick assessment. His entire body hurts like hell, but he doesn't think anything's broken. From the surveillance he'd done while he was supposed to be writing, Jason knows he has to head south and stay next to the cliff where it eventually gives way to a heavily wooded hill. *I'll climb that and cut across Pines & Quill using the darkness as cover to make my way down behind Thoreau cottage into the canyon.*

Exhausted and in pain, Jason crosses a patch of sand, skirting boulders and low rocks. Nearing Pines & Quill, the route roughens. Boulders are larger in spots, spilling at length into the Bay. Not one to discourage easily, he smiles when he thinks about the bottle of Jack and the Beretta that are waiting for him in the backpack he'd stashed in the canyon cave yesterday.

CHAPTER 18

*"Do not hoard what seems good for a later place
in the book, or for another book; give it, give
it all, give it now."*

— Annie Dillard

Emma pushes the door-activation button and rushes into Austen cottage, rolling straight through to the kitchen. Grabbing a hot mitt, she yanks the now-empty tea kettle from the flame and sets it on a cork trivet next to the stove, then turns off the burner.

Shuddering, she tips her head back in relief. *That could have been disastrous!* In her frantic state, she half expected to see flames from her fiery cottage roof licking treetops when she rounded the bend.

When Mick enters the kitchen of the main house, he's swarmed. Everyone wants to know everything about Cynthia. "Who, what, when, where, why, and how?" They pelt him with questions.

He looks around the room, his eyebrows knit in concern. "Where's Emma?"

Fran repeats what she'd told Libby. "She'll be right back. In her rush to get here, she thinks she left the tea kettle on a lit burner."

"Right," he says, nodding.

Shifting his gaze to Dr. Sutton, he asks, "How's Hemingway?"

"With Libby's assistance, he's cleaned, stitched, and sleeping comfortably. At least until the anesthesia wears off. He's going to be sore for a while, but he'll recover. I told Libby that when he wakes up in the morning to put the Elizabethan collar on him, so he'll leave the dressings alone."

Clearing her throat, Officer Chris interjects. "We hate to interrupt, but Mick, we need to ask you a few questions."

"Sure, but can I have some coffee?" His gaze turns pleadingly to his brother-in-law.

"You bet," Niall says. "Have a seat, and I'll bring you a mug of coffee and a plate of biscuits."

"And I'll bring you one of Niall's shirts," Libby adds.

Opening her notepad, Chris asks, "Do you recall what Ms. Winters said when she regained consciousness in the ambulance?"

"Yes, she said, 'It was Jason. He fell over the cliff, and he's dead.' And then she passed out again."

"Libby told us that Jason's last name is Hughes and that he's from Cleveland. Have you seen him since he left after dinner this evening?"

"No. When we finished dinner, we all went to The Ink Well for drinks and dessert where we had a pretty intense conversation. After that, I thought everyone went back to their cottages. I haven't seen him since."

Herb asks, "What was the 'intense conversation' about?"

"Cynthia explained that she'd done work as a forensic intuitive for several police departments throughout the southwest. Mostly cases involving missing children, and even a few cold cases."

Looking from Herb to Chris and back again, Mick contin-ues. "You're both aware that my partner's killer has never been caught. It's considered a cold case. As I'm sure you can imagine, Cynthia's expertise is of particular interest to me, so I kept asking her questions about how a forensic intuitive works."

Between bites of a biscuit, Mick asks, "Are you two ready to head out to the bluff?"

Chris and Herb look at each other, baffled, then back at Mick.

"What?" Mick asks. *If Sam and I had responded to this call, we wouldn't hesitate. We'd be out there in a heartbeat.*

Chris answers. "There's no point in going out tonight Mick. Not in this downpour."

"Our flashlights will barely make a dent," Herb adds. "They pale in comparison to the light of day."

"We should try to find him," Mick says.

"Ms. Winters said he fell over the cliff. There's no way he could have survived on a good day, let alone in a storm," Chris says.

Herb nods. "We'll send a team to the bluff tomorrow once things have had a chance to dry a bit. We'll also send a diving team to the base of the cliff where he fell over, and they'll search from there."

Chris stands. "Thank you. That'll be all for this evening." Closing her notebook, she adds, "If any of you remembers anything else that might be helpful, even the smallest detail, please call immediately."

Turning to Niall and Libby, she adds, "Thank you for your hospitality."

And with that, the two officers take their leave.

"I better get home, too," Dr. Sutton says. "And remember, put that Elizabethan collar on Hemingway when he wakes up." Then setting his cap, he follows Chris and Herb into the night, pulling the door closed behind him.

Wet, bruised, and chilled to the bone, Jason has one thing on his mind—the bottle of Jack Daniels he stashed in his backpack and left in the cave yesterday as part of his preparation.

A soft glow of light catches Jason's attention as his aching body steals through the wooded grove. Hugging trees for cover, he creeps closer. When he steps onto the smooth-tiled terra cotta patio, he presses his back to the cottage wall, then turns and peers through the sliding glass door. Like a bird of prey, his hooded, storm-gray eyes survey Emma.

There she sits, in front of the kitchen stove with her head tilted back, throat fully exposed. Its slender column brings to mind dozens of other throats in every shade of skin tone.

With his right arm still tucked up against his chest, the fingers of his left hand absently thrum the cargo pocket on his thigh. Pleased it's still there after his swim, he fishes out his knife. A Camillus, it's served him well on many occasions. It would have been a shame to have lost it on the cliffside or in the bay. His heart beats fast and hard, but not with fear, with fierce exhilaration. He feels a flow of heady exuberance.

Well-oiled, he knows the blade barely whispers when deployed. Tucking his thumb under the thumb-stud, he pushes it up and out, admiring its razor-sharp edge. Lost in reverie, he flicks it open and shut, tapping it against his thigh, again and again, with brooding deliberation as he imagines what he can do to Emma's lovely white throat with it.

Movement in his peripheral vision brings him back from his fantasy. When he realizes that Emma's rolling her wheelchair toward the front door, he runs around the side of the cottage and hides behind a large tree along the pathway.

As she passes him, unseen, he steps out behind her wheelchair and grabs one of the handles, halting it. "Where are you off to in such a hurry?" he asks.

Startled, Emma whirls her torso around and sees Jason, blade in hand. "What are you doing here?" she gasps, hands at her chest. "I thought you were dead."

"What made you think I was dead?" he asks, the slit eyes in his face bent so close she can see their acid gray color.

Emma's focus is on the knife. It's pressed against her left jugular, a superhighway of circulation. If severed, she'll bleed out in under a minute. Terrified, she struggles for breath, her heart beating fast. "Cynthia said she saw you fall over the cliff."

"Is that bitch still alive?" he asks, lip pulled back in a sneer. "I was hoping she was dead. I cut her pretty deep. If that goddamn dog hadn't interfered," he says, easing the knife slightly. "But I'm alive, and I'm here to pick up some bait. You see, I'm going fishing, and I know just the lure to catch what I'm after."

Trying to roll away, Emma says, "I don't know what you mean. I don't have any bait."

"Ah, but *you're* the bait," he says with a smirk.

Emma feels the blade press harder against her skin. Something slides down her neck. A drop of blood, but only a drop.

"And if you roll that chair one inch further," Jason continues, "I'll derive great pleasure from slitting your throat."

"But they're expecting me. I told them I'd be right back, as soon as I checked the stove. They're *expecting* me," she repeats in earnest.

The blade presses deeper against Emma's skin. Her jugular's exposed, right at the surface from the pressure. She feels another prick of the blade. Another drop of blood slides down her neck.

"I'm sure they are, but we'll fix that. Do exactly as I say. If you deviate from what I tell you, I'm going to kill you."

Closing the blade with his hip, he slips the knife back in his pocket, turns her chair around and rolls her back up the ramp. "I've watched you enough times to know exactly how to get in. Now push the goddamn button."

"You've been spying on me?" she gasps.

"I've been watching *all* of you."

Pushing Emma's chair toward the oak desk in Austen cottage, he continues. "You're going to use the house phone and let them know that everything with the stove is fine. Tell them that all of the excitement from this evening's events has caught up with you, and you've decided to go to bed. Keep your tone pleasant and don't add anything to what I've told you. Let them know you'll see them in the morning. Have I made myself clear?"

"Yes, I understand, but they're going to think it's unusual if I don't ask if Mick's back from the hospital and how Cynthia's doing. Can I at least ask that?"

His responding smile is menacing.

Taking a step toward Emma, he backhands her across the face. "Don't ever 'but' me," he says.

After thinking for a moment, he adds, "Actually, you can ask those two questions. The answers will help me to prepare. Now pick up the phone and say exactly what we discussed. If you deviate from the plan, I'll kill you."

Emma chokes down an unborn scream. Head reeling, she feels like her heart is beating in her face, but she knows it's not. Her cheek stings like fire where his hand left an imprint.

Tears held in check, she picks up the receiver.

The ringing phone in the kitchen of the main house startles everyone.

Picking up the receiver, "Emma?" Niall asks, concern in his voice.

All eyes are on Niall as he responds, nodding thoughtfully, "Yes. I understand. Thank you for letting us know. What's that? Oh yes, Mick's back and Cynthia's going to be okay. She's resting now. Yes, you too. Get a good night's sleep and we'll see you in the morning."

Raising his hands to ward off the sudden barrage of questions, he repeats what Emma told him. "Everything with the stove is fine. She said that all of the excitement from this evening's events has caught up with her and she's going to bed. She asked if Mick is back from the hospital and if Cynthia is okay. You heard what I said from this end."

"I'm exhausted, too," Fran says. "I'll see you all in the morning." Pausing, she adds, "If you hear anything about Cynthia or Jason before then, please call me."

Plowing finger marks through his hair, "I'm whipped too," Mick says. "Good night, I'll see you all tomorrow."

When he steps outside, Mick sees that the storm has given way to a clear night sky strewn with stars glistening like ice. His heart aches. He would like to have seen Emma, but he understands her exhaustion. He feels it too.

As he slips into bed, he thinks, *How is it that an auburn-haired, green-eyed woman has burst onto the scene and stolen my heart? I've fallen,* he tells himself. *I've fallen in love with her*

Knowing that he'll see her in the morning, he smiles and falls into a deep, bone-weary sleep.

Jason looks at Emma. As he watches her, he backs toward the front door and throws the deadbolt. "Now we're going on a little journey."

"Where are we going?" Emma asks, trying to keep fear out of her voice.

"You'll just have to wait and see. Let me remind you," he says, a grim smile of promise on his face. "If you say one word, or try to call attention in any way, I'll kill you."

Pulling the knife from his pocket, he presses his thumb under the thumb-stud, pushing out the blade so she can see its razor-sharp edge.

"Yours wouldn't be the first throat I've slit," he says baldly. "Do you understand me?"

Emma nods.

"I can't hear you," he taunts.

Looking straight into the twin eyes of evil, she says, "Yes, I understand."

Closing the blade with his thigh, he turns out the light, opens the sliding glass door, pushes her chair out onto the smooth-tiled patio, and then closes the slider behind them.

He can feel the blood pumping in his veins, and a thrill of excitement as darkness envelops them. He'd nearly forgotten the adrenaline rush. These days it usually only comes with the kill.

"Our destination isn't that far. If you work with me, we'll be there soon. If you work against me, you could—" He pauses, pretending to think of a suitable word. "*Tumble,* wheelchair and all—and break your pretty little neck. If you enjoy breathing, I suggest you work with me."

Surrounded by trees, Jason pushes Emma in her wheelchair through the stormy night.

Think Emma. Think.

"I'm scared," she whispers just loud enough for Jason to hear.

"Well good, then my plan's working," he replies.

Pretending to cry, she feigns sniffing. "Do you have a tissue—"

"Use the back of your hand."

Emma swallows and nods.

Covering her face with her hands, she tips her head forward, pretending to cry. The drape of her hair curtains the removal of a pearl earring she conceals in her hand.

Jason steps around the chair, juts his face into hers, and threatens, "If you don't stop crying, I'll give you something to cry about." And he slaps her across the face again.

Biting the inside of her lip to stifle a scathing remark, Emma tastes blood. Seething with anger, she pretends remorse. "I'm sorry," she sniffs.

When he steps behind her chair to continue pushing, she pretends to wipe her nose with the back of her hand. *There, I've got the other earring.*

She hides a self-satisfied smile and surreptitiously drops the first pearl on the ground.

A few dozen yards later, the terrain becomes even rougher, and though it's dark, she can feel the grade steepen sharply.

"It's going to get much rougher from this point on," Jason rasps, nearly out of breath from trying to keep the chair in his one-handed grip.

Unused to this point, Emma reaches for the handbrakes to help slow their decent, inconspicuously letting go of the second earring.

Tripping on a rock, Jason stumbles. "Fuck!" he shouts, releasing the wheelchair.

Emma, now on a wild ride, uses every ounce of her upper-body strength to pull the handbrakes. And though her wheelchair slows, it doesn't stop until one of the wheels strikes a boulder and she's thrown from her seat, landing face-down on the rock-strewn ground.

Dizzy and nauseous, she closes her eyes, trying to focus on the colorless void behind her lids.

Moving with stealth, Jason reaches Emma's crumpled heap. Her legs are twisted. She's laying perfectly still.

Toeing her body over with his shoe, moonlight reveals her mud-spattered face.

Leaning closer, he knows she's not dead because of the slight moan that escapes her lips. Straightening, he hisses a barked whisper. "Get up."

Emma opens her eyes slowly. Sharper than his razor-edged knife, Jason knows that if looks could kill, he'd be dead.

Speaking through clenched teeth. "Why do you think I use a wheelchair?"

"Oh, that's right, you're a *gimp*," he sneers, "but it's only your legs."

Panther-like he circles her.

"If I'm not mistaken, you were pulling on handbrakes during that unexpected little joy ride. Why didn't you say there were brakes when I was trying to keep us from barreling down the slope?"

"If you'll remember," she says evenly, "you told me to keep my mouth shut."

Jaw jutting forward, nostrils flared, Jason bends down and backhands her across the face yet again. "Don't get smart with me. The only reason I haven't slit your throat is that you're the perfect bait for what I'm catching.

"You happened to have landed almost on our doorstep. I'm taking your wheelchair in with me. If you want to use it again, you'll have to earn it back. Since you're only a gimp from the waist down, you can use your arms and crawl on your belly. Yes, I'd like that. And don't try anything clever, I'll be watching you from inside."

Using his left arm, he picks up the damaged wheelchair and disappears through an opening in the mountainside, leaving Emma, mouth agape, staring after him.

———

If my legs worked, I'd run and hide in the woods. But they don't.

Thoughts race through Emma's mind as she tries to formulate a plan.

I can stand, briefly, but Jason doesn't know that. He's never been present when I've done it. And the only place I've practiced in my cottage is in the bathroom when I'm brushing my teeth. Even if he's been spying on me, he wouldn't have seen that. I need to catch him by surprise.

She remembers playing with her brothers. They'd crawl on their bellies up and down the hallway mimicking the GI Joe character on television.

With my upper-body strength, I can do this, Emma resolves. *The alternative is unbearable.*

It takes a long, grueling while, but she does it. A shroud of moist darkness envelops her when she crawls inside the cave. The blackness is smothering. *It's like being buried alive, but above ground.*

Emma's breathing slows as she takes in the stale, humid air. Using the rough wall as a guide, she hears a faint dripping noise—*drip, drip, drip*—like dew sliding off rocks.

While her eyes adjust to the dark, a soft squeak alerts Emma to the presence of either mice or bats. The chilled air sends shivers down her spine.

Senses heightened, she smells Jason before she sees him. *Whiskey.*

She feels his gaze on her back.

Her brain registers the sound of a click, immediately followed by light.

"Welcome to Devil's Canyon," Jason says.

Turning, she sees the smile of a madman, uplit by a flashlight held under his chin.

Dazzled by the sudden bright light, thousands of bats form a cloud-like exodus, screeching as they leave a mud and blood-covered Emma hugging the ground in their wake.

Jason's maniacal laugh echoes long after their departure.

CHAPTER 19

"Write while the heat is in you. The writer who postpones the recording of his thoughts uses an iron which has cooled to burn a hole with."

—Henry David Thoreau

The main house is situated on a gently sloping hill. From upstairs the panoramic view of the surrounding forest makes Libby feel like she's in the Swiss Family Robinson treehouse.

This morning she stands at the window and watches the branches sway in the breeze. She doesn't miss the serrated skyline of San Francisco where she and Mick grew up, but she misses their parents who still live there. *I need to plan another visit.*

And though she can only hear it in her imagination because the windows are closed, Libby loves the frothy roil of the bay when it recovers from a storm. She also enjoys early mornings before the fog lifts, and the sun warms the house. With no tai chi today, she delights in the idea of a wood fire, wool socks, and hot chocolate made from scratch.

As she turns to look at her lightly snoring husband, she smiles at his hair, wild with sleep, and teasingly says, "Niall, it looks like you combed your hair with an eggbeater."

"What's that, wife?" he asks, pulling the pillow over his head.

"You heard me, husband." She pulls it back off. "Let's go check on Hemingway. Dr. Sutton said we have to put the Elizabethan collar on him first thing this morning. And I bet he's got to pee like a racehorse! By the way, where did that saying come from?"

Removing the pillow and the warm covers, Niall swings his legs over the bedside and puts on his slippers. Turning back, he looks at her from under shaggy brows and responds, "Trust me, Libby, you don't want to know." And with that, he heads to the bathroom.

Hemingway, wide awake in the mudroom, is busy licking salve from the stitches he can reach with his tongue, and desperately trying to get at those he can't. He'd need the tongue of an anteater to reach the ones on his back.

Hearing Libby and Niall enter the kitchen, he stands and body-wags a greeting.

"Good morning, fella," Niall says with exaggerated enthusiasm in his voice. "We've got a treat for you."

Turning to Libby, he stage whispers out the side of his mouth. "You get the collar around his neck while I distract him."

"Oh, hell no," she replies. "*You* get the collar around his neck while *I* distract him."

"All right," he says. "Let's think about this. Based on previous experience, we need a plan. We know that Hemingway has the advantage of speed, strength, and total lack of concern for our welfare."

"Yes, but we get to pick the battlefield," she says. "I say the mudroom."

"Mudroom it is," Niall agrees.

"Once Hemingway sees the Elizabethan collar, he's going to go berserk," Libby says.

"I agree, but the collar's in the upper-cupboard in the mudroom." Niall looks worried.

"I'll keep him distracted at the Dutch door with treats, while you get the collar," Libby assures him. "But I think you should change your clothes first."

"Change?" he looks at her curiously. "Into what?"

"Oh, let's see," she muses, tapping an index finger on her chin. "Overalls, construction boots, welding gloves, a football helmet, a hockey face-mask, and Mick's flak vest."

"Right," he says, laughing. "And that won't scare the daylights out of him?"

"Not if we use the element of surprise."

"*We?*"

"Well, *you,*" Libby replies, not one bit shame-faced. "Niall, once Hemingway's on to what's happening, speed is essential to your survival. And when it's all over, we know it's not—he'll be plotting ways to kill us in our sleep. Well, *you* anyway," she finishes, grinning wickedly.

Seeing the Bellingham Police Department number on the phone display, Mick sets down his coffee cup and picks up his ringing cell. "McPherson," he answers. "Good morning. Yes, I can be there in fifteen minutes." *Crap,* he thinks to himself. *I was hoping to see Emma this morning before heading out to the bluff.*

There in ten, Mick is the first to arrive at last evening's scene. Not wanting to jeopardize any potential evidence, he stays clear of the area.

Two cruisers pull up. Herb and Chris get out of the first one. Two other officers exit the other.

"Hey, Mick, it's been a while," Joe says, extending his hand. "I'm sorry it's under these circumstances." Turning to the officer next to him, Joe adds, "This is Toni, she just transferred in."

Stepping forward, Toni shakes Mick's outstretched hand. "It's a pleasure to meet you. We know you've already been over this with Chris and Herb, but would you mind telling Joe and me what happened, before we inspect the area? It'll help us to know what we're looking at and looking for."

Leading the four of them to the edge of the area, Mick points while sharing everything he knows—the same information he'd shared last night. "I stayed clear of the area so I wouldn't disturb anything."

Lifting up one of his feet, he continues, "I wore the same shoes as last night so you can tell my tread from the others."

"That's helpful, thank you. This isn't your first rodeo, is it?" Toni asks.

"No. I used to be on the force, too."

"Yeah, on the way over, Joe explained what happened. I'm sorry about that."

Shifting gears to the subject at hand, Chris says, "Even after the storm, we can see three sets of shoe prints. These impressions correspond in design, physical size, and mold characteristics to your shoes," she says, pointing at Mick's feet. "These," pointing to another set, "belong to a woman. See?" she continues, squatting near the ground. "This divot was made by a pointed spike like the heel on a woman's shoe." After snapping photos in rapid succession, she turns to Mick and asks, "Do you recall what shoes Ms. Winters was wearing last night?"

"When I lifted her into the ATV, I was trying to be careful not to bump any part of her, so I was paying attention. She was wearing fancy sandals, but I couldn't say with certainty if they had spiked heels, or not."

"Thank you. And these," pointing to the third set, "have a completely different design, mold characteristics, and are physically smaller in size than yours," she says, looking at Mick. "How tall would you guess Mr. Hughes is?"

"He's at least six inches shorter than I am."

"These," she says, pointing at paw prints, "must belong to your dog, the one who got hurt last night. How's he doing, by the way?"

"I haven't seen Hemingway yet this morning, but the vet assures us that he'll fully recover."

"By the size of these prints, he must be huge," Toni muses.

"He is," Mick says, smiling. "He's an Irish Wolfhound."

"I'm familiar with that breed. I sure wouldn't want to tangle with a dog that size."

"This slide or drag mark that goes to the edge is in keeping with a human body. And look, there are paw marks on each side, like the dog was standing over the person," Toni says.

"If he was," Mick counters, "it was to protect Cynthia. Hemingway's only aggressive when he's defending himself or someone else."

"It's hard to tell in the mud," Toni continues, "but this area is darker." She points. "It seems like it could be blood. And look at all of the glass shards. From what's left of this neck, I'd say they're from a wine bottle."

Slipping on a pair of thin latex gloves before bagging the broken glass, she continues, "I'll send these to the lab to see if they can lift any prints, even a partial might help. I'm going to collect some of this mud too. After all the rain I doubt they can test this potential blood for DNA, but it's worth a shot. It might not all be from Ms. Winters. From the looks of the scene, your dog may have done some serious damage to Mr. Hughes."

"Thanks, Toni," Mick says. "If it's blood, it's probably Cynthia's. Dr. Zimmerman said that her femoral artery had been nicked. She said that if it had been severed, she'd have bled out right here on the bluff."

"Can you think of any reason why Mr. Hughes would want to hurt Ms. Winters?"

"No, none. The guy arrived with what seems like a chip on his shoulder, and he likes his liquor. We have a well-stocked bar in the main house, yet he went to town and bought an additional stash. In fact, when Niall gave him a lift, he popped open a flask in the car. Niall made him walk the rest of the way. If he's angry about that, he'd be pissed at us, not Cynthia."

Joe says, "There hasn't been a mudslide here in a long time, but to be safe, let's not all walk to the edge. I'll take a look over the side to see if Mr. Hughes is down there."

Peering over, Joe lets out a long, low whistle. "Man, that's a long way down. I can't imagine anyone surviving that fall." Shaking his head, he continues, "We'll send a diving team to see if they can locate his body. It may have already gone out with the tide."

———

Finished with the unpleasant task at hand, a haggard-looking Niall stands back and presses both hands to his arched back.

Before he can suggest to Libby that they open the outer mudroom door to let Hemingway outside, she opens the Dutch door adjoining the kitchen.

Smiling at a pathetic-looking Hemingway, she says, "Oh dear, you do look like a cone—"

But before she can finish the sentence, he dashes past her, knocking into the doorframe on his way. With a reduced line of sight, Hemingway bumps blindly into chairs, the kitchen island, and the refrigerator door before bounding into The Ink Well.

"Come back here," Niall roars, as he and Libby make their way, hoping to trap him in that room.

A thundering crash announces that Hemingway just toppled the oak stand holding the retreat's journal.

Barreling back the way he'd come, the Elizabethan collar acts like a cowcatcher on the front of a train, clearing everything in its way.

Libby and Niall press their backs to the wall as Hemingway shoots past them.

"Quick Niall, open the front door before he destroys anything else."

———

Hand flying to her chest, Fran yelps, stopping mid-stride on the outside steps as Hemingway bolts past her.

"We're so sorry. We didn't know you were there," Niall apologizes to the stunned woman.

"I came to find out if there's any news about Cynthia," she says.

"The vet told us to put the Elizabethan collar on that hairy mongrel first thing this morning. Then we were going to call the hospital, but all hell broke loose," Niall says.

"Please come in and join us for breakfast," Libby invites. "I'll call now."

"Thank you. I'd like that."

After putting his apron on, Niall starts pulling items from the refrigerator.

Fran watches as he removes eggs, tomatoes, yellow peppers, mushrooms, a block of cheese, bacon, and sour cream.

"My stomach just growled. What are you making?" Fran asks.

"I call it 'The Farmer's Daughter.'" He smiles. "It's Libby's favorite. She loves avocados, so I finish it off with thick slices on top."

"Did I hear my name?" Libby asks, stepping back into the kitchen from the phone call.

"Yes. Niall says he's making 'The Farmer's Daughter,'" Fran replies.

"That's my favorite," Libby says with a smile.

"That's just what he was saying. What's the news on Cynthia? Is she okay?"

"She is. In fact, they're releasing her this afternoon. I think it would be nice if we all went in the van to pick her up. After I clean up the mess in The Ink Well, I'll head over to Austen cottage to see if Emma wants to join us."

Hemingway smells the delicious scent through the kitchen windows. Never one to pass up food, he barks at the mudroom door.

Pulling the lower half of the Dutch door closed behind her so he can't get into the kitchen, Libby lets Hemingway in. His paws are mud-caked, as is the bottom edge of the Elizabethan collar.

"I'm sorry, big guy, but the sooner your wounds heal, the sooner we can take that awful contraption off your head. If we remove it now, you'll just lick the salve off your stitches."

Laying down on his mat, Hemingway lets out a resigned *harrumph* and does his best to prop his head on top of his massive front paws.

While snipping bits of fresh parsley onto dollops of sour cream, Niall clears his throat and asks, "Ladies, do you really think Cynthia would want *all* of us there to pick her up?"

"Yes. Absolutely!" they say in unison. And with that, two battle-ready women launch into the merits of having *all* of them along.

A smart man, Niall knows to choose his battles. Clearly, this isn't one he'd win.

———————

"I'm stuffed. Thank you for such a lovely breakfast. It was delicious," Fran says. "What time should I meet you at the van?"

"Cynthia's going to be released after the doctor makes her one o'clock rounds. They suggested I call again before coming to make sure Dr. Zimmerman doesn't change her mind for any reason. I'll call the hospital at one-thirty, then ring you at Dickens cottage after I've confirmed her release."

"That sounds great," Fran says, patting her stomach. "In the meantime, I'm well-fueled and will write until you call."

Libby turns to Niall. "If you clean the kitchen, I'll take care of The Ink Well. Deal?"

"Deal." Niall smiles.

———————

It's not nearly as bad as it could be, Libby thinks. A couple of furniture pillows are tossed from overstuffed chairs, and a few books are knocked off the shelves. The crash they'd heard was from Hemingway knocking over an oak stand as he bulldozed his way through.

Once righted, Libby picks up the Pines & Quill journal and lays it flat, open to the most recent page. She smiles when she notices a fresh entry, delighted that one of this month's guests has written something.

Grabbing a pair of cheaters from the fireplace mantle, she reads the tight, precise script. *Look in the mirror and what do you see? An eerie reflection that looks like me.* It was signed, Andrew Berndt.

Foreboding wipes the smile off her face as if she'd been slapped. Heart-pounding alarm raises the hairs on the nape of her neck.

Libby recognizes the name from the newscasts and newspapers she'd watched and pored over after Mick's accident. Andrew Berndt is one of the ringleaders who was arrested in conjunction with the drug heist on the night of Sam's slaying. He was found hanging in his prison cell.

The other ringleader, his fraternal twin, is still at large.

CHAPTER 20

"In order to see a book through to the end, you have to have discipline, so carve out time every day—no excuses. When you get ready to write your novel, outline it first. There's nothing worse than getting halfway through and realizing you've painted yourself in a plot corner."

—JANET EVANOVICH

Mick is halfway to Pines & Quill when Libby's ringtone jangles in his jeans pocket.

"Hey sis, I'm just heading back from talking with the police team on the bluffs. I'm going to swing by Austen to see Emma—"

"Mick, come straight to the main house. It's urgent."

Not pausing to question the dread in his sister's voice, he bolts.

As she looks toward the mouth of the cave, Emma sees that day has just been born. With still-young light, she can just make out the shadowy shape of her wheelchair.

Nodding toward it, she asks Jason, "May I?"

It takes him a moment, but he finally responds. "Hmmm. I was thinking no, but since you asked so nicely, yes you may. I use positive reinforcement for training dogs. The look of astonishment when you inflict pain after a reward is extremely satisfying."

Sickened, Emma keeps her tongue in check and drags herself across the guano-covered, rock-strewn ground.

Reaching the wheelchair, she assesses it carefully, sets it to rights, locks the wheels in place, and begins the difficult task of pulling herself up and into the seat.

Hearing soft applause, she turns to see Jason's eyes locked on hers.

"Brava," he says, feigning interest in her accomplishment. "You seem to have quite the upper-body strength." Tapping his temple with his index finger, he says, "I'll have to keep that in mind."

"May I ask you a question?"

"It depends on what it is. Try me."

"Earlier you said you were going fishing and that you're going to use me as bait. I don't understand what you're trying to catch or why. Will you please explain?"

Libby and Niall are waiting for Mick when he arrives through the mudroom.

Passing Hemingway, he heads straight into the kitchen. His sister and brother-in-law appear to be okay, so he asks, "What's so urgent?"

Libby says, "I didn't want to contaminate any possible evidence, so I put the Pines & Quill journal down once I'd read the most recent entry. I left it open to that page so you can read it without picking it up."

"I don't understand."

"Follow me. I don't know what it means either," Libby says. "But whatever it is, it isn't good."

When Mick bends over the oak stand and starts reading, Libby and Niall both watch the color drain from his face.

"Ms. Winters, you had quite an extraordinary evening," Dr. Zimmerman smiles as she reaches out her hand.

Extending her hand to meet the doctor's, Cynthia smiles. "Please call me Cynthia. Everything's still a bit fuzzy. Can you help refresh my memory of what happened?"

"I don't have all of the details, but from what Sean McPherson tells me, you were attacked by someone on the bluff over the bay. You're fortunate that whoever did this to you only nicked your femoral artery. That was bad enough. If it had been severed, you would have bled out and died."

The pieces in Cynthia's memory start fitting together. And while she still doesn't have the full picture, she remembers that Hemingway saved her from Jason, and that a storm-driven gust of wind toppled him over the side of the cliff.

"Did they find his body?" she asks the doctor.

Wrinkling her brows in question, "Whose body?" Dr. Zimmerman asks.

"The last thing I remember is that a blast of wind slapped Jason Hughes over the side of the cliff."

"That's interesting," Dr. Zimmerman says. "There were no reported fatalities last night. I'd like to take a few of your vitals while we talk. Is that okay with you?"

"That's fine. When will I be released?"

"I'm determining that right now," Dr. Zimmerman says, smiling. "Libby MacCullough called and wants to know the same thing. Since you're staying at Pines & Quill, you must be a writer," she says, continuing her examination. "Please hold your head still and follow this pen light with your eyes."

"Yes," Cynthia answers. "I'm here working on a book."

"Now breathe deeply. That's it." A moment passes. "Again." Dr. Zimmerman takes gentle hold of Cynthia's wrist. Her thumb, where it rests on Cynthia's skin, is warm and soft. When she's satisfied, she takes a chart from the table and writes something. The doctor's cursive is precise and unexpectedly neat.

"Tell me about it. I'd like to hear." And while Cynthia gives her a thumbnail sketch of the book, Dr. Zimmerman finishes her examination.

"I'll dismiss you today if you will make, and *keep*,"—she emphasizes the word "keep" with a pointed look—"a promise."

"I'm sure that I can. What is it?"

"You've lost a lot of blood, but not enough for a transfusion. In other words, because your body's remaking blood, you have to rest. And by rest, I mean you need to remain still."

"Yes, I'll—"

"I'm not quite finished. You also have an impressive number of stitches on the inside of your upper thigh. They, too, need to rest."

Waiting to make sure the doctor has finished, Cynthia says, "Yes, I promise that I'll rest."

"Then I'll go call the MacCulloughs and let them know they can pick you up this afternoon. In the meantime, please lie still and get some rest."

"Thank you. Thank you for everything."

"You're welcome. I hope we don't meet again under these circumstances."

A deep quiet settles over the room. Cynthia rests her eyes and tries to reconstruct the events of last night. In her mind's eye, she sees herself being wheeled down a long corridor, and remembers ceiling lights flashing rhythmically through closed eyelids.

Mesmerized, she slips into sleep again.

"Niall, call the police and get them back out here. Let them know that Chris, Herb, Joe, and Toni are familiar with the case and we'd like one of them," Mick says before leaving.

Fifteen years his senior, Libby stays on Mick's heels as they run over the smooth walkway—fueled by fear—to Austen cottage.

Not bothering to knock, Mick pushes the door activation button. "The deadbolt's been thrown," he says over his shoulder to Libby as he rounds the corner of the cottage.

"Emma," he shouts, sliding the glass door open. "Emma!"

Libby's right behind him.

"Don't touch anything," Mick says, while his eyes drink everything in, looking for clues. "It doesn't look like there's been a struggle."

"I can't imagine where she's gone, or why she'd throw the deadbolt and use the sliding glass door to leave," Libby says.

"I don't think she would have," Mick answers, his voice laced with steel. "Please go back to the house and wait for the police. I'm going to my cabin, and then I'm going to Thoreau."

"Why are you going to your cabin?"

"To get my gun. Call me when the police arrive."

He pulls his phone from his pocket. "I'm putting my cell on vibrate so it's silent when you call. I don't want a ring to alert anyone of my presence."

"Oh, my God, Mick. Be careful."

From the tone of his people's voices and the way they're pacing the buttery pine floorboards in the kitchen, Hemingway knows that something is wrong.

He can smell their fear from the mudroom.

Alert to possible danger, Mick's adrenalin spikes as he loads and holsters his Glock 22, the same type of service weapon he'd been issued when hired by the SFPD. *Once a cop, always a cop,* he thinks. And though the clip holster is meant for ultimate concealment inside his waistband, he doesn't give a damn about that right now.

Stashing another magazine with fifteen rounds in his back pocket, he pulls on a pair of latex gloves and storms toward Thoreau.

The moist cave wall feels cool to his back as Jason positions himself so he can keep an eye on Emma and the mouth of the cave. Though the light is dim, he can see Emma take in his every move. *I don't give a damn. I have the upper hand.*

As he holds his right arm across his chest, fingers resting on his left shoulder, his other hand taps an empty bottle of Jack Daniels on top of his thigh. Now and then he raises it to his nose and inhales deeply, relishing the fumes. "So you'd like me to explain why I'm using you as bait. Is that right?" Jason sneers.

"Yes," she answers evenly, with no trace of emotion in her voice.

"It doesn't really matter what you know because you're going to be dead shortly, and I'm the one who's going to kill you."

Jason feels excitement tingle throughout his body. Just saying the words brings an explosion of pleasure.

"You're the ideal bait because I've seen how *Lover Boy* looks at you." His lips twist in a sneer. "Once he realizes that you're gone, he's going to come looking for you, and I'm going to derive a great deal of pleasure watching him crumple as I slit your throat. You'll be the second person I kill that he cares for."

"Who was the first?" Emma asks.

"His name was Sam. Poor, unfortunate bastard. He was McPherson's partner."

"I don't understand."

"A little slow on the uptake, aren't you?"

Shaking his head in derision, Jason continues. "Five years ago, my brother and I orchestrated a heist involving well over ten million dollars in heroin. The problem was, the goods were in the SFPD evidence lockup. But we had someone on the inside helping us—a dirty cop. Stay wary," he adds with a conspiratorial wink, "for treachery walks among you."

He watches with pleasure as Emma rubs the goosebumps on her arms, then continues. "The only thing we had to do was empty the station house. Police are predictable creatures. When an officer falls, they rally. Every one of them.

"All we had to do was kill a cop—*any* cop would do.

"We used a diversionary tactic to draw a squad car to a bridge. And that's when I got the driver in my sights and squeezed the trigger. *Boom!* Sam was out of the game."

"I don't understand why you want to kill Mick. He's off the force. And you got your drugs."

"Aah, but that's where you're wrong. I didn't get the drugs. My brother was one of three people who got caught. He's the one who stashed the drugs. He's the only person who knows their location."

"And he won't tell you where they are?" Emma asks.

"Dead men tell no tales," Jason retorts with an angry snarl. "My brother was killed in jail before he could tell me. So, I'm out ten million bucks, and McPherson's going to pay."

"But why Mick?" Emma asks. "You said *any* police officer would do, and you shot Sam. So why Mick? Why now?
Why five years later?"

Jason smirks and says, "Consider it tying up loose ends,
just like I'm going to do with you."

Emma closes her eyes and remembers a captivating article
she'd read on the flight from San Diego to Seattle. It discussed
the notorious "Golden State Killer" and the difference between
sociopaths and psychopaths. It said, "Psychopaths are more
dangerous because they don't feel shame or experience guilt
connected with their actions. They point blame instead." It
went on to say, "A psychopath is a human predator who wears
a mask of sanity, an aggressor who preys on others merely for
the pleasure of it, simply because they can."

Emma shudders.

Mick approaches Thoreau from the rear. With his weapon
drawn, he drops into a half squat and edges his face around the
corner. Peering into the solid glass wall, he does a tactical scan.
He can see everything inside the cottage except the bedroom
and bathroom.

Making his way to the front door, he tests the handle and
discovers that it's not locked.

He enters crouched. Ready.

Pivoting on his heel, he performs a 180-degree sight line.
Clear.

He listens for sounds. *Nothing.*

His senses are on high alert as he makes his way to the
bathroom and bedroom. His torso swiveling, his gaze sweeps
the space, drinking everything in like a dry sponge soaks up
water. *Empty.*

Satisfied, he stands for a couple of beats taking it all in.

The closet reveals that Jason hasn't hung any of his clothes.

Mick opens the first of two suitcases sitting on the floor next to the bed. It contains folded clothing, a pair of shoes, and a lightweight jacket.

The second one contains folded white towels that appear to be from a hotel. Divided into two stacks, the top two towels have rectangular name badges pinned to them. The one on the left says *Rose* and also bears the name and logo of a hotel. The one on the right says *Yolanda* with a different hotel name and logo.

Lifting those towels, Mick discovers that each subsequent towel in the suitcase also has a name badge affixed. *Linh, Teagen, Mai, Teresa, Amala, Veronica, Devi,* and *Silvia.*

The two common denominators that he can readily see are white hotel towels and badges with female names. But each badge belongs to a different hotel.

Racking his brain, Mick recalls dropping Jason off at Thoreau on that first day. In his mind, he pictures him with a suitcase in each hand, and a backpack slung over his shoulder.

Where's the backpack?

Back in the central part of the cottage, Mick finds numerous empty bottles of Jack Daniels. He also sees the empty boxes UPS delivered with Jason's manuscript—the pages are nowhere to be found.

I wonder what was really in these boxes?

The cell phone in his pocket vibrates. Mick sees Libby's name on the screen and answers.

"The police are here," she says.

"I'll be right there."

When the vehicle sensor buzzes in the main house, signaling the arrival of the police, Niall buzzes them in and Libby phones Mick as he requested.

The cruiser pulls into the roundabout just as Fran arrives.

"Is everything okay?" she asks the officer who steps out of the car.

"Mr. MacCullough asked me to come out," Joe offers. Extending his hand, he continues, "And you are?"

"I'm Fran Davies, one of the writers staying here this month."

All heads turn as Libby opens the front door.

"Oh, Fran," she says, looking surprised. "You're here too. In all of the commotion, I forgot we were going to pick up Cynthia."

Stepping out of the way, she continues, "Come in everyone, please."

Fran and Joe follow Libby to the kitchen.

"My God it smells good in here," Joe says. As he extends his hand, Niall says, "I bake when I'm upset."

"He bakes regardless of the emotion," Libby says smiling. "Please have a seat."

"Did the hospital say they would release Cynthia today?" Fran asks.

"With the recent developments, I haven't called yet."

Niall sets a plate of freshly baked scones on the table, and Libby pours coffee for everyone. After taking a bite, Joe says, "Seriously, what is this? I'm in heaven."

"They're chocolate-drizzled chocolate scones with chocolate-and-orange-speckled clotted cream and orange marmalade," Niall answers. "Chocolate is my drug of choice."

"What developments?" Fran interrupts.

Before anyone can answer, Mick arrives. After thanking Joe for coming back, he says, "First and foremost, we've got to find Emma. Emma Benton.

"When Libby and I went to Austen cottage this morning, the front door was bolted, so we went around back and entered through the sliding glass door. She wasn't there, and we didn't see any signs of a struggle.

"It's important to note that Austen cottage is specifically designed around the needs of a person in a wheelchair. I lived there myself, that's where I recovered."

His look is grave as his eyes travel from face to face around the table. "I'm point on this case." His tone brooks no discussion as he leaves to get the journal.

Returning from The Ink Well, his glove-clad hands set the book on the table. Before opening it, he brings them up to speed on the towel-filled suitcase he found in Thoreau.

"When we're done here," Joe says, "I'll retrieve the suitcases. They could be evidence. I'll run the names on the hotel badges against the hotels to see if we get any leads. From what you said, I don't recognize any of those hotels as being from around here."

Turning back to the book, Mick says, "Each of our guests has access to and is encouraged to write something in the Pines & Quill journal. This morning, a newly coned Hemingway," he nods in the direction of the Dutch door, "knocked over the stand this sits on," he says, tapping the edge of the book.

Nodding toward Libby, he continues, "When my sister picked it up, she saw a new entry." Pointing to it he reads out loud. "'*Look in the mirror and what do you see? An eerie reflection that looks like me.*' It's signed, Andrew Berndt. He's one of the two ringleaders in the drug heist that killed my partner, Sam.

"I think that Jason Hughes is the other ringleader. I think he's Andrew Berndt's fraternal twin."

CHAPTER 21

"This is how you do it: you sit down at the key-
board and you put one word after another until
it's done. It's that easy, and that hard."

— NEIL GAIMAN

When Libby and Fran arrive at St. Joseph Hospital, the cacophony of institutional sounds and intrusive fluorescent lighting stirs unwelcome memories of long, white hospital hours that Fran has spent searching for answers to her infertility. A sinking sensation fills her chest. She blinks, swallows down a wave of nausea, and makes herself focus. Hands fisted at her sides, she keeps it to herself as the two women walk with purpose to Cynthia's room.

Cynthia has never been happier to see two people in all of her life. "The cavalry has arrived," she says, beaming. "Thank you for coming to get me."

"Paddy, what are you doing here?" Libby asks her brother-in-law who's sitting in the chair next to the bed that Cynthia's sitting on.

"I'm at St. Joseph's on chaplaincy duty and discovered Ms. Winters. She just brought me up to speed on the recent events."

"Well, it's good to see you. Please come out to the house later this week for a visit. Niall and I were just talking about you."

"So that's why my ears were burning." He winks. "I will. Thank you for the invitation." Turning to Cynthia, he continues, "I wish it had been under different circumstances, but it was a pleasure to see you again."

Libby and Fran step away from the doorway so Paddy can leave. As he steps out, an orderly with a wheelchair steps in.

Libby turns to Cynthia. "Hospital discharge policy dictates that patients be wheeled to their ride home."

"But I can walk." Cynthia shakes her head.

"If you want Dr. Zimmerman to change her mind—" the orderly says.

"No, I don't," Cynthia interjects.

———

Leaning forward between the two front bucket seats, Fran asks Cynthia, "How do you feel? Are you *really* okay?"

"The only thing that's wrong with me is that I'm out of the loop. What happened while I was in the hospital?"

In rapid-fire succession, Libby and Fran fill her in on the recent events.

"Let me see if I've got this straight," Cynthia says. "I saw Jason fall over the cliff, but the diving team hasn't found his body, at least not yet.

"When you went to check on Emma in Austen cottage, you had to enter through the glass slider because the front door was bolted shut. She wasn't there, and there were no signs of a struggle. Yet she hasn't been seen or heard from since last night when she remembered she'd forgotten to turn off the flame under the tea kettle.

"Mick found one of Jason's suitcases filled with towels that have hotel name badges pinned to them.

"And poor sweet Hemingway is wearing an Elizabethan collar because of the wounds he got while saving my life."

"Whew! That about sizes it up," Libby says, turning to sigh at Cynthia.

Officer Joe is walking to the squad car, carrying a suitcase with a gloved hand when the Pines & Quill van pulls into the circular drive by the front door.

Cynthia pushes the button that lowers the passenger window and calls out, "Please wait."

"What's up?" Fran asks.

"I want to see those towels and name badges," she says. "I might be able to get information from them."

Curiosity piqued, Libby and Fran get out of the van with her.

Joe has a perplexed look on his face as three women—who look like they mean business—approach him.

"Joe, you haven't met Cynthia Winters yet," Libby says. "She's the one who was taken to the hospital last night. Will you please come into the house for just a few minutes?"

"It's a pleasure to meet you, ma'am," Joe says, touching the bill of his cap. "But I'm on my way to the station with potential evidence."

"Yes, but there's something important you should know. Please." Libby's eyes plead. "It'll just take a moment."

Niall, who just finished wiping down the kitchen counters, looks up, surprised to see the women enter the kitchen with Joe in tow.

"Now, what's this all about?" Joe asks the women, his empty hand resting on his hip.

Cynthia steps forward. "I've helped several law enforcement agencies solve cases. You see," she continues, "I'm a forensic intuitive."

Brows knit together, Joe looks to the others for confirmation. "Is that so?"

Wiping his hands on a dish towel, Niall steps forward. "Yes, she is, Joe. And if she can help in any way, shouldn't she be given a chance?"

After a moment's consideration, Joe says, "I can't see any harm in that."

Turning to Cynthia, he continues, "But you'll need to wear crime-scene gloves, so nothing gets contaminated."

"Certainly," Cynthia agrees.

After she slips on a thin pair of latex gloves that Joe hands her, he opens the suitcase.

Before touching anything, she looks at Joe and asks, "May I?" After a quick nod of his head, she lifts the top towel from the left stack. It has the name badge "Rose" pinned to it.

All eyes are on Cynthia.

Holding the folded towel on her left palm, she touches the badge with her right hand and traces each engraved letter: R-o-s-e.

Putting it back in place, she looks at Joe again, points to the towel on the top of the right stack, and asks, "May I?"

Again, he nods assent.

Everyone leans toward Cynthia in wide-eyed anticipation and a collectively held breath.

She does the same thing, this time tracing the letters Y-o-l-a-n-d-a.

After returning it to the suitcase, she says, "Death. These two women are dead. And I suspect you'll find that the other name badges belong to women who are dead as well."

Astonished, and not knowing what else to say, Joe closes the suitcase, clears his throat, and says to the group at large, "I'll let you know the results I find at the station."

As Libby walks him to the front door, she says, "Thank you, Joe. If you hear anything more from the diving team, you'll let us know?"

"Yes. And if Mick, or anyone else," he says, raising his eyebrows and pointing his head toward Cynthia, "discovers something more, please call me."

"I will," Libby assures him.

After placing the suitcase in the cruiser's trunk, Joe gets into the car and radios Toni.

"Yep," comes her response.

"Where are you?"

"I'm near the entry gate. I've been scouring the woods and haven't found a thing, except for mosquitoes."

Joe hears a sharp swat in the background. "I'll be there in a minute."

"Make it fast," she responds.

Joe laughs, shakes his head, and puts the cruiser in gear. Not one to miss details, he looks up as he drives down the long lane beneath a canopy of leaves, and muses. *The tree limbs look like wrinkled alligator skin.*

I wish Hemingway was with me scouring the woods around Emma's cottage, Mick thinks as he swats mosquitoes away. *Niall's right, that dog's got a nose for news.* But wounds have his four-legged companion in temporary confinement—otherwise known as the mudroom.

Mick comes across short, unblemished sections of tire tread marks in the now-drying mud from last night's storm. Thin and evenly spaced, he knows they're from a wheelchair. *It looks like someone's made an effort to cover them. But who? And why?*

Using the camera on his cell phone, he takes photos, and a few more when he finds a partial shoe print. *I don't know if they'll match the images that Chris took on the bluff earlier, but I intend to find out.*

With mud, twigs, and decomposing leaves, the ground is covered in dark camouflage, so when something light is added to the mix, it stands out, making it easier to see.

Approaching the back side of Thoreau cottage, Mick squints as he focuses on something a few feet ahead on the ground.

Careful where he steps, he finds a pearl earring.

Recognition floods his mind. He remembers twin pearl earrings peeking from the deep red curtain of Emma's hair. He also recalls expressive eyes that brought to mind the deep bottle-green Bahamian pools he'd scuba dived in.

I'd give anything to drown in those eyes again.

On the drive from Pines & Quill to the station, Joe doesn't mention his conversation with Cynthia to Toni. He isn't one to buy into mumbo-jumbo, hoodoo-voodoo, or superstition, and he doesn't want to cause embarrassment to himself or anyone else.

At the Bellingham police station, Joe pours a cup of black coffee before sitting at his desk computer and connecting to the homicide database. Indispensable, this resource helps police from multiple jurisdictions to coordinate their respective investigations.

The next step is to fill in the parameter fields. Not knowing a specific location, Joe leaves that field "national." In the "first name" field, he types in "Rose" and leaves the "last name" field blank. The only other piece of information he has is the name of the hotel that's printed above the logo on the rectangular name badge. Once he keys that in, he presses "enter," sits back, puts his hands together like steeples on his stomach, and waits.

Toni untucks her legs from the chair, pushes to her feet, and then walks to Joe's desk with a fresh cup of coffee in hand. She looks over his shoulder and asks, "Do you need any help?"

"No, but thanks for offering. Hey, why don't you work on the Mitchell case? We'd all love to see that one put to rest."

"Okay." She nods and returns to her desk. Once there, she swivels in her chair and watches Joe. Her eyes are narrowed, and her eyebrows pulled down in intense concentration. After a few moments, she twists her mouth and bites the inside of her bottom lip. Then with a slight shrug, she turns back around to focus on the Mitchell case.

Joe leans forward, his arms braced on his thighs. He stares at the computer screen when the information that Cynthia shared—*death*—comes back confirmed. A coldness runs across the back of his neck.

Rose Gonzales was part of the housekeeping staff at a hotel in New York, New York. Her body was found in the bathtub of room 313. It was rolled in a shower curtain that had been removed from the rod. Her throat had been slit with precision and accuracy. The room had been registered to an Edgar Wycoff. There were no fingerprints. Everything had been wiped clean.

The description of the vehicle Wycoff used to check in at the hotel was a rental car they found abandoned ten miles away. The security cameras at both the rental car agency and the hotel had been disabled in advance, so the murderer wasn't caught on camera.

The autopsy determined that Rose had been raped before and after her death.

In her comments, the medical examiner, Dr. Felicia Simmons, annotated, "There are three basic types of rape—anger, power, and sadistic.

"Rose Gonzalez was kept alive on purpose. Her larynx and laryngeal nerves were slit, while avoiding her trachea. And though she could still breathe, Ms. Gonzalez couldn't make a sound during the frontal rape. A power rape. Afterward, both of the carotid arteries in her neck were severed. Once dead, she was raped again. This time, anally. A sadistic rape.

"We know a few things for sure. The killer didn't wear a condom. We were able to collect semen from the victim. Unfortunately, after running the data through CODIS, we came up empty-handed—no DNA match. Why he'd leave semen but wipe his prints clean is beyond me. But whoever it is, knows his anatomy."

The cold serrated edge of police work cuts jags across Joe's heart. Sickened, he shakes his head and repeats the search process in the database with Yolanda. He discovers the same brutal pattern.

Yolanda Davis had been part of the housekeeping staff at a hotel in Jacksonville, Florida. Her body was found in the bathtub of room 224. It was rolled in a shower curtain that had been removed from the rod. Her throat had been slit in the same manner as Rose. Twice. And she'd been raped the same way. Twice. The first time, supine—face up—while still alive. The second time—prone—face down, postmortem. The room had been registered to a Philip Gray. There were no fingerprints. Everything had been wiped clean.

The description of the vehicle Gray used to check in at the hotel was a rental car they found abandoned ten miles away. The security cameras at both the rental car agency and the hotel had been disabled in advance, so the murderer wasn't caught on camera.

The term "serial killer" turns over and over in Joe's mind. A third murder will earn the killer the monstrous title.

Typing each name from the rectangular badges in the suitcase into the database, Joe finds murdered housekeeping staff from differing hotels across the country. He methodically runs through each case, the highlights of which are on his computer screen. Teagan Lewis in Chicago, Illinois. Mai Lee in Los Angeles, California. Teresa Mendez in Boston, Massachusetts. Linh Wong in Dallas, Texas. Amala Banik in Portland, Oregon. Silvia Miller in Kansas City, Kansas. Veronica Alvarez in Denver, Colorado. And Devi Chandra in Philadelphia, Pennsylvania.

Joe slumps back in his chair, reeling from the information that's fastened like a tick in his mind. He squeezes his eyes shut and takes a breath. As he exhales upward through his lips, he thinks, *This is the work of a serial killer.*

He thinks back to one of the department's mandatory classes taught by a forensic psychologist, Dr. Elizabeth Hamilton. Pulling a file from his desk drawer, he reads his notes. She'd explained the difference between narcissism, sociopathy, and psychopathy, saying, "A narcissist is someone who lacks empathy, is grandiose, entitled, seeks validation, and is arrogant. They have trouble regulating their self-esteem. When a narcissist does a bad thing, they feel a fair amount of guilt and shame. More shame than guilt, because they're concerned about how other people will view them. Shame is a public emotion. They don't like being viewed negatively in the public eye. As a result, they're held hostage by the opinion of others."

Joe sets his notes on his lap, closes his eyes, and thinks about something his dad told him years ago when they'd been discussing pride. "Son," he said, "people often value their reputations more than their integrity." Joe nods his head in silent agreement.

Picking up the paperwork, he continues reading. Dr. Hamilton went on to say, "Psychopathy is a different animal. Psychopaths are all of the things a narcissist is, except there's no guilt and no shame. They don't feel remorse when do they something terrible. They make great serial killers, assassins, and people who are hired to go in and gut a business. They don't care who gets hurt."

Not wanting to rely solely on his notes, Joe opens his drawer again and digs through paperwork to find the handout from Dr. Hamilton's class. He flips through the stapled pages until he gets to the part that he's looking for, and then reads, "And while sociopathy and psychopathy are both antisocial personality disorders—some clinicians even class them together—criminologists differentiate between them based on their outward behavior. For instance, sociopaths tend to be disorganized, while psychopaths can be almost obsessively organized.

"Sociopaths aren't able to maintain normal relationships with family, friends, or co-workers, while psychopaths can maintain normal social relationships. They may even take care of aging parents or be married with children.

"Sociopaths are often unable to keep steady employment or housing, while psychopaths are often very successful in their careers.

"Sociopaths often live on the fringe of society. Studies of homeless people show that a disproportionately large number of them are classed as sociopaths. On the other hand, psychopaths often live in a typical house or apartment, and are indistinguishable from healthy people.

"A psychopath's ability to charm and manipulate people is one of the hallmarks of their disorder. The psychopath is an award-winning liar, gaslighting is second nature, the threat of punishment doesn't faze them, and they thrive on other's constant praise. Because the psychopath doesn't possess real empathy—although they are adept at faking it—their ability to see consequences of their actions is limited to the furtherance of their own agenda.

"Violence in sociopaths is erratic and unplanned. They're easier to identify and apprehend as they generally leave behind a large trail of clues. Psychopaths often plan for years to exact revenge. They're difficult to catch because they calculate each step of the act to ensure they will commit their crime undetected.

"When a normal person does something wrong (mean, bad, embarrassing, rude) our autonomic nervous system causes our heart to race, we sweat, and we look around. A psychopath doesn't have the same response. That's why they're able to lie on polygraph tests and get away with it—they literally don't care.

"PET scans reveal that the part of the brain that exhibits empathy doesn't light up in psychopaths. They have glib, shallow charm, and tend to be intelligent. They learn behavior to assimilate into society, but it's all a facade."

Joe sets the paperwork down and walks across the room to a large map of the United States tacked on the wall. Although his gait is sure and measured, he is grim-faced and pale. With his index finger, he traces a line from location to location of the hotel murders in the order they occurred. Crossing multiple state lines, the killer is spider-like, weaving an intricate web. Brilliant about covering his tracks, he never strikes in the same state twice.

Joe walks back to his desk, grabs a pen and recreates the path on a piece of paper to see if there might be a recognizable shape, a symbol of some sort. No such luck.

In each case, the killer used a different alias, but his MO remained the same—hotel rooms, rental cars, and disabled cameras. His method of rape and murder were identical with one exception—the wrists of the last eight women had been bound together with zip-tie restraints. But the most chilling consistency is the killer's psychopathic predilection for premeditated violence—what Dr. Hamilton referred to as an "intra-species predator who preys on humanity."

Joe feels the onslaught of information stretching about inside his brain, unfolding its many tentacles. Picking up the handout again, he continues reading. "When a psychopath goes to jail, he doesn't get upset. It's viewed as 'the cost of doing business.'

"Most people who commit domestic or intimate-partner violence are either narcissistic or psychopathic. The psychopath will simply dispose of you if you get in their way."

Joe scrubs his hands over his face. *I've been on the force long enough to know that given the right motivation, we're all capable of murder.*

He continues to read. "*Empathy* is a positive emotion. A psychopath isn't empathetic, but they're very understanding. They can read and understand a person's vulnerability and use it to leverage their power."

Shaking his head, Joe puts the handout back in his desk drawer. With the information he's gathered, he wonders, *Why haven't the police put these murders together? Why aren't they linked?*

He realizes that the answer is on the computer screen in front of him. The crimes had been committed so far apart—in time and distance—that up until now, each one was viewed as a one-off crime, not as part of a series.

Patterns and connections. They were there all along, just waiting to be made.

"This discussion isn't open for negotiation," Libby says to Cynthia as she leads her down the hall to the guest bedroom.

"But I can rest just as well in Brontë cottage as I can here," Cynthia counters.

"You heard Dr. Zimmerman just as well as I did," Libby continues. "She said that if we were 'back in the day,' you'd be in the hospital for at least a week. But times have changed. And though you're medically fit for discharge, that doesn't mean that you're well. It merely means that the hospital needs the bed."

Libby continues, pointing first to herself, then to Cynthia. "And Dr. Zimmerman put *me* in charge of *you* because she doesn't want you to get 'revolving door syndrome.' She doesn't want to see you back in the hospital. Her orders were for you to come home with me, stay put, and get well." And though she's smiling, Libby's statement brooks no argument.

Entering the guest bedroom, Libby can't help but notice Cynthia's eyes widen in appreciation. "It's beautiful," she says. Admiring the sun-weathered beige with hues of aqua, rose, and ochre, she continues, "I love the colors and fabrics you chose."

"I do too," Libby says. "Sometimes I hope Niall's snoring gets so loud that I have to come in here to sleep. I love the serenity in this space."

Walking toward the distressed white plantation shutters, an accent piece in the corner, Cynthia touches the nightgown draped over the top. "This looks like my nightgown."

"Yes, I hope you don't mind. I went to your cottage and gathered a few things, including your toiletries," Libby finishes, pointing to the ensuite bathroom.

"You've thought of everything." Cynthia smiles. "Thank you."

"Rest now. Niall's just started making a pot of his world-famous chicken noodle soup." Pressing her hands together in prayer-like fashion, Libby emphasizes, "It's delicious!" Then she leans in conspiratorially and whispers, "I've pretended to be sick just so that I can have some."

Cynthia places both hands on her stomach. "I love his cooking. I can't imagine him making anything that's not delicious."

"Well, I can vouch that his chicken noodle soup will cure anything that ails you, regardless of what it is."

As she returns to the kitchen, Libby says, "Fran, Cynthia is resting now. You might as well get some rest too. I'll ring you in Dickens cottage if anything new transpires."

"Promise?" Fran asks.

Raising her little finger, Libby smiles. "I'll pinky-swear if that'll make you feel better."

Fran laughs and hooks her little finger around Libby's. Entwined, they make a swift downward movement and together say, "Pinky swear!"

"Okay." Fran smiles. "I believe you."

Libby gathers her wind-tangled hair into a loose bun and then shifts to face the bird feeders. While filling them with seed, she notices the lengthening shadows and knows that dusk is on its way. She hasn't heard from Mick. *I'm not going to worry. At least I'm going to try not to worry.*

Long ago her mother told her, "Worry is like sitting in a rocking chair. It gives you something to do but doesn't get you anywhere." She smiles, knowing there's wisdom in that adage.

"Did you pick some basil for me?" Niall asks over his shoulder when Libby steps into the kitchen.

"I sure did. Oh, that smells good!" Feigning illness, she holds the back of her hand to her forehead and bats her eyelashes.

"You'll get some too," Niall laughs.

Libby watches as Niall bathes the chicken in Chardonnay. When it's almost cooked off, he tops the golden meat with sautéed artichoke hearts and sprinkles it generously with the basil that Libby had minced while he was making egg noodles.

Niall turns the flame as low as it will go. "I'm going to hold off on anything further until the troops gather. Once I add the noodles, these bad boys won't take long," he says, pointing a flour-covered finger toward fat golden strips draped over a wooden rack.

They turn in unison as Mick bolts through the door, Fran not far behind.

―――――――――

"Fran told me that Cynthia's here," Mick says. "I need to speak with her."

"I was just about to wake her up," Libby says.

"Who, me?" Everyone turns as Cynthia enters the kitchen.

"Cynthia, I'm so glad that you're alive and safe. Here—" He leads her to a chair at the enormous pine table. "I need to show you something."

As he steps up to the table, Mick turns so that his right thigh is against the edge, then reaches into his pocket and pulls the interior fabric until a pearl earring drops onto the table. Everyone leans forward for a closer look.

"This is one of Emma's earrings," he says. "I haven't touched it. When I found it near the back side of Thoreau, I staked the spot with a stick, then scooped it up with a leaf and slid it into my pocket. I'm not sure what you look for when you tune into the energy of an item, so I didn't want to contaminate it."

"Not many people are as thoughtful as you," Cynthia says, looking up into Mick's eyes, tight with worry. "Now if one of you will get a pen and paper, it's a good idea to write down what I say."

"I'll write," Fran volunteers.

"I'll get a pen and paper," Libby says.

"Would it be okay if I use the recorder on my cell phone as a backup?" Mick asks.

"Yes, that's a great idea." Cynthia smiles.

As Libby hands a tablet and pen to Fran, Niall asks, "Are you going into a trance?"

"That's a good question, Niall. The answer is no." Cynthia looks around the room and continues, "I'm just going to close my eyes and sit with Emma's earring for a bit. If I receive any energetic pictures, I'll state them out loud. I say this in advance because it might seem disjointed."

"What do you mean by energetic pictures?" Fran asks.

"An impression. It could be something I see or hear. It might be something I feel, smell, or even taste."

"You said *if*," Mick notes, an unasked question hanging on the end of his statement.

"That's right, Mick," she says gently. "It doesn't always work." And with that, Cynthia picks up Emma's pearl earring, lays it on her left palm, covers it with her right palm, then rests both hands on her lap.

All eyes are on Cynthia as she closes hers.

CHAPTER 22

*"Cram your head with characters and stories.
Abuse your library privileges. Never stop looking at the world, and never stop reading to find
out what sense other people have made of it.
If people give you a hard time and tell you to
get your nose out of a book, tell them you're
working. Tell them it's research. Tell them to
pipe down and leave you alone."*

—JENNIFER WEINER

Jason's hands are trembling. His whole body is jittery.
Damn, I need a drink, and I'm out of Jack. He wonders
what else will soothe him. Patting the knife in his pocket he
muses, *Should I kill Emma now?* Excitement tingles through
him at the prospect. *What a great blow that would be to
Mick. But devastation should be paced. It should build—
slowly—until the final eruption. No,* he tells himself, *keep to
the original plan.*

Jason removes a small, battery-operated lantern from his backpack and turns it on. It casts light on the damp walls. Bat guano glistens on the rock-strewn ground.

Emma observes Jason's face surreptitiously. The threatening emotions that play across his face raise the hair on the nape of her neck. Everything in her is coiled tight, ready to shatter. She can taste her dinner in the back of her throat. It's been hours since she's emptied her bladder and it feels like it's going to burst. *I'll be damned before I take care of something that personal in front of him.* The heavy knot in her stomach is dread.

"They say anticipation makes pleasure more intense," Jason says to Emma. "I saw you watching me."

Looking toward the mouth of the cave, Emma ignores his comment. "It'll be dark soon."

Darkness is safer. I'm at home in the dark, Jason thinks. "What's the matter, are you afraid of the dark?"

"No," she answers, her voice steady.

"You should be. All of my disposals happen at night."

She can't help herself. "Disposals?"

Leaning forward, he looks into her eyes. "My kills. The ones I've done with my knife. It takes a great deal of stealth and intelligence to accomplish what I have," he continues, pride lacing his voice.

Heart pounding, mind racing, Emma knows she needs to buy time. *Keep him talking.*

"What have you accomplished?" she asks.

"Sliding his back down the rock wall he seats himself on the ground, wincing as he makes himself comfortable. "Let's see now, there was Rose, Yolanda, Tegan, Mai, Teresa, Linh, Amala, Silvia, Veronica, and Devi."

He pauses for a moment. "There was also Sybil, but she doesn't count. She was my mother. She never counted."

Watching him inhale deeply from the mouth of the empty bottle, Emma is filled with a mixture of horror, anger, and fear.

He leans toward her a little further. "That's ten, in case you weren't counting. You're number eleven."

———

Cynthia says, "Dark. Dank. Foul. Slippery." She feels imminent danger in each word.

The pen in Fran's white-knuckled grip captures each word.

"Emma is above ground, yet under. She's alive. I hear a word, but it's so faint I can hardly understand it. I think it's *burnt*." Cynthia listens harder than ever to the universe. "Jagged edges."

Minutes pass, but nothing more comes. When Cynthia opens her eyes, she hears a collective exhale. "Did you get everything?"

"Yes," Fran says, setting the tablet on the table so everyone can see it.

"I think you just described a cave," Niall says.

"I agree," Libby and Mick say in unison.

"Where do you keep the brochures for our guests?" Niall asks Libby. "Isn't there one with locations for spelunking?"

"You're right," Libby says, "I'll get it."

"What's spelunking?" Fran asks.

"It's the sport of exploring caves and caverns," Mick interjects. "Several years ago, Sam and I did it with one of our buddies."

Libby returns and hands the brochure to Mick.

Opening it, he reads out loud. "Ape Cave at Mount St. Helens. Blanchard Hill Bat Caves and Oyster Dome in Bellingham, WA. Big Four Ice Caves in Snohomish, WA. Gardner Cave at Crawford State Park. And Paradise Ice Caves at Mount Rainier's Paradise Glacier."

"It has to be Blanchard Hill Bat Caves," Niall says. "It's the closest."

Turning to Cynthia, Mick says, "You saw Jason Hughes fall over the cliff in the storm. It's hard to imagine anyone surviving that fall, but the divers didn't find a body. And we know that Emma wouldn't have left willingly without at least saying goodbye."

Studying the words Fran wrote on the tablet, Niall picks up Mick's line of deductive reasoning. "All of the words from the impressions Cynthia received have a common theme— caves—except for one, the word *burnt*."

"*Berndt!*" Mick and Libby shout at the same time, eyes wide with excitement.

"It's not burnt, like burnt toast," Mick explains. "It's b-e-r-n-d-t." He spells it out. "Like Andrew Berndt, the signature in the journal, and he's dead. Jason Hughes has to be his fraternal twin."

Toni's morning has been chewed up with paperwork and warrants. Frustration crawls over her, its needle-like claws digging under her skin. She stands next to Joe's desk as he makes a phone call. She can only hear his side of the conversation.

"Hello, Niall. It's Joe Bingham at the station. Cynthia Winters was right. The name badges pinned to each towel belong to housekeeping staff at hotels strewn all across the country, and each one of them is dead. She said what?" he barks into the receiver. "I think you're right, it's gotta be. Wait a sec. Let me grab a pen."

Toni watches him scribble five lines.

Ape Cave—Mount St. Helens
Blanchard Hill Bat Caves and Oyster Dome—south
of Bellingham
Big Four Ice Caves—Snohomish
Gardner Cave—Crawford State Park
Paradise Ice Caves—Mount Rainier, Paradise Glacier

"What's going on?" Toni mouths, pointing to the list.

Shaking his head, Joe continues, "We're on our way. Be there in fifteen," and hangs up the phone. Turning to Toni, he says, "Bianco, grab a jacket and your tactical bag, I'll fill you in on the way."

Cynthia looks at Mick in the chair next to hers. "Okay," she nods. "I'll tell you everything that happened on the bluff, even if it seems inconsequential."

As she closes her eyes, Cynthia pictures the violent scene. "First he told me he'd been watching me. Then he said, 'You know about me, don't you?' I told him that because he hadn't let me look at his palm, I didn't know anything about him. I asked, 'What is it you think I know about you?' and he said, 'You're the psychic, you tell me.' I repeated that I didn't know anything about him. That's when he said, 'Don't toy with me,' and smashed a bottle of wine against a boulder."

Cynthia continues. "Holding the neck of the broken bottle with the jagged edges facing me, Jason backed me toward the cliff's edge. When I asked him why he wanted to hurt me, he said, 'I don't want to *hurt* you, I want to *kill* you. But it's got to look like an accident. Anything, a gust of wind, could cause you to keel over the edge and plunge to your death.' That's when Hemingway arrived."

Niall ladles the soup that he made. They eat and listen as Cynthia paints a vivid word picture of what happened on the bluff.

"Jason said he thought I was a sorceress. I played on his fears and told him that I'd beckoned him out there intentionally. I could see he was scared. That's when he cut me. Hemingway jumped into the fray and knocked him down."

At the sound of his name, Cynthia hears Hemingway's tail thump the floor on the other side of the Dutch door.

"Even though he'd been cut, Hemingway got Jason's wrist in his jaws and clamped down until he let go of the bottle. I'd be surprised if his wrist isn't broken. As they continued to wrestle, Jason tried to scoot himself away from Hemingway. I don't think he realized he was heading toward the cliff. He managed to get to his knees, then maneuvered to his feet just as a strong gust of wind came tearing from the north. He was so close to the slippery edge, he lost his footing and plunged over the cliff."

A quick siren blast announces Joe's arrival. Taking one of her warm hands in both of his, Mick says, "Thank you, Cynthia."

Walking over to the Dutch door, Mick looks over at Hemingway. "And thank you, too, you big lug."

"Be careful," Libby calls after his retreating back.

"I will. I'm going to stop at my cabin and then head out. I'll keep you posted when I can."

Approaching the cruiser, Mick sees Toni in the passenger seat. Leaning down he speaks to both her and Joe through the open passenger window. "I'll be right back. I just need to grab my go-bag."

The still air in the cave has an eerie kind of clarity. Jason watches Emma in the darkness. His eyes have a crazed intensity.

Raising his eyebrows suggestively, Jason says, "I think we should enjoy a little prelude before the real fun begins." He stands and starts to walk toward her.

Sweat beads across Emma's hairline. Her fingers curl into her palms; the muscles along her arms tighten, shorten, ready to strike. She looks at Jason. His eyes are stones of hatred, polished evil. *I know he can see the terror I'm hiding.* The primitive center of her brain screams—*Run!*

A sharp stench fills the air—urine.

"You disgusting bitch, you peed yourself!" Jason backhands Emma across the face. "You should be ashamed." Covering his mouth and nose with his good hand, he backs away.

I'd rather die than be raped by that loathsome pig. Shaking from frayed nerves, Emma turns her head toward the opening and intentionally redirects her thoughts. She wonders when the bats they'd displaced earlier will return. She remembers reading that humans owe bats a considerable debt of gratitude because every night each one consumes hundreds of insects. Without them, the insect population would grow to unmanageable proportions.

Pretending she's outside looking up at every star imaginable pricking the black sky, Emma wonders, *What's happening at Pines & Quill? Do they know I'm gone? Do they know I'm being held captive by Jason?*

Wondering what's captivated her attention, Jason's gaze follows Emma's to the mouth of the cave. His eyes widen in panic as a billowy whiteness floats into his line of vision. Icy fear twists his heart. As in the woods, the shimmering form floats toward him and then goes slightly out of focus, like an old-time photograph.

Scrambling across the rock-strewn cave floor, Jason slips behind Emma in her wheelchair. Grabbing the knife from his pocket, Jason tucks his thumb under the thumb-stud, pushes it up and out, releasing its razor-sharp edge.

"Take one step closer, and I'll slit her throat," he shouts.

Emma doesn't hear or see who Jason's speaking to, but she knows that he's using her to shield himself from whatever it is. She remains still.

"Come now, Alex," the woman with brilliant white eyes and silver skin says. "That's not any way to treat a woman."

"How do you know my name?" he yells.

"What mother doesn't know her own child's name?" the apparition asks. And while slowly backing out of the cave it sings, "And here comes a chopper to chop off your head! Chip chop, chip chop, the last man is dead." On the final note, the foggy, white mass disappears.

Jason slumps to the floor in relief. "You stink," he growls at Emma before crawling back to the other side of the cave. He grabs the empty bottle of Jack and holds it to his nose. Inhaling deeply, he wonders, *Was that a hallucination from withdrawal?* He knows the tremors are. *I haven't gone this long without alcohol since I can remember.* Feeling bolstered that it was a hallucination, not a ghost, he shoots a glance at Emma and sneers, "What are you looking at?"

Mick slips into the squad car behind Joe on the driver's side so they're able to see each other in the rearview mirror.

Before they head out, Joe brings Mick and Toni up to speed on his findings in the homicide database.

In the rearview mirror, Joe sees Mick's face turn ashen. If they weren't blocked from view, he'd also see that his work-worn hands are balled into fists.

Joe turns to Toni. He sees her sitting rigidly with her eyes trained straight ahead. *If I touch her, she'll break.*

"A serial killer who crossed several state lines," Mick says. "Officially, this just became an FBI case. But before I make the call, I want to find Emma. Are you with me?"

"Yes," Joe says, without hesitation.

The only response from Toni is a curt nod.

"I know right where it's at," Mick says.

"Where what's at?" Joe asks.

"Blanchard Hill Bat Caves," Mick responds to Joe's eyes in the rearview mirror.

"Right," Joe says. "Me, too."

Breaking her wall of ice, Toni chimes in. "Well, I don't. Can you let me in on the secret?"

"I'm a big fan of hiking," Joe begins. "I don't do it nearly as often as I'd like, but such is life. Blanchard Hill has it all. Views, lakes, forest, and open areas."

Mick picks up the thread. "It's located on Chuckanut Mountain and is one of this area's most beautiful natural landscapes. The hikes range from relaxing to grueling," he finishes, rubbing his leg.

"There are several access points," Joe continues. "You make your selection based on the level of difficulty and distance you're looking for."

"Well it's dark, and I'm not familiar with this area," Toni says, "so I vote for the one that gets us closest to the destination."

"Then we'll drive to a lookout about halfway up and continue to the peak from there. There are a couple of small lakes along the way, depending on which trail we take. From the parking area, the trail—part of the famous Pacific Northwest Trail—winds upward to the bat caves, and then continues up to the top, Oyster Dome."

Once parked, Mick pulls a pair of night optics from his go-bag.

Toni and Joe exchange glances.

"Night vision goggles?" Joe asks.

"Yes," Mick responds, securing them. Even with the goggles, it's still dark, but with this technology he can see a person standing over two hundred yards away on a moonless, cloudy night.

"I wish they'd issue those to us," Toni says.

"You can buy them online at most sporting goods stores," Mick says.

"I'll remember that." She nods.

Hemingway rests his head, cone and all, on the closed portion of the Dutch door and whines. The hope of table food is evident in his eyes.

"You want to join us, don't you?" Libby says, sending his tail into propeller mode.

Looking from Cynthia to Fran, Libby asks, "Do you mind if I let him in?"

"Not at all, please let him join us," Cynthia says.

"Yes," Fran agrees. "After all, he's a hero."

"You're shameless," Libby says when she lets Hemingway in, but her eyes are full of admiration.

Wagging furiously, Hemingway eats up the praise as readily as he eats his, or anyone else's food.

Fran asks, "Do you think they'll find Emma?"

"I have every confidence," Niall answers.

"But what if the bats hurt her?" Fran continues.

"The bats up there are Townsend big-eared bats. It wasn't long ago that they were nearly extinct. Local conservation teams have taken great pains to keep them off the extinction list, because we need them to play their part in maintaining ecological balance."

"Why are they called big-eared? Do they really have big ears?" Fran asks.

"As a matter of fact, they do," Niall says. "When Libby and I attended a presentation at Western Washington University a few years ago, we learned that when their ears are laid back, they extend all the way to the middle of their body."

"Is that what made you think of a cave right after I finished reading the energy in Emma's earring?" Cynthia asks.

"Yes, it is. We watched a slideshow at that presentation, and you described many elements of a cave."

Conversation is sparse after that as each person entertains their own thoughts about what Mick and the officers will find at the bat caves on Blanchard Hill.

———

As she lowers her gaze to her feet, Emma's eye catches a shape on the guano-covered rocks. Her heart thunders in her ears. *Oh, my God. Is that what I think it is?*

"What was that?" Emma asks. The fear in her voice brings Jason fully alert.

"What?" he asks, sitting upright.

"I thought I saw someone at the entrance," she whispers.

"What did they look like?" he asks. A sense of urgency staining his voice.

"It's hard to tell, but I think it was a man."

A surge of relief flows through him. *It's not the ghost.* Grabbing his Beretta, he slips a second magazine with thirteen rounds into his back pocket. *They think I'm the prey, but I'm the predator.* He smiles as the familiar combination of tension and exhilaration grips him. He's on the hunt.

Pressing his face to Emma's he whispers, "Stay here. Oh, that's right, you can't walk. And keep your mouth shut," he warns through clenched teeth.

With phantom elusiveness, Jason crouches and moves forward in the stygian blackness toward the mouth of the cave.

———————

Emma takes her chance. She leans forward and picks up the knife Jason dropped when he'd crumpled in relief after whatever he thought he'd seen had left. She has no idea how to operate it and doesn't want to make any noise, so she slips the open blade under her right thigh, working hard to wipe the smug look off her face before Jason turns around.

CHAPTER 23

"Write. Rewrite. When not writing or rewriting,
read. I know of no shortcuts."

—LARRY L. KING

S hrouded in darkness, the smell that had caught them in whiffs as they neared the cave, is now a presence.

"Bat guano," Joe states the obvious.

"Let's make it quick," Toni says, pinching her nostrils. "It reeks in here."

The high-powered beams from their flashlights illuminate rough, damp walls all the way to the back of the enclosure. "There's only one chamber in this cave," Joe says as Mick studies the ground looking for possible clues.

"There's another cave," Joe says. "It's less known because of its well-hidden entrance. Follow me."

Outside the air is chilly. Darkness almost obscures their view of the town and the bay beyond. The only telltale sign that gives it away are the pinpricks of light. From this vantage point, it looks like a faerie village.

"It would be easier with a machete," Joe says while leading them into the next cave. The interior is colorless and strained. Mosquitoes whine around their ears and land on their cheeks and hands.

"You're right. I wouldn't have known this was here if you hadn't shown the way," Mick says to Joe. The combined intensity from their SureFire flashlights reveal yet another empty cave.

"It's kind of freaky how Cynthia Winters gets those 'impressions,'" Joe says.

"What impressions?" Toni asks.

"She's a 'psychic intuitive.' In fact, she's been instrumental in helping several law enforcement agencies solve crimes."

"Oh, come on," Toni says. "Quit pulling my leg. Just because I'm a new transfer doesn't mean you've got to bust my chops."

"I'm not kidding," Joe says. "Apparently, Ms. Winters receives energetic impressions from items associated with a case."

"I can't explain it." Mick shakes his head. "I did a little checking, and Cynthia has a tremendous accuracy rate. She also reads people."

"What do you mean by that?" Joe asks.

"When I picked up this month's group of authors at the airport, she read their palms. Her accuracy was dead on." He didn't tell them that she'd read his palm, too.

Showing a sudden interest, Toni asks, "Is that why Jason Hughes fought with Ms. Winters on the bluff?"

"He's the one guest who wouldn't let her read his palm," Mick says.

"Maybe he has something to hide," Toni suggests.

"The only thing I know," Mick says, "is that Blanchard Hill's a bust. Let's head to the next one on the list."

Swatting at her neck, Toni agrees. "Yes, let's get out of here."

Libby picks up her cell phone when she hears Mick's ringtone.

"Mick?" she answers, her voice filled with hope. "Well crap!" she says, shaking her head to let Niall, Fran, and Cynthia know that they hadn't found Emma yet. "Which one?" she asks. "Okay. Thank you for letting us know. Please be careful." Then she disconnects the call.

"There isn't any sign of Emma or Jason at Blanchard Hill, so they're heading to the Big Four Ice Caves in Snohomish, the next set of caves on the list. They're about an hour and fifteen minutes from here, but Joe's taking I-5 with cherry lights and sirens to shave off time."

"Hey, big fella," Niall says to Hemingway when he comes over and nudges his leg. "You've had your dinner, so you must need to go out. Hold on just a minute while I grab my jacket and torch. You might be able to see in the dark, but I can't."

"Torch?" Fran looks at Niall inquiringly.

"That's right," Niall says with a smile. "Outside of North America, flashlights are commonly known as torches."

"They say you learn something new every day. That's my 'something new' for today," Fran says with a laugh.

The women can hear "the boys" getting ready for Hemingway's evening routine. "We'll be back shortly," Niall calls over his shoulder before pulling the mudroom door shut behind him.

"You hit the jackpot with that one," Fran says to Libby.

"Yes, but Niall hit the jackpot with Libby too," Cynthia says, pointing to Libby.

Laughing, Libby says, "We are fortunate to have each other, foibles and all."

Niall takes a deep breath and looks up. The moon is a well-manicured crescent between the clouds in the sky, and the night is wafting a salt-laden breeze from the bay. Every now and again a flurry of wind dispenses a sprinkling of rain that never amounts to anything more than that.

Hemingway tries to poke his head in a bush to get a better sniff, but the Elizabethan collar makes it difficult. Niall smiles as an orchestra of startled crickets becomes instantly silent. "Hey buddy, you know you wouldn't have to wear that thing if you'd stop licking the salve on your wounds."

Their continued meandering brings them close to Austen cottage. And though he can't see them, Niall knows from Hemingway's stance that his ears are perked. Tipping his head back for a better sniff, Hemingway catches a scent on the air. He looks at Niall, at least six feet away. Never slow on the uptake, he sees his chance and takes it.

"Come back here!" Niall shouts, bolting after Hemingway.

———————

Hemingway keeps his nose as close to the ground as he can, but the blasted cone doesn't help. He picks up his best friend Mick's scent, and Emma's too. Then he discovers two more. One is from the man he doesn't like. The other is a human scent, but from a person he's not familiar with. He keeps going.

———————

Niall finds Hemingway standing statue still, head to the ground. "There you are, you stinker. What's gotten into you?" he asks.

Hemingway doesn't move. When Niall approaches, Hemingway still doesn't move, nor does he look up.

What the heck is he so intent on? Niall wonders.

Aiming his torch on the ground in front of Hemingway, the beam picks up an object. Bending over to get a closer look, he says, "Well I'll be damned." It's the matching pearl earring to the one Mick had dropped from his pocket onto the kitchen table earlier in the day.

"Good boy, Hemingway. You're such a good boy!" When Hemingway sees Niall pick up a stick, he thinks they're going to play, a reward for finding the prize.

"Not just yet, mister. I'm going to use it as a stake to mark this spot in case we need to find it again." After that, Niall scoops up Emma's earring with a leaf just like Mick had done and slips it into his pocket. "Race ya home," he says to Hemingway and takes off at a dead run.

———

When the mudroom door flies open with a bang, it startles all three women.

Libby jumps. Her hand flies to her chest where her heart races. "What on earth?"

Niall bends over, both hands on top of his thighs, trying to catch his breath. He raises his head slightly. "Someone, please give Hemingway a biscuit. You're not going to believe what he found."

Happy to assist, Fran gets a biscuit from the jar and gives it to Hemingway.

Once he catches his breath, Niall makes his way to the kitchen table and turns so that his right thigh is up against the edge. He reaches into his pocket just like Mick had done, and pulls the interior fabric until the pearl earring tumbles onto the table.

"I didn't touch it. When Hemingway found it, I scooped it up with a leaf like Mick did and slid it into my pocket."

Wide-eyed, Fran asks, "Do you think Emma's dropped her earrings on purpose, like a trail of breadcrumbs?"

"I wouldn't doubt it," Libby says. "She's an intelligent woman."

"I'd like to see if I get the same energetic impressions from this earring," Cynthia interjects. "Would that be okay with everyone?"

"Yes," comes their unanimous response.

Fran asks, "Does each object—even if they're the same thing and belong to the same person—have different stories to tell?"

"I've never worked with two objects from the same person before," Cynthia answers. "So I haven't had the opportunity to find out. But I'd like to try."

Cynthia picks up Emma's pearl earring, lays it on her left palm and covers it with her right palm. Then just like before, she rests both hands on her lap and closes her eyes.

Fran has the tablet and pen ready.

"Dark. Dank. Canyon. Foul. Slippery." As before, there's a long pause between each word. "Emma is above ground, yet under. She is alive. Burnt, or Berndt," Cynthia corrects herself. "Devil." Another long pause is followed by, "Jagged edges."

When Cynthia opens her eyes a few minutes later, Fran bursts out, "There are two extra things on the list, canyon and devil. The rest of them are the same."

"What?" Fran asks Niall and Libby who had both just gasped and are looking at each other with incredulous looks on their faces.

"I think she's right under our noses," Niall says. "Thoreau cottage sits on the ridge overlooking *El Cañón del Diablo*— The Devil's Canyon."

A surge of anger flares through Jason as he marches back to Emma. Grabbing her by the hair, he yanks her head back, and says, "Don't pull a stunt like that again." Through clenched teeth he continues, "I could kill you now, and I'd feel nothing but pleasure. But I won't because I want to watch McPherson's face when I slit your throat."

"Shouldn't we go outside? You're trapped in this cave. Unless there's a back door, there's no way out. You're going to get caught."

Jason pronounces each word carefully so she can't possibly mistake his meaning. "Risk is shrouded in complacency, and I'm never complacent."

———

Mick's cell phone vibrates in his pocket. Pulling it out, he views the screen and sees it's his sister. "Libby," he answers. "What's up?"

"Mick, you're never going to believe it. Hemingway found Emma's other pearl earring. Niall marked the spot like you did when you found the first one. When he brought it home, Cynthia read its energy. In addition to the previous impressions, there are two more."

"What are they?" Mick asks, hope filling his heart.

"Canyon and devil," she answers. "Mick, we think they're in The Devil's Canyon."

"We're on our way," he all but shouts into the phone. "Call the station and have them radio Herb and Chris. Tell them it's a Code 2—urgent, no emergency lights or siren." Then he ends the call.

"Joe, turn the car around. The other earring's been found. Cynthia read its energy, and there's a good chance that Emma's being held captive in The Devil's Canyon, right below Thoreau cottage, the one that Jason Hughes was staying in."

Joe punches the gas, "I'll switch to Code 2 when we're ten minutes out. If Hughes fell over the side of the cliff, and with Ms. Benton in a wheelchair, it would have been difficult to make it this far. It makes a lot more sense that they're closer to Pines & Quill."

Toni offers, "It feels like a bit of a wild goose chase to me. I find it hard to believe that we're chasing Hughes and Benton all over kingdom come based on 'impressions'"—she places air quotes around that word—"a psychic gave us."

"I'm not one to buy into the hoodoo-voodoo realm either," Joe says. "But if you'd seen what I saw, you'd be much more inclined to believe what she has to say."

They ride in silence; the pursuit lights bathing the night in blue and white hellfire.

———————

Beyond the cave's mouth, the evening sky is the color of a bruise. Backwashed in the dim light, Emma sees Jason cock his head. *He heard it too.*

Turning toward her with menace, he hisses, "Don't make a sound."

———————

Returning to the kitchen, Libby says, "I just phoned the station. They put me through to Herb. He and Chris are on their way."

"Do you think Emma's okay?" Fran asks the room at large.

"I do," Cynthia says with confidence, both of Emma's pearl earrings still nestled in her palm.

"I do too," Niall says to a large bowl of over-stirred dough he's taking his worries out on.

To shift his and everyone else's mind from what might be happening in The Devil's Canyon, Fran says, "Niall, tell me how you learned to cook."

Looking up with a smile from a distant memory, he says, "My *seanmháthair* taught me."

"*Seanmháthair,*" she repeats, trying to pronounce it the way Niall had done. "What does that mean?"

"It's Scottish Gaelic for grandmother." He then describes the hours he'd spent in the restaurant with his *seanmháthair*, the herbs and spices that had developed his nose, the aromas wafting from the kitchen out to the street. His heart swells and squeezes with the memories.

"Thank you," Libby mouths to Fran.

———————

The vehicle sensor buzzes, notifying them that Herb and Chris have arrived.

Pushing a button on the wall by the intercom, Libby swings the entrance gate open remotely.

A few moments later, headlight beams wash across the kitchen walls as the patrol car pulls into the curved drive in front of the main house.

Libby opens the door as they're about to knock. "No lights, no sirens. Thank you for honoring Mick's request. He, Joe, and Toni have their radios off, and their cell phones on vibrate so they don't make a sound."

"What's going on?" Herb asks. And the four of them—Niall, Libby, Cynthia, and Fran—bring the two officers up to speed.

"I want night vision goggles," Joe whispers to Toni after tripping, sliding down the slope, then tripping again.

Jutting her chin toward Mick's back, she answers, "Yea, he moves like a mountain goat with those things."

Mick waits for Joe and Toni to catch up. Leaning in, he whispers, "Once we're on level ground, don't make a sound. I'm lead on this case, and I can see." He indicates the night optics on his eyes. "If Jason Hughes is Andrew Berndt's brother, he's probably armed, definitely dangerous, and I don't want any harm to come to Emma."

"We'll be careful," Joe assures him. "If Hughes is the guy who slashed the throats of those women, he's deadly."

"I'm going ahead, *alone*," Mick emphasizes. "Wait here until I come back or yell for you." And with that, he vanishes into the foliage.

"He's a good cop," Joe says, admiration in his voice. "He knows what he's doing."

"*Was* a good cop," Toni reminds him.

———

"What in God's name was that?" Fran asks, wild-eyed.

"Those were gunshots," Herb and Chris say simultaneously, scraping their chairs back as they rise to their feet.

Everyone sprints through the front door. Hemingway on their heels.

CHAPTER 24

"You don't actually have to write anything until you've thought it out. This is an enormous relief, and you can sit there searching for the point at which the story becomes a toboggan and starts to slide."

—MARIE DE NERVAUD

Through the green monochrome tint of his night optics, Mick sees the jagged edges of an opening in a wall of rock. *It's wide enough for Emma's wheelchair, plus a foot on either side.*

Looking down, he sees footprints, and what looks like drag marks, leading in. *If I step out from cover, Jason will shoot me. If I stay here, he'll kill Emma.*

Mick picks up a rock and tosses it into the opening.

"What took you so long?" comes the voice of Jason Hughes.

"Is Emma Benton with you?" Mick asks.

"Mick, I'm—" Emma's voice is cut off by the sound of a sharp slap.

Anger flushes through Mick, slow and burning. The muscles in his arms tense. "Hughes, or should I say, *Berndt,* this is between you and me. Let me trade places with Emma."

"You'd like that, wouldn't you?" Jason laughs. "No. You're going to join us. And if you don't, I'll send her out— one piece at a time—until you do."

Mick sends a text to Joe: *Found cave. Jason has Emma. Going in or she dies. Move forward fifty yards. Stop. Remain quiet. Stay under cover.*

"How do I know you're not going to shoot me when I step in?" Mick asks.

"You don't." Jason laughs. "You'll just have to trust me. Throw your weapon in first, and then enter with your hands above your head."

Mick sets the safety, then throws in the Glock, grateful for his ankle carry.

He enters the cave and sees Emma in her wheelchair. His heart gallops at the sight of her. His mind floods with relief, dousing the nightmare images he'd imagined. *She's alive.* He exhales slowly to make his breathing slower and more effective.

As Emma leans toward Mick, Jason pulls her body back.

Crouching behind her, he sneers. "You look like a bug-eyed frog. Take off those night vision goggles. And while you're at it, turn around. I want to see if you were stupid enough to tuck a gun in your waistband."

Mick does what he's told.

"Okay. Turn back around."

Jason shoves a flashlight into Emma's left hand. "Hold this on your lap and aim it up. I want Mick to have a good view when I slit your throat." He yanks Emma's hair, pulling her head back, exposing her neck. "Don't move."

Exhilaration soars through him. The power of life and death is his, and he's drunk with the taste of it. Before starting his handiwork, he crouches behind Emma, rests his chin on her shoulder, and smiles tauntingly at Mick.

Emma hears his breathing. Slow and measured—no panic, or lack of control. His breath is foul. The smell sweeps into her nostrils, nearly making her gag.

Except for his face, no other part of Jason is exposed. Reaching into his left cargo pocket, he feels for his knife. "What the fuck?"

When Jason turns his head to check his pocket, Emma slips her hand under her right thigh and fists the knife, blade down.

Knife-less, Jason grabs his gun and stands up behind the chair. Emma feels his stomach at her back as he leans forward toward Mick.

Adrenaline surges through her veins, accelerates her heart rate. *I've got one chance.* Standing fast, Emma catches Jason hard under the chin with the top of her head.

She hears a primal, guttural sound ring throughout the cave. It takes a second for her to realize it's her as she slams the blade back into Jason's right thigh and twists it.

Mick has a look of disbelief on his face as Emma flinches before toppling forward, face down on the ground.

Then a bullet rips into Jason's chest and joins the echo of Jason's Beretta.

Jason's gun drops to the ground.

"No, I wasn't *stupid* enough to tuck a gun in my waistband. It was in my ankle carry."

Jason falls backward and hits the ground.

"What the hell?" Weapons drawn, Joe and Toni enter the cave—each in a half squat, their torsos swiveling—to find Mick bent over Emma's blood-stained back with two fingers on the side of her neck checking for a pulse.

"She's still alive," Mick shouts. "Joe, radio Herb and tell him we need LifeFlight. There's not enough clearance on the property, tell them to land at the entry gate. Then call Niall and tell him to get the ATV as close to the back of Thoreau cottage as he can. Toni"—He nods toward Jason's body. "Check to make sure he's dead."

As Toni kneels over Jason, he whispers, "I told her." Then he loses consciousness.

Pressing two fingers on his carotid artery, she feels a weak pulse. "He's still alive."

"Lucky son of a bitch," Joe says. "He's already escaped death once. Mick, do you want Herb to get an air ambulance for him, too? Or should he just wait for a meat wagon?"

"I'm not through with him. I want that bastard to live," Mick growls. "Order another lift."

Herb and Chris try to keep up with Hemingway as he races toward the back of Thoreau cottage. "Wait up, Buddy," Herb shouts.

Libby answers on the first ring. "Yes. Yes. Okay, behind Thoreau. He'll be right there."

"Who was that?" Niall asks.

"Emma's hurt. Mick needs you to bring the ATV to the back of Thoreau, then drive them to the front gate. LifeFlight's on their—" She finishes her statement to Niall's already-retreating back.

Mick lifts Emma, cradling her in his arms as gently as he can. Stepping out of the cave into the fresh air, he feels her blood ooze down his arms, slow and insidious. The moonlight is tangled in Emma's dark auburn hair. *Please God, let her be okay.*

Joe joins Mick. "I'll shine the light on the ground in front of you 'til we get to the top. It's rough going under the best of circumstances, but if we both try to carry her, we'll jostle her too much."

"Thanks, buddy. Did you call Niall?" Mick asks.

"Yes, he's on his way. Can you tell where she was hit?" Joe asks, worry evident in his tone.

"He shot her in the back. It hit the left side, between her scapula and spine. When I first heard her breathe, there was a sucking sound. I think a bullet may have hit a lung. I plugged the wound so she can breathe easier."

"So that's why you're missing a sleeve," Joe says, nodding toward Mick's bare arm.

Just then they hear Hemingway bark. "We're almost there, Emma. Hang on," Mick whispers.

When they reach the top of the canyon, Herb, Chris, Joe, and Niall lift Emma from Mick. Once he's seated in the back of the ATV, they transfer her back to his waiting arms. Mick's heart thrashes against his sternum as he looks at her. *Please don't die.*

From the side of the ATV, Hemingway tries to nudge Mick. "It's going to be okay, boy."

Turning, Mick says, "Chris, will you please take Hemingway up to the main house? I know Libby, Fran, and Cynthia can use your assurance."

Motioning for Joe to step closer, Mick says, "Now's the time to call the FBI. Bring them up to speed on the situation, and then you and Herb head back down to Toni. I'm sure she'd appreciate it."

Joe nods his agreement.

And with that, Niall drives toward the front gate.

"Herb, you head down to Toni," Joe says. "I'll be right there."

Whump-whump-whump. They hear the sound of rotating helicopter blades long before they see the chopper. As they drive through the front gate and stop, it swiftly sheds altitude and lands about a hundred feet away. Its prop wash pummels them and bends the tall grass back.

Two first responders exit the bird with a stretcher and make the expert transfer look easy. "We're taking her to St. Joseph's. It's the closest hospital with a helipad," one of them shouts.

As Mick makes to join them, one of the guys shakes his head. "There's only room for the triage unit," he yells.

Mick nods in understanding. "I'll be there as soon as I can," he yells back.

The noise is deafening as the turbine gears up for liftoff.

Niall says, "Mick, if you let Libby call Emma's parents while you shower, you can be on your way to St. Joseph's all the sooner. I'll have a fresh pot of coffee ready by the time you head to the hospital. You're a little on edge to be the one to call her folks."

"You're right," Mick agrees. "I almost killed a man tonight, Niall."

Resting his hand on Mick's forearm, Niall says, "We were wondering what happened in The Devil's Canyon. But from the bits and pieces we've put together, it sounds like the world would be a safer place without him."

Mick runs his hands through his hair and down his face. He exhales deeply through his mouth and inhales through his nose, trying to wrap his mind around what's happened.

Above them, the stars seem weary in a sky bleached thin by the neighboring city's lights.

"Jason was going to slit Emma's throat," Mick says. "Everything happened at once. She stood up fast and caught him under the chin with her head and stabbed him in the leg. He shot her in the back. I shot him in the chest."

"Emma stabbed him?" Niall asks, impressed. "Where'd she get a knife?"

"I think it was Jason's. When he reached for it in his pocket and it was gone, he pulled a gun instead. That's when Emma stood up. He didn't expect it. She blindsided him. Remember, he wasn't in the kitchen the night she showed us what she's been working on—that she can stand."

———

Toni slaps on a pair of latex gloves and rummages through "Jason's" backpack. She shakes her head at the number of aliases she's known him to use. She checks every compartment but doesn't find anything of use.

Turning her flashlight onto Alex's body, her eyes are drawn to the knife sticking out from his right thigh. *Emma, you're one smart cookie.* She nods with admiration.

Picking up an empty bottle of Jack, Toni looks at Alex's motionless body and says, "Everyone has an Achilles heel, and this is yours."

She starts pacing—back and forth, back and forth. *I can punch his ticket right now, and no one will be the wiser. Just pinch his nostrils, cover his mouth, and it'll be over.* She pauses and turns around, directing the beam at Alex's face. *He's one of the most dangerous and volatile men I've ever known.* She draws in a long breath, then blows it out, giving herself a moment. *He's got a hole in his chest. It would be a "mercy" killing.* Her brief smile is followed by a frown. *But I want to know what he meant by, "I told her." Who, Emma? And just what did he say?*

As she walks over to the wheelchair, she's impressed that it's still upright. *But that makes sense. Emma fell forward when she was shot in the back, and Alex fell backward when he was shot in the chest.*

With nothing else to do, she peels off the gloves, sits in the chair, and waits for the others, callous to the fact that someone is dying a few feet away.

"I'll meet you in the kitchen with a thermos of hot black coffee," Niall says as he pulls away from the front of Mick's cabin.

"I'm just going to shower and change. I'll be right over."

The wind kicks up, howling its worry as Niall pulls around to the mudroom entrance. "Hey, where's Hemingway?" he calls out, expecting a greeting from his companion.

"He bolted when Chris and Herb opened the front door," Libby says. "How's Emma and where's Mick?"

"We don't know about Emma's condition yet. They've taken her to St. Joseph's."

What exactly happened?" Libby asks.

With mutual concern, Fran and Cynthia step over to join the conversation.

"Jason shot Emma in the back, and Mick shot Jason in the chest," Niall says. His expression is grim. "As you know, Emma's been life-flighted to St. Joseph's."

Slack-jawed, Libby's and Cynthia's hands fly to their chests. Fran buries her face in her hands. Through parted fingers, she asks, "Is Jason dead?"

"Close to it, but no. There's another LifeFlight on its way," Niall says.

"This is a terrible thing to say," Fran says, "but I wish he had died."

Niall nods and continues. "Mick will be here in a minute. He's showering and changing his clothes, then he'll swing by to grab a thermos of coffee on his way to the hospital. Libby, will you please call Emma's emergency contact. Mick and I both assume it's in her registration paperwork and that it's her parents."

"You're right on both counts, this is going to be a difficult phone call," she says, heading to her office.

Niall starts a fresh pot of coffee then puts on his apron and begins pulling ingredients out of the refrigerator and cupboards.

Seeing the look of devastation on Niall's face, Cynthia says, "Fran, let's give them some space. You haven't seen the gorgeous guest room yet. I'd love to show it to you." And with that, the two women head down the hall.

——————

Mick arrives at the main house and finds Libby in her office, wrapping up the conversation with Emma's parents. "Yes. St. Joseph's. Okay. Sean McPherson is my brother. He'll be at the hospital waiting. No. No. It's no trouble at all. You can stay in Emma's cottage. Yes. Uh huh, text me your flight details, and I'll see you in Seattle. Ok, bye." And she ends the call.

"You're driving to Seattle?" Mick asks Libby.

"Well, the Benton's—Maureen and Philip," she corrects herself, "said it'll be much faster to catch a flight to Seattle than Bellingham. They've got to get to St. Joseph's from Sea-Tac somehow, and it'll be emotionally better for them to ride with someone who knows Emma rather than with a stranger."

"Has anyone ever told you that you're the best sister ever?" Mick asks.

"Maybe a time or two." She smiles. "By the way, are you going to finish getting dressed?"

Mick looks down and shakes his head. He tugs his shirt closed, then his fingers march up the buttons, fastening them.

Libby and Mick enter the kitchen together and share Libby's plan with Niall.

"You're right," he agrees. "Mick, while you're at the hospital, I'll keep the home fires burning. I imagine it'll be like a revolving door around here until the dust settles. And most people like to eat when they're stressed." Brandishing a wooden spoon, he continues, "And I can meet that need. Speaking of which, here's that thermos of hot coffee I promised. Please keep us posted on any updates."

Turning to Libby, Mick asks, "Are you taking the van?"

"That's what I had in mind."

"That's great, I just filled it. I'll take my Jeep. Thank you for the coffee," Mick says to Niall as he heads toward the door. "I'll call or text when there's news about Emma."

When Joe enters the cave, flashlight in hand, he sees latex gloves crumpled on Toni's lap. "Did you check the backpack?" he asks, nodding toward it on the ground.

"I did, but nothing looks important. I left everything where it was. Do you want me to bag and tag it?"

"Yes, please."

Pointing with her chin, she continues, "I removed the knife from the guy's thigh before they carried him out of here. I bagged and tagged it, along with the empty bottles of Jack. They might have prints we can lift."

"Good work, Bianco. Thank you."

Carrying the evidence bags up the side of the canyon, Joe turns to Toni. "There are ten unsolved murders we think this guy's responsible for. The autopsy findings from the first two victims show that each medical examiner recovered tissue from under their fingernails. And while the DNA tissue scrapings match each other, they don't match anything currently on file in CODIS."

Bianco listens intently, as she always does, sometimes grunting or nodding in encouragement, occasionally requesting clarification.

Joe continues, "At the hospital, we'll be able to get DNA from Hughes or Berndt, or whatever the hell his name is."

"I wonder why only the first two women had tissue under their nails?" Toni asks.

"The eight women after them had zip-tie restraints around their wrists," Joe says. "It appears the killer got better at subduing his victims."

They trudge for a while in silence, each one thinking their private thoughts.

"I'm meeting with Sean Rafferty at the hospital in the morning," Joe says.

"Who's Sean Rafferty?"

"Oh, that's right, you're a new transfer. Rafferty's an FBI agent from the Seattle office. We've worked cases with him before."

Toni's step falters and she catches herself. "When did *they* get involved?"

"About thirty minutes ago."

CHAPTER 25

*"My aim in constructing sentences is to make
the sentence utterly easy to understand, writing
what I call transparent prose. I've failed
dreadfully if you have to read a sentence twice
to figure out what I meant."*

—KEN FOLLETT

Toni enters the hospital, wearing her uniform. *Everyone
trusts a cop.* At the reception desk, she inquires about
Alex's post-op condition.

"I'm sorry, but we don't have a patient by the name of
Alex Berndt, listed," the woman says.

Toni thinks about which fake ID he's carrying and
amends the question. "I'm sorry, that's his pseudonym." She
smiles. "He's an author. He'd be listed as Jason Hughes."

The receptionist runs her finger down the page. "Ah, yes.
Here's Mr. Hughes. He's in intensive care, but stable. That's
on the fourth floor. The elevator's right over there." She points
to polished metal doors with fake greenery in large terra cotta
pots on either side.

From the panel of lights above the doors, Toni sees there are twelve floors and that the elevator's descending.

"Thank you."

On the way to the hospital, Mick's cellphone buzzes. He answers it, cupping it against his ear with his shoulder as he drives toward a sky that promises more rain. The inclemency of the weather doesn't faze him. He has other things on his mind as he listens to the person on the other end of the call. He thanks them and puts his phone away.

The rain falls harder, causing a thundering drum on the roof of the Jeep. Mick's view is reduced to a blur. He turns the wipers to full power. If there were any oncoming traffic, his face would be distorted to them by the rainwater on the windshield. They wouldn't be able to see that he's crying.

I used to feel a lot of things before Sam died. Up until I met Emma, I mainly felt grief, rage, and guilt, devouring each other like tail-eating serpents. Emma's presence in my life shattered the numbness I felt. Those feelings are still there, but now they're overlaid by a rich, quiet glow.

When he pulls into the parking lot of St. Joseph's, he rolls down his window and punches a button. A ticket pops out, and he tucks it in the visor.

Like the aching tug of an ocean current, Mick's feelings for Emma run deep. Looking in the rearview mirror, he brings his hands up and rubs his face. *Please, God, don't let her die.*

The lights are dim on the fourth floor of the hospital. The nurse's desk is a visible glow at the end of the corridor.

Toni has a grim twist to her mouth. She can feel the hospital's central heating breathing as quietly as the patients in the calm of the night shift.

As she approaches room 401, she sees a man—his back to her—sitting in the guest chair. It's pulled up close to the hospital bed. The man is bent over Alex Berndt, a.k.a. Jason Hughes. She can't hear the whispered words, but it sounds like a prayer. *Well, I'll be damned. It's Father Patrick Mac-Cullough, Niall's brother. I bet he's on chaplain duty.*

Toni leans in further trying to hear what's being said, but the hushed words are muffled. *Is it just the priest who's talking, or is Jason responding?*

Aware of the security cameras, Toni casually walks down the corridor and leans against the wall in an alcove, ostensibly to check her phone. From here, she watches Alex's door. When she sees Father MacCullough leave, she heads back down the hall and enters room 401, shutting the door behind her.

The ICU waiting room is warm and comfortable with pale ochre walls, woven yarn hangings, and sage corduroy chairs. The buzz humming through the hospital almost drowns out the beeps and hisses of the machines. A low murmur comes from other people in the waiting room awaiting news of their loved ones.

Mick observes that the more life-threatening the prognosis, the quieter the doctors and nurses become, their calmness balancing the hysteria around them.

Nearing the breaking point himself, Mick links his fingers behind his head, stretches his back, and continues pacing. His mind wanders back to the day he picked up this month's group of writers at the airport. *The moment I saw Emma rolling toward me in her wheelchair, she kept rolling, right into my heart.*

There's a low hum of activity in the hallway—a doctor being paged by the oncology department, the wheels of a gurney bouncing off the wall, a cry silenced.

"We've got to stop meeting like this."

Mick whirls around to see Dr. Zimmerman.

"What are you doing in the intensive care unit, Mr. McPherson?"

"I'm waiting for news about Emma Benton. Do you know how she is?"

Tilting her head to the side, Dr. Zimmerman says, "Just the other day you were here for one of your guests, Cynthia Winters. Is Ms. Benton another guest, or is she a family member? You know I can't give out infor—"

Mick doesn't hesitate. "She's my fiancée. We're engaged."

Dr. Zimmeerman thrusts her hands into the deep square pockets of her white lab coat and stands still. She raises an eyebrow and gives the slightest of smiles. "She's not my patient, but I'll see what I can find out."

Toni adjusts the drip rate on the IV bag hanging above the patient's head. *Until now you've been known as Jason Hughes. But the cops, the FBI, and everyone else is going to find out—if they haven't already—that you're really Alexander Berndt. And I'll be damned if you take me down with you.*

Turning to Alex, she says, "I increased the med flow, so the pain will lessen soon."

As she sits in the still-warm chair, she leans over him. When she notices the cannula threaded under his nose, force-feeding him oxygen, she removes it.

"It's your own damn fault that you're in this position. You've been sloppy, Alex, and now I'm forced to clean up the mess. I don't have a choice."

Alex slits an eye open. His hand moves toward the call button.

Toni shakes her head. "Uh, uh, uh. I'm sorry, but we can't have any interruptions. Now let's see." She pauses for a moment. "When we were in the cave you said, 'I told her.' Did you mean Emma Benton?"

Alex nods his head yes.

"What did you tell her?

He tries to speak but can't. It's increasingly hard for him to breathe.

"Did you tell her that I'm a dirty cop?

Alex gives another affirmative nod. And though he can't speak, he makes a poor excuse of a smile.

"Does anyone else know?"

He gives her another weak smile and whispers, "Yes."

"Who else did you tell?"

He still can't talk.

Toni threads the cannula back under his nostrils and waits. It's barely audible, but she hears, "I told the priest."

Toni opens her jacket and extracts two syringes. She lays one on the bedside table.

"Now let's see just how good of a teacher you were when you taught me this clever little trick of using two drugs to mimic a heart attack. Correct me if I'm wrong," she smiles, "but you said, 'It's virtually undetectable as a murder.' Let's find out, shall we?"

She uncaps the needle and continues. "If I understood this accurately, calcium gluconate is a drug used to counter-act the effects of *hyperkalemia*—too much potassium in the body—that can produce heart arrhythmias. An injection of too much calcium gluconate, however, initiates lethal elec-trolytic imbalances that disrupt the normal levels of sodium, potassium, and chloride in the body's cells. These electrolyte imbalances interfere with and slow the heart to dangerously low levels, eventually creating a heart attack."

After inserting the needle into the IV's access port, Toni pushes the plunger. She stands, walks over to the biohazard box mounted on the wall, and drops the syringe in among the rest of the used needles.

In a short while, Alex begins exhibiting the initial symptoms of a toxic dose of calcium gluconate—flushed skin and profuse sweating.

As Toni gets the second syringe from the bedside table, she says, "Alex, when you taught me how to kill someone and make it look like a heart attack, you said that if I was in a hurry—if it was an 'impatient disposal'—that I could add a second medication."

Looking at the now-uncapped needle, she says, "This one is potassium phosphate. The calcium and phosphate in the two solutions will interact and form an insoluble bond that creates aggregate anaphylaxis—severe hypertension and right ventricular heart failure."

Toni inserts the second needle into Alex's vein. While pressing the plunger, she adds, "You were a good teacher, Alex. Oops. Did I use the past-tense? Sorry about that, but it won't be long now." She smiles. "I'm a good student. I remembered what you said. 'When calcium gluconate and potassium phosphate solutions are mixed together, they form an insoluble precipitant. That's why they've got to be injected separately—to prevent precipitate formation until they're in the victim's bloodstream.'"

Toni stands by the bed, listening to Alex's moans weaken.

The second syringe joins the others in the biohazard box.

Toni walks out the door and is halfway down the corridor when Alex—known until now as Jason—flatlines.

⸻

Emma feels like she's floating out of her body. She looks down on the shell of herself laying prone on a hospital table. Doctors and nurses in surgical masks and scrubs surround her. She hears someone's shoes make gasping little sucks at the floor when they move. *There's a white sheet propped up over the lower part of my body. It reminds me of one of those temporary tents thrown up at an archeological dig.*

She has a fleeting sense of something drifting up from her subconscious, almost within reach, but too fragile to grasp. A faceless man hovers like a specter at the margins of her mind's eye, refusing to go away.

All heads in the ICU waiting room lift at the call of "Code Blue" over the intercom. Their exhausted faces now fully alert. Everyone's aware that a patient—possibly their loved one—is having cardiopulmonary arrest and needs immediate resuscitation.

Mick notices a grandmotherly woman across from him fingering her rosary beads, eyes closed, her lips moving silently.

Please, God, don't let Emma die.

As Toni leaves the hospital, she looks up at the night sky scattered with dense clusters of sparkling stars of every size and intensity and stretches languidly with her arms above her head. *An agent from the FBI will be here in the morning. At least he won't be able to get any information from Alex.* She smiles.

I've got two more loose ends to tie up—the padre and Emma. She's probably still in surgery, so my first priority is Father MacCullough. It's been a long time since I've darkened the doors of a church. I'll swing by St. Barnabas on my way home and acquaint myself with the lay of the land.

Dr. Zimmerman sees Mick before he sees her. She watches him pace the tension-filled room. When he turns toward her, she sees hope fill his face. She also sees shadows under his eyes, a healthy growth of stubble on his face and neck, and spikes in his hair from raking his hands through it.

He rushes over to her. "How's Emma?"

"I'm happy to tell you that Emma has a good prognosis. The surgeon who removed the bullet and repaired the damage, Dr. Martin Timms, is one of the best thoracic surgeons in the Pacific Northwest. But Emma still has a *pneumothorax,* a collapsed lung. She also has some broken ribs, both front and back." Dr. Zimmerman didn't tell Mick that before they were able to get her stabilized—when her blood pressure was still all over the place—she'd flatlined. They'd lost her.

"Miss Benton is going to be monitored in the ICU for the next few days, maybe even a week, to make sure she doesn't develop ARDS—acute respiratory distress syndrome. And there's another thing you should know. The man who shot Miss Benton, Jason Hughes, is dead. He died from a massive heart attack while he was in recovery."

"Jason Hughes is an alias," Mick says. "His real name is Alexander Berndt. The FBI will be here in the morning. They'll want DNA samples from him so they can match them against ten rapes and murders."

"Oh, my God. I'll let Dr. Marshall in the hospital morgue know."

"Thank you. I appreciate it. I'd like to go sit with Emma now," Mick says. "I won't say a word. I'll just sit quietly in a chair."

Dr. Zimmerman looks into his pleading eyes. "I'm sorry, Mr. McPherson, but there are no visitors, except for clergy, while she's in recovery."

A light goes on over one of the patient's doors, followed by a low ping. A nurse in pink scrubs and white crocks that squeak with every step, approaches Dr. Zimmerman and Mick. "You're needed on the floor, Dr. Zimmerman."

"Thank you, Sarah. I'll be right there."

Turning to Mick, she says, "If there's anything else I can do for you, please let me know. I've told Emma's surgical team that her fiancé is in the waiting room or the hospital chapel."

She gives him a pointed look. "And to let you know of any further news."

"Thank you so much, Dr. Zimmerman. I appreciate your help."

As Dr. Zimmerman heads to her patient, Mick heads to the chapel on the first floor.

———

Expecting resistance, when Toni pulls the ornate handle on the door of St. Barnabas, she marvels. *It's true, the doors on Catholic churches are never locked.*

As she steps in, she closes her eyes and inhales the incense and beeswax scented air, letting the peace of the place soak into her. After buying three candles—one for Alex, one for Father MacCullough, and one for Emma Benton—she steps into the dark interior of the church.

Turning full circle, she takes in her surroundings. Not surprising, it appears that she's the only "worshipper" at three o'clock in the morning. At the far end of the vaulted nave, a shrine of Mary is backlit with hundreds of tiny lights. As Toni draws near, she can make out the flesh-tinted face. Even though it's only plaster, lit from beneath it has an eerily lifelike look.

She takes a seat in the front pew and continues to examine the space, looking for anything that might help her. She checks each direction for doors. Most of them are visible in the dark because current laws mandate a lit exit sign over them making them easy to find in the event of an emergency. Experientially, she knows that many laws are overlooked. Wondering if the church has cut any corners, she gets up and walks the perimeter to verify the location of each door. When she comes upon the confessional booth, she smiles. *This is it.*

The "booth" looks more like a massive wooden cabinet. The area on the left is where the priest enters, pulls the door shut, and waits. The area on the right side—separated by a wooden partition with a small ornate screen—is where the penitent enters, pulls their door shut, and sits or kneels. *Now all I need to do is check the outside perimeter for security cameras, and then find out when Father MacCullough takes confessions.*

———

Mick looks up when Joe enters the small chapel.

"I thought I might find you here. How's Emma?"

"The good news is, they got the bullet out. The bad news is, she has a collapsed lung and some broken ribs. They're keeping her in ICU for a few days to monitor her."

"Speaking of ICU," Joe says, "Rafferty from the FBI is upstairs in the waiting room.

"I thought he wasn't coming until morning."

Joe nods. "He arrived early." Continuing, he says, "We know that Hughes, or rather, Berndt, is dead. Rafferty wants the three of us to go to the morgue together. Is that okay with you?"

Mick stands then runs a hand down his face; his fingers stop at his chin. "Yes. And then, once I check on Emma's status, I need to go home to shave. I showered but forgot to mow this stubble, and Emma's parents are due to arrive soon."

———

After introductions are made, Rafferty, Bingham, and McPherson fill out the necessary forms, then take the elevator to the small basement morgue.

Dr. Marshall is standing at a steel table in her lab coat and gloves, her hair tucked under a cap, with a female body laid out in front of her, draped from the neck down.

Nodding at the men, she says, "Dr. Zimmerman told me I could expect the FBI. Gentlemen, may I see your identification, please?"

While she checks their identification, Rafferty explains that he's FBI, Bingham's a police officer, and McPherson's a civilian here to ID the body. After they sign in, Dr. Marshall opens a refrigerated body drawer. In it is a sheet-covered corpse.

When the doctor pulls back the sheet, Mick steps forward and looks intently at the face. *I'm glad that one evil man, at least, is no longer at large upon this earth.*

He turns to Rafferty, Bingham, and Marshall. "This is Jason Hughes. We've since learned that's an alias. His real name is Alexander Berndt."

———

A new day greets Mick when he steps out of the hospital. The morning air is moist and cool enough to turn his breath to vapor. In his mind's eye, he imagines rafts of seagulls rise off the water, making their way in the first misty light with the whale-watching boats bound for the San Juan Islands in the Salish Sea, the Caribbean of the Pacific Northwest.

On the drive home, Mick's mind takes a one-eighty. He thinks about death. About how close Emma came to it. He thinks about the morgue and Alex Berndt, a.k.a. Jason Hughes. He also thinks about Sam. *Sam's death is as fresh now as it was five years ago when it occurred. Not just the visuals, but the emotional hatchet attached to the mental images as well.*

His therapist told him he has "survivor's guilt." *I survived, and Sam didn't.* Mick was grappling with grief, of course, but it was grief marred by guilt. *We flipped a coin to see who would drive. Sam "won." It could just as easily have been me in the sniper's scope that day.*

Now though, when he shuts his eyes, he hears gunfire, then sees Emma's body flinch and fall forward onto the ground. Mick processes the gut-wrenching scene in slow motion—over and over again.

Some shrinks might interpret this as being afraid of another significant loss. And they might not be far off the mark.

CHAPTER 26

"When you are describing a shape, or sound, or tint: don't state the matter plainly, but put it in a hint; and learn to look at all things with a sort of mental squint."
— LEWIS CARROLL

Hemingway hurls himself—cone head and all— at Mick when he steps through the mudroom door. "I missed you, too," Mick says. As he strokes Hemingway's chest and back, the dog whines with pleasure. Mick can't help but smile.

The top of Niall's apron-clad body almost fills the space above the Dutch door. "Welcome home. How is Emma?"

Like bookends, Cynthia and Fran appear, one on each side of Niall.

"The surgeon removed the bullet from Emma. She has a collapsed lung and a few broken ribs, but they assured me she has a good prognosis. When I left, she was still in recovery. I'm just going home to shave, then I'll head back."

"Her parents will be so glad to hear that news," Fran says.

"Have you heard from Libby?" Mick asks. "Do you know when they expect to arrive at the hospital?"

Niall wipes his hands on the front of his apron. "She called about ten minutes ago. You must have just missed each other."

Rubbing a hand over his face, Mick says, "I'm glad to have a chance to shave before I meet Emma's parents."

"You *are* looking a little scruffy," Niall teases. "Almost as bad as Hemingway."

"What's the word on Jason?" Cynthia asks.

"He died. He had a heart attack when he was in recovery. This morning, Joe Bingham, Sean Rafferty, an FBI agent, and I went to the hospital morgue where I identified Alex Berndt, who we know used the alias, Jason Hughes. It's now a joint federal–Bellingham law enforcement investigation."

"Why did the FBI get involved?" Niall asks.

"Cynthia was right about the towels in the suitcase. It turns out there are ten unsolved rapes and murders. The trail is geographically disparate. Each one took place in a different state."

"Crossing state lines, is that the reason for the FBI?" Fran asks.

"That, and because there are over three almost-identical killings, it makes the murderer a serial killer."

Niall takes in a long breath, then blows it out, giving himself a moment to calm down. "It's hard to wrap my head around the fact that he was here as our guest. Emma is a fortunate young woman."

"Yes, she is," Mick says. "I'm so grateful she's still alive. One of the things Agent Rafferty told Bingham and me this morning is that rape isn't about sex. It's about power and control and humiliation. He also said that serial killers leave certain trademarks. Some they're aware of. Others they're not. In this case, the killer—quite possibly Alex Berndt—was methodical, and his methods were informed by his knowledge of anatomy."

"What do you mean?" Fran asks.

"Trust me, you don't want to know. But I will say this. They're getting Berndt's DNA right now to match against the DNA they collected from the victims."

Niall shakes the dishtowel. "Enough about that. I know you're anxious to shave and get back to the hospital. Would you like a quick cup of coffee and a bite to eat before we head out?"

"Yes, please." Mick smiles. "I was hoping you'd ask."

———

Dr. Zimmerman is passing by when Mick, Niall, Cynthia, and Fran step off the elevator on the fourth floor. "You're just the person I'm looking for," she says to Mick. Taking him by the arm she leads him down the corridor—like ducklings, the others following behind. "Emma's parents are here. They filled her surgical team in on her condition—*Transverse myelitis.* That's where I come in. It's one of my areas of practice."

Stopping outside a closed door, she looks into Mick's eyes. "This is Emma's room." She leans in and whispers conspiratorially. "We're breaking the rules a bit with the number of visitors she has, but then we all break the rules now and then, don't we?" she says, pointedly. "I'll leave you now, but I would like to speak with you later."

After patting him on the arm, she turns and walks down the hallway.

Am I in some kind of trouble? Mick wonders, as he watches her white lab coat disappear around a corner.

———

When he pushes the door open, the first thing Mick sees is Emma. She seems heartbreakingly frail amid the array of tubes, racks, and monitors. Because of the incision in her back, she's propped up in a medical unit that keeps pressure off the dressing. He feels a rush of joy so big it almost stuns him. He realizes his heart is pounding.

Niall, Cynthia, and Fran slip around him into the room. They join the others around the bed.

The second thing Mick notices is that all of the original people surrounding Emma—Libby, Bingham, Rafferty, and a man and woman he suspects are Emma's parents—are looking at him.

"What?" he asks.

They continue to stare.

In his mind, he quickly goes through a mental checklist. He looks down, his zipper's closed. He reaches up, his hair is combed. He wipes the front of his teeth with his finger.

They continue to stare.

"What?" he asks again.

"We understand that congratulations are in order," his sister, Libby, says.

In unison, Niall, Cynthia, and Fran turn to him incredulously, and say, "What?"

Mick feels a flush creep across his cheeks. His ears get hot. Grimacing, he says, "No wonder Dr. Zimmerman wants to speak with me later. I *am* in trouble."

Looking directly at Emma now, he says, "I realize that it's probably too early to ask you to marry me, but it's not too early to tell you that I *love* you, that I'm *in love* with you, and that I want to be part of your life."

Turning to her parents, he says, "Mr. and Mrs. Benton, your daughter means the world to me."

"Well, that took a lot of guts," Joe says.

"I'd rather be in a firefight," Rafferty says.

Niall starts clapping, and the rest chime in.

Eyes glistening, Emma beckons Mick over. "I love you, too," she manages to whisper.

With a no-nonsense look from Dr. Timms as he checks on Emma, the visitors in her room dwindle down to three—Mick, Rafferty, and Bingham.

Rafferty flashes his badge at the doctor, and says, "The moment we get a statement from Ms. Benton, we'll leave." Nodding toward Joe, he says, "This is a joint task force effort, FBI and BPD—Bellingham Police Department." Suppressing a smile, he turns to Mick. "And this is Sean McPherson, Ms. Benton's *fiancé*."

Joe coughs.

Emma's wide grin turns into a wince from the pain of the effort.

Dr. Timm's face shifts from no-nonsense, to a smile. Turning to Emma, he says, "Congratulations. I'll give you ten more minutes, and then visiting hours are over. You need your rest." And with that, he leaves the room.

After agent Rafferty tells Emma what he needs to know, he turns on his recorder.

Emma begins. She tells them that Jason bragged to her that she was going to be his eleventh "disposal"—kill. "He said it didn't matter that he was telling me, because I'd be dead, and the information would die with me." She lifts a hand up to her throat.

Mick holds a glass of water with a straw to her lips, and she drinks.

"Thank you," Emma says. "He named ten women that he killed, but I can only remember one. Rose Gonzales. He said that I was going to be number eleven. I asked him what I had to do with any of it. He said that I was bait." Turning to Mick, she continues, "He said that he was fishing for Sean McPherson." Emma's eyes pool.

"I asked what Mick had to do with any of it. He told me that five years ago, he and his brother orchestrated a heist involving over ten million dollars in heroin. It was in the San Francisco Police Department evidence lockup. But he said that wasn't a problem because they had someone on the inside helping them—a dirty cop. He winked at me and told me to 'stay wary, for treachery walks among you.'"

The three men exchange questioning glances.

After another sip of water, Emma continues. "Jason said the only thing they had to do was empty the station house. He said, 'Police are predictable creatures. When an officer falls, they rally. Every one of them.' All they had to do was kill a police officer. He said, '*Any* cop would do.'"

Emma closes her eyes for a moment. "He said they used a diversionary tactic to draw a squad car to a bridge. And that's when he got the driver in his sights and squeezed the trigger." She covers her eyes with her hand and continues. He said, "'*Boom!* Sam was out of the game.'"

Emma takes her hand down and sees the three men looking at each other, stunned.

"I told Jason that I didn't understand why he wanted to kill Mick, that Mick's off the force and he got his drugs. He said that's where I was wrong. He said, 'I didn't get the drugs. My brother was one of three people who got caught. He's the one who stashed the drugs. He's the only person who knows their location.'"

After taking another sip of water, Emma says, "I asked him why his brother wouldn't tell him where the drugs are. Jason said, 'Dead men tell no tales. My brother was killed in jail before he could tell me. So, I'm out ten million bucks, and McPherson's going to pay.'"

Emma feels like she might shatter and blow away. She covers her face with both hands. Her shoulders are shaking. The men can barely hear what she says.

"Jason said, 'It would be too easy, too quick, to just kill Mick. I'm going to make him suffer first. He's going to watch as I slit your throat. That way, he'll die twice.' I was in the dark, listening for a footstep. But my heart was beating so loud in my ears, I wasn't sure if I could hear an elephant approaching. I was afraid that Jason was going to shoot Mick the moment he stepped into the mouth of the cave."

After a quick rap on the door, Dr. Timms steps into the room. "Your ten minutes is up. Ms. Benton needs her rest."

"Thank you, doctor," Rafferty says. "We got what we need."

Bingham, Rafferty, and McPherson follow Dr. Timms to the door. "I'll catch up with you guys in just a minute," Mick says. "I want to say goodbye to Emma."

Rafferty chuckles and shakes his head.

Bingham winks encouragingly and smiles like a fool.

Dr. Timms' face puckers as he warns, "A minute."

When Mick turns around, Emma's eyes are closed, her eyelashes resting gently on pale cheeks. Exhausted, she's fallen asleep.

In the waiting room, elbows on knees leaning toward each other, voices low, the men debrief.

Sean Raferty says, "I spend my days hunting people who couldn't care less, who have little or no empathy, to whom conscience is a foreign entity."

"The fact that Hughes, or Berndt—or whatever the hell his name was—left DNA on his victims, makes me wonder if he wanted to get caught," Joe says.

"I don't think it was carelessness or lack of control. I think it was intentional—like he was marking his territory," Mick says. "He acted like he was invincible."

Rafferty agrees. "Most serial killers are arrogant, sure of themselves. They enjoy every hoop law enforcement jumps through in order to catch them. In their own minds they *are* invincible. They view themselves as the master of their victims' fate."

Joe thinks back to the department's mandatory course he took. "When I took the department's class taught by a forensic psychologist, she said, 'Serial killers are likely intelligent, of at least average IQ, charming, possibly married, outwardly optimistic, manipulative, and will appear to function very well within the boundaries of society.'"

Mick laces his fingers together. "That's what I'm afraid of," he says. "We can't tell who they are. Berndt told Emma, 'Stay wary, for treachery walks among you.' What do you think he meant? Do you think there's a dirty cop involved?"

Mick sits in his Jeep in the hospital parking lot. So much—so very much—is going through his mind. He thinks about agent Rafferty. *He's a good listener, and the way he respectfully considers everyone else's ideas takes the sting out of his occasional pushbacks.*

His window's rolled down, and he takes a deep breath. He looks up. *I swear the light is different. Crisper. It seems bluer, and the edges of everything are more defined.*

A bevy of emotions run through Mick's mind. He thinks of Emma upstairs in intensive care, grateful that she's alive. And now that he's learned the "why" behind Sam's death, he also feels a sense of satisfaction at Alex's death. *I've never felt this emotion before at the death of another human being.* As he starts the Jeep, his chest, heart, and shoulders feel lighter.

CHAPTER 27

"In the planning stage of a book, don't plan the ending. It has to be earned by all that will go before it."

—Rose Tremain

During the next two weeks, Mick works on carving a beautiful pendant for Emma. Before he began, he put a lot of thought into what it would be and why.

When he picks Emma up at the hospital, Mick notices that her hair is tucked behind her ears, revealing a single pearl dangling from each lobe. He smiles.

After wheeling her down to the parking area, he lifts her and transfers her gently onto the front passenger seat of the Jeep.

A new wheelchair is stowed in the back, waiting for her to use when they reach Pines & Quill.

Before starting the ignition, Mick turns to Emma and splashes a broad smile all over her. His eyes drink in her auburn hair, sparkling green eyes, the smattering of freckles across her nose, and her cheeky grin.

Reaching into his shirt pocket, he says, "I made something for you." He pulls out a small black velvet bag and hands it to her.

She looks up, into his eyes.

"Well, go on. Open it." He encourages.

Emma loosens the drawstring at the top of the small pouch and pours the contents into her left palm. She inhales fast and deep. She picks it up and runs her fingers along its carved lines. "Oh my gosh, Mick. It's beautiful."

"I'm glad you like it, Emma. It's a 'Honu,' a Hawaiian green sea turtle. It symbolizes good fortune, endurance, and long life. When lost, turtles are excellent navigators and often find their way home—in your case, I hope it's always to me."

Leaning over to put the leather cord over her head, he whispers, "Emma, I love you," along her cheek, and draws closer still.

Emma lifts her head to look up at him. "Tell me again."

His voice is low and husky with emotion. "I love you." His mouth crushes down on hers, smothering any more words, any more thoughts.

When they arrive at Pines & Quill, Mick presses a button on the remote attached to the visor over the driver's seat. The huge entrance gate swings open and the vehicle sensor buzzes in the main house, notifying the occupants that Mick and Emma have arrived.

Inside the main house, it sounds like someone poked a hornet's nest. There are all kinds of whispered hushing, shushing, and jockeying for position in good hiding spots.

As the Jeep pulls into the circular drive, Libby stays behind the front door, opening it just enough for Hemingway, sans Elizabethan collar, to race out and greet them—a diversionary tactic on their part.

Hemingway's jumping and barking with excitement. Mick has to honk the horn to keep from running him over.

Mick puts down the driver's side window. "Hold your horses, big fella. I'll have her out in just a minute."

Once the Jeep has stopped, Mick comes around, gets the wheelchair, and transfers Emma from the passenger seat to the chair.

Hemingway yelps with joy at the sight of his friend, Emma. He nudges her hand with his wet nose.

Emma coos and scratches behind his ear.

Hemingway pushes his warm body against Emma's legs. She bends down and buries her face in his fur.

As Mick checks his watch, he says, "I'm sure Niall has brunch ready. Let's go inside."

"I've missed his cooking. And after all that hospital food, I'm starving!"

———————

The moment her wheels cross the threshold, Emma's nostrils fill with a delicious scent. She turns to Mick. "It smells like Thanksgiving!"

"It sure does," he agrees, rolling her down the hall.

When they enter the massive kitchen and dining area, people jump out of the woodwork and shout, "Welcome home!"

With her hands to her checks, Emma looks through tear-filled eyes and sees Niall with his arm around Libby, her parents with their arms around each other, Dr. Zimmerman standing next to Cynthia, Sean Rafferty standing next to Joe Bingham, and Fran standing next to a man in a police uniform. Emma has yet to meet him—Officer Herb who'd been on duty the night Cynthia was hurt.

"Oh, my gosh, you scared the living daylights out of me," Emma says as the crowd of people surrounds her.

"I see Mick gave you your pendant," Libby says.

Emma reaches up to touch it. "I love it."

Niall raises a wooden spoon. "Your timing couldn't have been better, you two. Brunch is ready."

"What are we having?" Emma asks.

"A celebration feast," Niall answers. "We have turkey breast with sausage and apricot stuffing, roasted Brussels sprouts, sweet potato pan dumplings, strawberry spinach salad, and soft yeasty rolls. I've paired it with a D'autrefois Reserve Pinot Noir from Vin de Pays, France. I chose it because of its rich undertones of vanilla and spice, and accent notes of cherry and cassis. It'll go nicely with the pear cake we're having for dessert."

The volume around the table rises and falls as they bring each other up to date on the current happenings.

Niall says, "Officer Toni and my brother, Paddy, would have joined us this afternoon, but Paddy has mass and confessions today, and Toni has a pressing family matter. She said it just can't wait any longer."

Mick says, "I'll pull the van around shortly. I know some of you have outbound flights this evening."

Mr. and Mrs. Benton are catching an evening flight back home to San Diego. They're ecstatic about Emma's relationship with Mick.

Cynthia is catching a flight back to Tucson. She doesn't miss the look that passes between Fran and Herb and smiles—a look that promises a multitude of air miles being racked up between Seattle and Boston.

"Will I see you tomorrow, Dr. Zimmerman?" Emma asks.

Emma's mom looks up. "See her for what, dear?"

Emma clears her throat. "Well, you all had this lovely surprise gathering for me. I have a little surprise for you, too." She scoots her chair back and stands up. Then, to everyone's astonishment, she takes three steps before plunking down on Mick's lap.

Emma's mom covers her face with her hands and bursts into happy tears.

Even Cynthia didn't see this coming.

Dr. Zimmerman looks at the group and says, "When Mr. and Mrs. Benton shared the details of Emma's *Transverse myelitis* with me, I started doing some tests of my own. Each day the sensation in her lower extremities gets stronger and more capable. Just as *Transverse myelitis* can develop in a matter of hours—Emma's happened overnight—it can leave just as quickly. I'm not certain, but I think her recovery has something to do with the trauma she experienced. Not only in being shot, but in the surgery afterward."

Niall starts to move to the big urn for coffee, then changes his mind. On impulse, he opens the refrigerator and pulls out two bottles of champagne. It isn't every day a nightmare has a happy ending. "Mick, will you get some champagne flutes, please?" And with that, he sends the cork cannoning to the ceiling.

There are toasts all around.

Cynthia walks over to Mick and whispers. "When you need help with future cases, please call me."

"What do you mean, 'help with future cases?'"

Cynthia smiles and pats his arm. "You'll see, dear. You'll see."

Turn the page to read an excerpt from
Iconoclast: A Sean McPherson Novel, Book Two

PROLOGUE

"There is only one plot—things are not what they seem."

—Jim Thompson

"Forgive me, Father, for I'm about to sin."

A suppressor muffles the sound of six consecutive rounds fired below the screen through the thin wooden partition separating saint from sinner in the confession booth.

As Father Paddy's body slumps to the floor, the iconoclast slips out a back door.

Rounding the corner, she does a tactical scan to ensure there's no one around. *All clear.*

She looks up to make sure the black sock she put over the security camera is still there. *In place.*

She removes the oversized trench coat and pulls off a short gray wig, mustache, and beard. She rolls them, along with her gun and suppressor, into the coat, and tucks everything into the briefcase. Before getting into the car she borrowed from Vito, she places the briefcase on the floor behind the driver's seat.

As she pulls away from the curb, she smiles. *I entered St. Barnabas as an old man. I left as a woman. Now if that's not a miracle, I don't know what is.*

Thirty minutes later, she drives down a gravel road to The Scrap Heap. On the surface, to innocent passersby, it's a wrecking yard where vehicles are brought, and their usable parts are salvaged and sold, while the unusable metal parts are sold to recycling companies. In reality, it's a place where people and things who've outlived their usefulness pass through.

The tips of Toni's nails, polished in "dagger pink," tap the steering wheel through thin, nitrile gloves. Usually, it's a fifteen-minute drive, but she takes a route devoid of street cams.

Two snarling Dobermans greet her through an eight-foot chain-link fence topped with triple concertina wire. The result is an extremely effective barrier.

Tapping the fence, Toni muses. *This is the second barrier I've dealt with today—first, the screen in the confessional, now the chain-link fence. If I had a shrink, they'd probably conclude that I enjoy keeping barricades between the men I don't like and me.* She smiles. *And they'd be right. I can always see them from the outside, where I stay safe and maintain control. They're defenseless and easily manipulated on the inside.*

A huge bald man in oil-stained coveralls steps out of the doorway of a small shack by the gate. He smiles. "Hey, Toni."

"Hey, Vito. Did you wait as I asked?"

"I did. Just a sec. Let me get these guys."

After shutting the dogs behind the door of the shack, Vito opens the gate.

Toni drives through, opens the back passenger door, and retrieves the briefcase.

Before they head into the central part of the yard, Vito closes and locks the gate.

Toni follows him to a waiting pile of wrecked cars. She hands him the open briefcase, peels off the nitrile gloves, and tosses them in, then tucks her hands into her back pockets. *Such a waste. That was a sweet Smith M&P22 compact and .22LR suppressor.*

After closing the briefcase and giving it a speculative weight check, Vito shrugs his massive shoulders and tosses it through the air into the top car's open trunk. Then he climbs up a ladder into a rig next to the pile of cars and starts the engine. When he pushes a black-knobbed lever, the car crusher begins its descent, closing the top car's trunk as it does.

Toni notices two words spray-painted on the side of the machine. "Big Bang."

She looks up at Vito. His face is red, and his head is glistening with sweat. He wipes the moisture from his forehead with the front of his hairy arm.

He looks down at her, gives her a thumbs up and smiles.

When it's all over, he climbs down. "How about dinner sometime?"

"I'd like that." She mentally applauds herself for not finishing the sentence with *idiota*—Italian for idiot.

Nodding toward the pile of crushed cars, Vito holds out a hand.

Toni looks at his waiting palm. *If his fingers were laced together, his hand would look like a baseball mitt.*

"That'll be five hundred bucks," Vito says. "But when we go out, it's on me." He smiles.

"It's a deal," she says.

After paying Vito in cash, he unlocks the gate and opens it.

Toni thanks him again, then gets in her own car and drives away. Looking in the rearview mirror, she sees Vito. *I'd rather die.*

Clutching her glasses in one hand and a crumpled tissue in the other, Carol Stapleton, an elderly penitent, steps into the confession booth. She's crying because she knows she has to tell the priest the hateful thoughts she's entertained about her neighbor. She sits down, closes her eyes, and tries to compose herself as she waits for the priest's usual greeting.

After tucking the tissue in her sleeve, her now-empty hand fingers the string of pearls at her neck. After a few minutes tick by in silence, she retrieves the tissue and blows her nose. Clearing her throat, she says, "Father MacCullough?"

When he doesn't answer, she wipes her lenses with the hem of her cotton dress and puts her glasses on. That's when she notices the splintered wood. *What on earth?*

She presses her wrinkled face to the small ornate screen in the partition that divides them. Red oozes down the wall where the priest should be seated. Her nose wrinkles at the faint coppery smell. Her forehead furrows. *Is that blood?*

Heart pounding, she pushes her ashen face forward a little more to look down. It's hard to see, but it seems like Father MacCullough's crumpled on the floor. Carol crosses herself.

Calling his name again, she steps out of her side of the booth and opens his.

Panic rips her chest, clawing to climb out of her mouth when she sees the bloodied, hole-pocked vestments. The door on the priest's side of the confessional had been blocking the pool of blood Father MacCullough is laying face down in. Now unblocked, it slowly spreads, inching toward the tip of Carol's black orthopedic shoe.

A primal scream pierces the sanctuary.

I hope you enjoyed reading *Indelible* and the sneak peak of *Iconoclast*.

If you did, please consider leaving a review for *Indelible* on Amazon, Goodreads, or BookBub.

A review can be as short as one sentence and your opinion goes a long way in helping others decide if a book is for them.

ACKNOWLEDGMENTS

First and foremost, thank you for choosing to read *Indelible,* book one in the Sean McPherson series. I hope you enjoyed it. If you did, please tell everyone!

To be the first to hear about *Iconoclast,* book two in the series, please subscribe to my quarterly newsletter at www. lauriebuchanan.com, where you're always welcome to stop by and say hello.

To my publisher, Brooke Warner, and editorial manager, Lauren Wise, at SparkPress, thank you for trusting in my vision for *Sean McPherson* and for allowing me to turn my dream into reality yet again. I'm proud to be listed among your authors.

Thank you to Vickie Gooch, a detective in the Major Crimes Unit of the Idaho State Police. I now know more about sex crimes, the production and sale of drugs, violent offenders, "suicide by cop," probable cause affidavits, ViCAP (the FBI's violent offender program), human trafficking, Touch DNA, cold case homicides, and serial killers than I ever dreamed of.

Thank you to Rylene Nowlin, DNA specialist at the Idaho State Police Crime Lab, for sharing with me your knowledge about processing rape kits and cyanoacrylate fuming to develop latent fingerprints.

Thank you to Dr. Glen Groben, forensic pathologist, for the fascinating discussion about forensic pathology, the early changes of death, gunshot wounds, blunt force trauma, and sharp force injury.

Any inaccuracies in law enforcement or medical processes and procedures are my own.

In particular, I want to thank Christine DeSmet, author and *tour de force* for all things literary. *Indelible* would be a lesser book without your insights, mentorship, encouragement, and unfailing support—gifts beyond measure. Thank you for making me a stronger writer.

Thank you to my sister, Julie, who listened to multiple early drafts, and shared her best ideas and opinions. You know my characters at least as well as I do and are always willing to help me dig deeper to get the plot unstuck. My stories are better because of you.

Thank you to Willa, my four-legged companion, who is the real-life inspiration for Hemingway.

Last but not least, thank you to my husband, Len, for helping me negotiate the minefield of modern technology and for making me laugh, especially when I'm ready to scream bloody murder! Which, if you think about it, fits hand-in-glove (no fingerprints) when writing a suspense/thriller series.

ABOUT THE AUTHOR

photo © Len Buchanan

Across between Dr. Dolittle, Nanny McPhee, and a type-A Buddhist, Laurie Buchanan is an active listener, observer of details, payer of attention, reader and writer of books, kindness enthusiast, and red licorice aficionado.

Her books have won nine awards, including the *Foreword* INDIES Book of the Year Gold Winner and the International Book Award Gold Winner.

She and her husband live in the Pacific Northwest, where she enjoys long walks, bicycling, camping, and photography—because sometimes the best word choice is a picture.

To learn more, please visit Laurie's website at
www.lauriebuchanan.com.

ABOUT SPARKPRESS

SparkPress is an independent, hybrid imprint focused on merging the best of the traditional publishing model with new and innovative strategies. We deliver high-quality, entertaining, and engaging content that enhances readers' lives. We are proud to bring to market a list of *New York Times* best-selling, award-winning, and debut authors who represent a wide array of genres, as well as our established, industry-wide reputation for creative, results-driven success in working with authors. SparkPress, a BookSparks imprint, is a division of SparkPoint Studio LLC.

Learn more at GoSparkPress.com

SELECTED TITLES FROM SPARKPRESS

SparkPress is an independent boutique publisher delivering high-quality, entertaining, and engaging content that enhances readers' lives, with a special focus on female-driven work. www.gosparkpress.com

Watermark: The Broken Bell Series, $16.95, 978-1-68463-036-3. When Angel Ferente—a teen with a dysfunctional home life who has been struggling to care for her sisters even as she pursues her goal of attending college on a swimming scholarship—doesn't come home after a party on New Year's Eve, her teammates, her coach's church, and her family search the city for her. The result changes their lives forever.

So Close: A Novel, Emma McLaughlin and Nicola Kraus. $17, 978-1-940716-76-3. A story about a girl from the trailer parks of Florida and the two powerful men who shape her life—one of whom will raise her up to places she never imagined, the other who will threaten to destroy her. Can a girl like her make it to the White House? When her loyalty is tested will she save the only family member she's ever known—even if it means keeping a terrible secret from the American people?

Pursuits Unknown: An Amy and Lars Novel, Ellen Clary. $16.95, 978-1-943006-86-1. Search-and-rescue agent Amy and her telepathic dog, Lars, locate a missing scientist who is reported to have an Alzheimer's-like disease—only to discover that someone wants to steal his research for potentially ominous purposes.

Tracing the Bones: A Novel, Elise A. Miller. $17, 978-1-940716-48-0. When 41-year-old Eve Myer—a woman trapped in an unhappy marriage and plagued by chronic back pain—begins healing sessions with her new neighbor Billy, she's increasingly drawn to him, despite the mysterious circumstances surrounding his wife and child's recent deaths.

The Goodbye Year: A Novel, Kaira Rouda. $17, 978-1-940716-33-6. Told from the points of view of both the parents and kids, *The Goodbye Year* explores high school peer pressure, what it's like for young people to face the unknown of life after high school, and how a transition that should be the beginning of a parents' second act together—empty nesting—is often actually the end.